BEARIED TREASURE

TED MULCAHEY

Publishing services provided by  **Archangel Ink**

ISBN: 978-1-950043-15-6

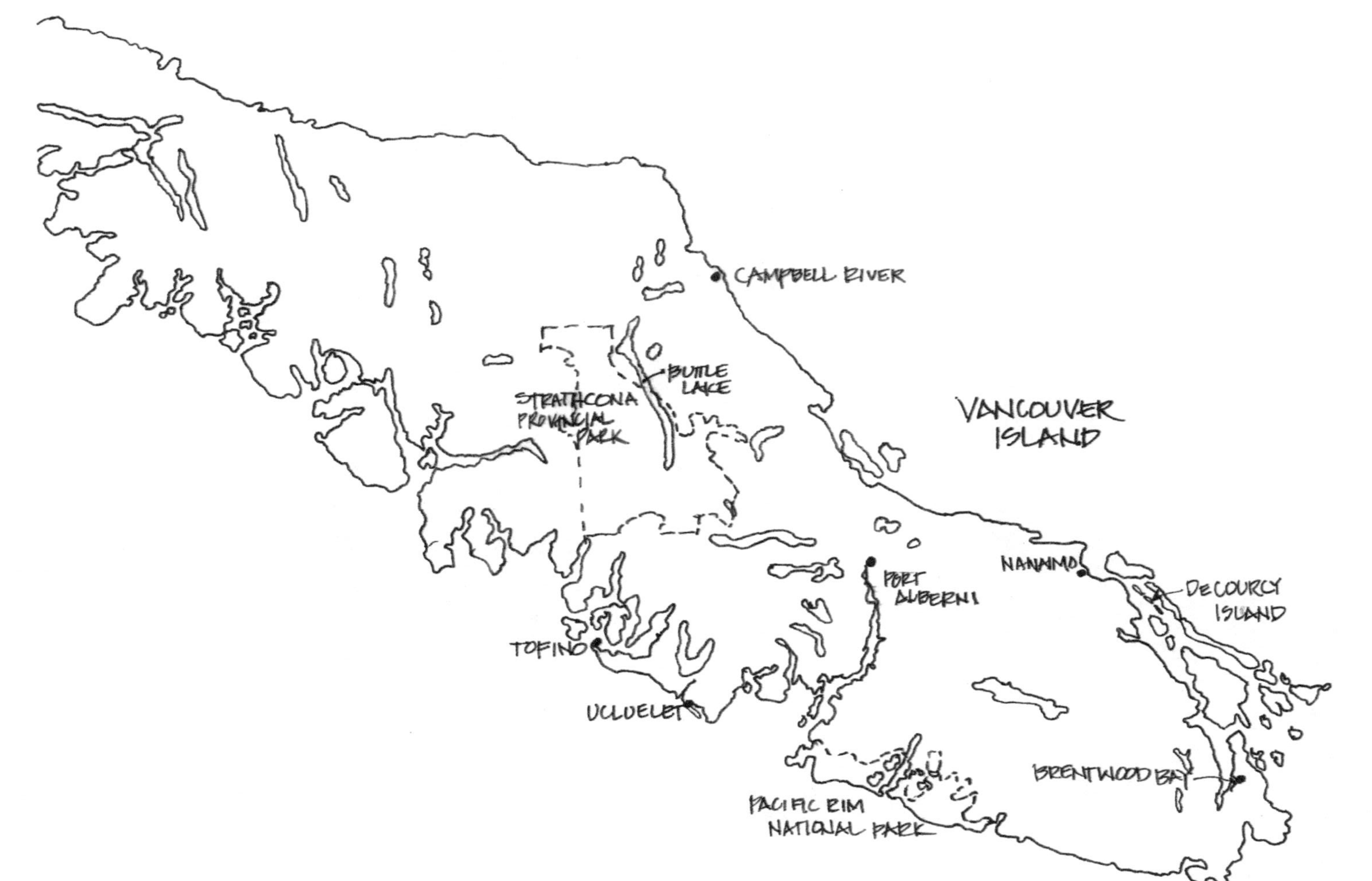

CAMPBELL RIVER
STRATHCONA PROVINCIAL PARK
BUTTLE LAKE
VANCOUVER ISLAND
PORT ALBERNI
NANAIMO
DE COURCY ISLAND
TOFINO
UCLUELET
BRENTWOOD BAY
PACIFIC RIM NATIONAL PARK

ACKNOWLEDGMENTS

I'd like to thank the folks at Archangel Ink for shepherding me through the publishing process. I owe my love of reading and writing to my folks, especially my dad, whose entire working days were spent as the sports editor for our hometown newspaper. My sense of humor I owe to my mom and my wife, with special thanks to the spouse for putting up with me for "lo these many years" (for you, MF, thanks for the first read). My brother Rick gets a thanks for asking me incessantly, "What the hell is happening with Marty?"

I could never have finished without the constant and selfless encouragement from my wife. If it's any good, it's her doing, if not it's all mine.

CONTENTS

Chapter 1 1

Chapter 2 5

Chapter 3 10

Chapter 4 16

Chapter 5 22

Chapter 6 30

Chapter 7 37

Chapter 8 43

Chapter 9 48

Chapter 10 52

Chapter 11 56

Chapter 12 67

Chapter 13 71

Chapter 14 75

Chapter 15 83

Chapter 16 96

Chapter 17 103

Chapter 18 112

Chapter 19 122

Chapter 20 131

Chapter 21 142

Chapter 22 152

Chapter 23 158

Chapter 24 165

Chapter 25 174

Chapter 26 179

Chapter 27 189

Chapter 28 196

Chapter 29 203

Chapter 30 212

Chapter 31 219

A Small Favor 226

"Teed Up for Terror" 227

About the Author 229

CHAPTER 1

"Two more days and we'll be able to get the hell out of this place."

Roger and Tiny were in the middle of a furniture installation on the west coast of Vancouver Island in the province of British Columbia. They had been receiving, arranging, and rearranging sofas, chairs, tables, lamps, pianos, drapery, and artwork for the better part of a week now and were in far deeper than they had any business being. The enormous Roger and the petite Tiny comprised the installation division of Interiors by Martin, a design firm known more for its brazen founder and owner than anything remotely resembling competence or talent in interior design or installation. It was Thursday morning and the grand reopening of the Tofino Inn and Spa was exactly three days away. There was a greater possibility of Burton, the hotel mascot, solving Rubik's Cube than Marty and his troops getting the overly ambitious—considering the budget—project completed on time.

The nine-foot Steinway Grand, which was to be the focal point in the main restaurant of the hotel and spa, was the subject of their consternation at the moment. Evidently the formidable entrance to the lodge-styled dining room was designed and built two inches narrower than would accommodate the valuable piano. Martin, in an attempt to shave a few bucks from the cost of the project, had selected the lower cost stock doors rather than go to a custom manufacturer. This would not normally have been a problem, but Howard Bories, the owner/operator of the resort, was an aficionado of classical music and insisted it be played during the evening meal on only the best piano money could buy. Bories had allowed Interiors by Martin to furnish every stick of furniture in the hotel but the Steinway—this he saw to himself. Steinway & Sons had delivered, assembled, voiced, and tuned it just this morning. Unfortunately for Howard, Martin's installation division had been contracted to relocate the delicate instrument and had not the slightest inkling how to disassemble it or move it. And now it appeared the piano could become somewhat less than a nine-foot grand.

"I think if we angle it diagonally and give it a shove from about three feet away we can force it through the jambs. We might screw it up a little but, you know, a little caulk and paint and nobody'll know the difference."

Roger's solution to the problem was a fate accomplished save for the intervention of Mr. Bories: "I'll not have you damaging that beautiful piano, gentlemen. You'll just have to find some other way to get it into the dining room."

"Mr. Bories," Tiny whined, "if we hafta find another way, we won't have all the stuff in place for the openin' on Sunday."

"You'll find another way, and you'll do it in time for Sunday. We're sold out and we'll not be refunding twelve thousand dollars in deposits just because that bloody Martin asshole screwed up again. And, you *will* get him here this morning or your miserable little lives will become even more wretched. Is that understood?" Little specks of spittle were now flying from Bories' puffy, pouty lips, his generous mustache limp with streaks of perspiration.

Although only five foot five inches tall, his total lack of patience and his ability to go on the offensive immediately placed Howard Bories somewhere near the bottom of the list of people you'd like to confront. His snow-white frosting of hair created the appearance of a halo, from which erupted his glistening cherry-red dome. The bushiness of his brows might have been hacked closely with a hedge trimmer and, on the plus side of the ledger, his forty excess pounds smoothed out whatever wrinkles there otherwise would have been. He could easily have been the model for the banker on the Monopoly game board.

Problem was that most people took him for a kindly old soul. On the other hand, experiencing firsthand the degree of ineptitude that Martin Menucci could bestow upon a project as complicated as the total refurbishment of the Tofino Inn had pushed Howard to depths of frustration.

Martin had promised Bories to be "on site" during the entire installation at the inn, but that had been during the contract negotiation phase. As it turned out, the designer had made only one site visit during the schematic, design/development, and project management stages and had stopped in three days ago, conveniently, when the hotel owner was in Seattle.

Roger had now convinced Tiny that if they took the piano in the oversized freight elevator up to the mezzanine level, where the meeting and conference rooms were located, it would be possible to move it down the hallway and through the timbered cedar arch that overlooked the central dining area. Then, with any luck, it could be lowered via block and tackle into the foyer of the room.

The easy part had been getting it to the forged iron railing that surrounded the mezzanine. Tiny then scaled the hand-hewn beams that rose three and half stories to the rectangular glass enclosure that served as roof and skylight for the restaurant below. The pulley was fastened to the uppermost horizontal member of one of the beams, and the ropes were doubled and redoubled through the block. After thoroughly securing the Steinway with ample coils of two-inch nylon rope, the movers hoisted the instrument inches at a time until it just eased over the railing and floated surrealistically into the vast airspace. A guideline to keep the piano from spinning while it hung over the restaurant had been forgotten and, with nothing to hold it secure, it swung back and forth in a thirteen foot arc, all the while twirling counterclockwise. Several painters doing touchup work in the restaurant gasped as the 1200-pound heirloom, thirty feet above their heads, gave the impression of an enormous wind chime caught in a funnel cloud.

Gravity will cause any swinging object to eventually cease its motion. Unless, of course, two morons begin lowering the object, thus increasing its arc and perhaps adding just a tad more stress to an already fatigued fifty-cent chrome-plated block pin. The stainless replacement pin, a dollar-fifty item, was much too expensive to use in a "stupid" pulley even though the shear strength was ten times the cheaper version. With all the forces of nature and the universe working against them, it was inconceivable that Roger and Tiny could manage to lower Howard Bories' Steinway concert grand piano to the foyer. Yet they did. The first ten feet it was lowered in a twisting swinging motion and the last twenty were straight down at great speed as the two-inch securing pin ripped in half. The echo of 260 piano strings snapping and reverberating within the marvelous acoustics of the room is a story that became legend among the Vancouver Island Painting and Faux Finishing Corporation and truly became the strings that broke Marty's back.

CHAPTER 2

The Kenmore Air Otter, perhaps the most dependable seaplane in the world, finally nudged up against a battered fuel dock—they had arrived in Nanaimo. Bags in hand, the two trudged up the gangway (it was a very low tide) to a dilapidated metal building. The spartan nature of the hangar was in direct contrast to the smartly bedecked, if elderly, chauffeur holding the "O'Malley" placard just outside the baggage area. With a quizzical glance at Jenne, Kevin strolled up to the driver.

"I'm O'Malley. What can I do for you?"

"Sir, my name is Tony. I've been instructed to escort you and your wife up to the inn."

"Why and by whom?"

"Sir, Mr. Bories has insisted that whatever your needs may be, it is my duty to attend to them."

With a look of confusion, Kevin turned to his wife. "First he says no to our proposal, then he invites us up here and provides transportation. What gives?"

"Sir, if I may, I really can't speak to my employer's motives. It's my job to see to it that you and your wife are safely transported to the inn and that your stay is a most pleasant experience."

"Tell him we thank him for his generous offer. We had planned to rent a car here at the dock. They assured us they'd have one ready.

We thought we would drive across the island on our return and take the ferry back to the mainland."

Kevin's curiosity at this sudden largesse had been tickled, but never one to give up the privacy and independence of his own set of wheels, he turned his back on the chauffeur and navigated Jenne to the solitary car rental counter in the hangar.

"My name is O'Malley. We have a car reserved."

"I'm thorry, Mithter O'Malley, we are unfortunately out of carth at thith time." The gum-snapping, spike-haired young woman at first engendered sympathy at the perceived speech difficulty. Upon closer inspection however, this impediment could be seen to be the result of the rather large silver bauble that was speared through her tongue, and the condition was no doubt amplified by the half pouch of Big League Chew bubble gum that somehow managed to coexist in the same mouth.

With the seeds of frustration beginning to sprout along the fringes of Kevin's consciousness, his response was slightly delayed as he absorbed the impression imparted by Callie, evidently just at the beginning of her career in the auto rental industry.

"We made the reservation yesterday, a Land Rover for the week. We were assured it would be here. Why isn't it?"

"I'm thorry thir, the only information they gave me wath that all our carth, the four of them, were tranthferred latht night to Port Alberni. It mutht be thum thort of emergenthy."

"I really don't care whether there's been an emergency. We'd like our car!" O'Malley's voice had risen by several decibels.

"Thit, thir, what do you ecthepect me to do, I jutht work here!" Callie's voice began to crack.

Had it not been for Jenne's intervention, raised voices followed by tears followed by apologies would surely have been the result. As it was, she led Kevin by the arm over to the corner of the airport containing the newspaper racks. "I know you'd like to throttle little Hanna Hertz, Kev, but we both know it won't help. Why don't we take advantage of this guy with the sign and figure out what to do after we get settled at the hotel." O'Malley never ceased to be amazed at his wife's ability to say the right thing at the right time, often short-circuiting an otherwise embarrassing situation. Perhaps because it had taken him the better part of a lifetime to find her among the throngs of also-rans, he was much more willing to listen and play along with her suggestions than he might have been at an earlier, less-informed stage of life. Perhaps, too, it was because she was almost always right.

The limo was a Mercedes stretch version, a relatively new one at that. The quiet hum of the powerful twelve cylinders, the rich smell of the leather seats, and the late morning sun warming him through the automobile's windows all contributed to a significant drop in O'Malley's blood pressure. The last flurry of deadlines and the thrill of small-plane air travel had taken almost all the energy from the two designers. The frustration at the rental counter served to consume whatever little was left and, as lovely as the scenery on this rugged coast was, the O'Malleys' nodding heads soon resembled those of the little dog statues seen in twenty-year-old autos throughout the south.

At this time of the morning on the Pacific Rim Highway, where it serpentined through thousand-year-old firs and cedars, the sun filtering through the trees occasionally caused blind spots in the road ahead. Tony, the driver and a devoted servant of the Bories family for over thirty years, was used to this phenomenon and understood that if he waited a split second or so his vision would adjust to the intermittent flashes of sunlight. As the six-thousand-pound vehicle accelerated, pulling out of a switchback in the two-lane highway, an eight-point whitetail vaulted into the center of the road. Tony's very brief battle with the sunlight resulted in a slower than normal reaction to the big animal. He swerved mightily, successfully avoiding the creature. Unfortunately, the right side of the vehicle skittered on the gravel shoulder, resulting in a 180-degree spin out. When the dust settled, the engine had stalled, and they were facing the direction from which they had come. Fate was smiling on them. If the automobile had veered right, it was a fifty-foot drop to a rugged, rocky creek. The O'Malleys were slammed against their shoulder straps and thrown into each other when the rear end of the car swerved to the right. Now they were fully awake, and the only sound was the ticking of the heat off the stalled engine.

"That was close, Tony. What happened?" Kevin finally said when he'd found his voice.

"I damn near hit that buck back there and fishtailed when I swerved to miss it."

"Well, let's get this thing turned around and get out of here before someone comes around the curve and drills us."

Tony did not have to be asked twice, but in his haste to get going, he managed to flood the engine.

"Tell you what, Tony." This from Jenne. "How about we go back to the other side of that curve, and we'll flag down anyone who's on the road to make sure we don't get hit."

The couple hopped out and, keeping to the inside of the curve, hurried back in the direction they had come. Kevin removed his orange vest just in case he needed to get a driver's attention.

Monty Jennings normally loved driving the Rim Highway. He especially loved it while piloting his six-month-old fire-engine-red class-eight Peterbilt 587 sleeper. Not today, though. He was in a hurry. He had topped off his tanks when coming through Port Alberni and, while filling up, a couple of road warriors had admired his rig. Naturally he couldn't be rude to fellow truckers, so he'd taken the better part of an hour touring them over, under, inside, and out of his new tractor.

Now he was late. The trailer full of furnishings for the lodge was supposed to be there in time for them to be installed for the grand opening. That Bories character was not the kind you'd like to piss off so now he was texting him a fabricated story as to why he might be a few minutes late.

Texting him. While driving a fire-engine-red tractor trailer that, loaded up as he was, weighed eighty thousand pounds. He knew about the upcoming curve, so, no problem, he'd slow down enough to steer through it safely. Thing is, he was sitting up tall in the saddle and he too had to battle the sunlight—when he wasn't looking at his phone. Which is why he didn't see two people frantically waving an orange vest. Which is why those two people had to dive into the roadside brush to avoid imminent death. Which is also why he rounded the curve a little faster than he should have and promptly plowed into Antonio Scola and his beautiful Mercedes limousine.

CHAPTER 3

The Tofino Inn opened its doors in 1947. It became world famous because of its attention to detail, its superb continental cuisine, and the level of hospitality it provided. As often happens, the hard-working couple who had established the property and taken pride in what they'd created ultimately passed on the property to their three children. As also often happens, the three were incapable of managing the property. They were never on site, treated it like a cash cow, and chose to defer any improvements or even basic maintenance until it eventually fell into total disrepair as the twenty-first century turned the corner.

Howard Bories loathed passing up a bargain. He'd made his substantial fortune during the tech boom in the Pacific Northwest as Microsoft, Amazon, Nintendo, and Starbucks grew up and prospered beyond belief in the Seattle area. The proliferation of multiple millionaires and the M&M's (millennials with money) provided all the population needed to take up residence in the mixed-use high-rise complexes developed by the Bories Corporation.

Howard was a very wealthy man and he bored easily. With his real estate portfolio solid and most of the available property already developed, built-up, and leased, he needed a project. He had just finished *The Vancouver Wiccans*, a creepy history of a coven of witches living on the west coast of Vancouver Island. In the exploration of the island witchcraft practices, there was mention of a dilapidated hotel hugging the rocky coast in the small artist community of Tofino.

After the floatplane trip to Ucluelet and the short drive north to Tofino, Bories had surveyed a very pathetic Tofino Inn. Rooms that had previously gone for three to four hundred bucks a night back in the nineties were now offered at rates similar to Motel 6. The kitchen was not operable, and the staff was deplorable. No wonder the occupancy rate had tumbled to twenty-eight percent. There was no longer any reason to consider the Tofino Inn a destination resort. The venue, however, was spectacular.

Bories could easily imagine tourists visiting during the summer months when the weather was stunning and the night sky bright with a million stars, the gurgle of soft waves lapping up against the rocky coast. It was his genius, though, that allowed him to promote the inn during the stormy winter months. The new brochure offered guests the prospect of hunkering down in $500-a-night suites to enjoy the storm-battered coast, the thundering waves crashing into the rocky cliffs.

The thirty-million-dollar refurbishment was now almost complete. The general manager had been recruited from the Fairmont Group and the head chef had been coaxed away from a world-famous restaurant in the heart of Napa Valley. The new kitchen had the finest equipment, and the menu, already previewed by the critics, was earning praise in both Canada and the States. Advance bookings were off the charts. All Howard had to do now was make certain the damn place opened on time. Marty Menucci was inexorably edging his way to the top of Howard's shit list.

The last load of furniture should have been there hours ago. A partial text from the driver offered the prospect that all was not on schedule or perhaps something amiss.

It seemed like minutes, rather than the one or two seconds it took for the grisly sounds of the ripping, twisting, and splitting of steel and aluminum to reach Kevin's ears. Both vehicles thrashed down the steep rocky hillside and eventually rumbled to a deafening stillness.

Jenne found her voice first, although it was more of a groan than a distinct verbalization.

"What do we do now," she managed to get out.

"I don't know. Maybe we can help Tony or the guy who was driving the truck." Kevin moved a little closer to the edge of the cliff, attempting to see if there was any movement below. The view was enough to cause his stomach to lurch. The tractor trailer had flipped over. The cab had hit the rocky creek bed first, and the trailer had compressed it to almost a quarter of its original length. Only the front headlights and the distinctive Mercedes hood ornament peeked out from beneath the big rig's wreckage. Smoke, dust, and debris, still suspended in the air above the creek bed, cast a surreal haze through which he observed the devastation.

"Even if we can get down there without getting killed, I'm not sure anything we can do will help either of them now. Do you still have your cell phone with you?"

Jenne pawed through the leather pack she'd managed to drag from the limo and found it, flipped it open, and punched in 911 without a word. No service. Perfect! Fortunately, it was only minutes before another car on the way to the inn pulled up to the O'Malleys. Unfortunately, the occupants were a little suspicious of a dazed couple standing in the middle of the road ten miles from civilization without visible transportation. After convincing the two thirty-somethings, their candy-apple-red Porsche Macan Turbo strangely out of place in the prehistoric forest, that something very bad had indeed happened, it was decided Jenne would proceed to the hotel to get help. Kevin would stay behind. She climbed into the smallish back seat, thankful her two new friends, Darcy and Darryl, were kind enough to provide a lift the rest of the way.

Still a little dazed and staring as the trees whizzed by, she recalled that morning's trip from Seattle from a few short hours ago.

They had taken off from Lake Union at dawn. It was an unusually sunny day for October and the drone of the plane's engine, muffled by the mandatory earplugs, had her visualizing all that had transpired since Kevin had come into her life. As the small floatplane droned northward toward Ucluelet Harbor, the splash of early October foliage emerging from the autumn morning ground fog was truly breathtaking. While the fall colors in the Pacific Northwest couldn't hope to match those of the deciduous forests in New England, the hundreds of Puget Sound Islands added another dimension. The greens and oranges, golden khakis, lemon yellows, and burgundian purples that dotted the landscape a thousand feet below allowed the overwhelming midnight greens and blues of the firs, cedars, and sound waters to create a canvas of infinite depth. With the tapestries and textures of nature's palette slowly crawling by, Jenne's thoughts meandered back to Dr. Janet Lee, her mentor during the years she had spent at the University of Washington in their interior design program.

"The surest way to balance your color palette is to emulate what you see in nature. You'll never see two colors that don't work together if their adjacency occurs in a natural state." Dr. Lee's field trips and classes were among the most popular at UDub, and Jenne still used her teachings as the foundation for her nationally recognized work.

During the past four years, her life had taken a decided turn for the better. Maybe all that crap about "good things take time" was finally coming true. It wasn't as though she hadn't paid her dues. An on-again, off-again sixteen-year marriage to a nice but wandering guy was not a prescription for lifelong happiness and, while she had realized it somewhat early on, the pressures of career, a strong Catholic upbringing, and the fear of what was around the corner had led her to accept the status quo for all too long. Interior design had been her life. The futility of trying to become a full partner in a male-dominated, nationally recognized architectural firm hit home when she was passed up for promotion for the third time. Forget the fact that all the interiors work done by the firm was brought in by

Jenne and forget the fact that fully thirty percent of the architectural fees were driven by the client's desire to have Jenne handle the interiors portion. It was a "boy's club," after all, and the thought of having to split the profits with a touchy-feely "designer type" woman, albeit a very talented one, was beyond the comfort level of even the most liberal of the firm's partners. This rejection had planted the seeds of a commitment to leave some six years ago.

Coincidentally, or maybe not so, Jenne began visiting Ruth Loeb on a weekly basis just around the time the proverbial shit hit the fan on both the personal and the professional fronts. It had been at the suggestion of a friend who said she should "talk to someone who won't tell you only what you want to hear." Ruth turned out to be not just a therapist but a true friend who seemed really to care and had a genuine interest in the outcome of Jenne's life. It wasn't that big a stretch to learn that Jewish guilt was almost the same as Catholic guilt. The "Big Lesson" was in learning when it was a good thing and when it wasn't. Ruth had the ability to be a kind listener, when required, and, if need be, would speak her mind, almost daring Jenne to "get off your ass and make something happen."

Change came slowly at first. A separation from John—not that big a deal, he was rarely at home anyway. Lots of work, long hours, anything to make the alone times shorter. Then she'd met Kevin. He'd seemed like a nice guy, for a contractor who practiced design on the side. Scary thing was it had been two years since she'd been out with anyone not business related, and Jenne was very much afraid. To listen to her folks, going out with a divorced man was most certainly a mortal sin. A twice-divorced Catholic like Kevin, who went to church and received communion only occasionally, well hell, dating a guy like that was grounds for instant excommunication.

Not only did Kevin turn out to be a wonderful guy, he was a soul mate in the truest sense of the word. His first marriage had ended because his ex felt the grass was a little greener elsewhere and the second because he'd been on the rebound and had made a terrible mistake, fortunately a short one. Neither Jenne nor Kevin had been very anxious to get back into a relationship and so, naturally, it had happened.

Their partnership had turned out to be all that she and he had hoped one could be—natural, loving, independent, passionate, and irreverent. It was the first time in her life she'd come across someone that had the same bizarre take on life that she had. It was not uncommon for them to be out in public, clowning and laughing, and have people staring and thinking they were stoned even though they'd had nothing to drink or smoke. Even today she marveled at their good fortune in finding each other.

Coincidentally, her newfound independence had given Jenne the courage to leave her comfortable dead-end position at Marcus & Associates. The idea of Kevin and she starting a business together was discussed over dinner one night and implemented the following day. That had been three years ago, two and a half years before they were married, and they had never looked back. Business was good, almost too good. They both really needed this vacation.

"Jenne, Jenne, we're almost there, snap out of it." Darcy's shove brought her back to the present, refocusing her attention on getting some help for the crash victims. She couldn't recall a thing of their thirty-minute drive to the inn.

When they finally emerged from the rain forest, the view of the inn was breathtaking. If it hadn't been under such serious circumstances, she would have relished the panorama. The Tofino Inn was perched upon a rocky outcropping on one of the most storm-battered coasts in North America. The late afternoon sun backlit the huge rollers that exploded twenty to thirty feet high as they slammed into the slabs of stone erupting from the sand.

The manager on duty was told of the situation and hurriedly dispatched two of the on-staff security personnel and alerted the authorities. The team from the inn would get to the site much faster than the rescue brigade. Jenne chose to accompany the security men to the site of the crash.

CHAPTER 4

The only sound now was the occasional rustle of fir boughs. The adrenaline rush he'd experienced during the crash was finally easing. His down jacket was at the bottom of the cliff along with the rest of their baggage. This far north the late afternoons brought quickly dropping temperatures, and O'Malley felt a chill. The scorched tire smell was still strong in the air, and not knowing whether the two people at the bottom of the ravine were alive or dead was unnerving. He felt helpless.

The first vehicle that passed him was a '78 Ford Ranger pickup, rusted burgundy, that had oxidized over the years in large patches. The gold and orange racing stripes had peeled away except for a small tattered area on the passenger side, by the front fender. The truck tires squirted rubber as they slowed quickly coming into the curve. The driver knew the road. There were two of them. They screeched to a stop fifty yards past him and exited the cab quickly. At least someone to keep him company until help arrived. He jogged up to the driver's side of the truck.

"What are ya doin' way out here?" the driver asked.

"There was a crash, a bad one. Help is on the way but if you guys have a rope maybe we can get down to the creek and see if anyone is still alive." The driver, a short man sporting terrible acne scars, looked at his companion. The passenger, a skinny guy with week-old fuzz on his face, seemed uneasy.

"Why don't you check the toolbox in the back, Jeff. I'll take a look under the seat." It seemed like more of an order than a suggestion. The short stocky guy bent over the seat and reached under.

"How about we use this to help out." If Kevin had been able to see the driver's face, he would have seen the sneer. His entire focus, though, was on the shotgun with the large barrel that was thrust into his chest."

"Get in!"

"We need to help those people. What are you doing? Is this a robbery?"

"Get in, asshole." Another jab in the sternum with the gun.

O'Malley was squeezed into the middle of the cab. Jeff drove, and Bad Skin rode shotgun, literally, the business end stuffed into Kevin's kidney.

After making a three-point turn in the road, they headed east for five miles. Jeff slowed to a stop when they came to a logging road. Judging by the overgrowth, it was little used. He got out, dropped the cable that was used to deter off-roaders, then pulled the truck in behind the old growth until it couldn't be seen from the highway. After securing the cable once again, they continued for at least thirty minutes. The going was slow. Deep ruts, large fir limbs, and the occasional mudslide kept the effective speed to less than ten miles per hour. The trail wound severely through the big trees and undergrowth to the point where no light seemed to penetrate the canopy.

At one point O'Malley tried once again to find out what was happening, but the inquiry was met with an elbow in the gut. He was afraid, worried about his wife, and still concerned about the accident victims. But he was mostly just afraid.

When Jenne and the crew from the inn arrived back at the scene of the accident, there were several parked vehicles pulled to the side.

A few gawkers peered over the edge of the cliff to survey the carnage below.

"Did you see my husband? We left to get help and he stayed behind," Jenne asked an elderly man who appeared to be guiding the sporadic traffic around the bystanders.

"There were some folks here on the side of the road with an old pickup when we got here. When we stopped to see if they needed help, they hopped into the truck and took off. I'm pretty sure there were three of them. Then we looked over the cliff and saw the accident. Geez, what a mess! Then a couple more cars came by, so we stopped them and tried to figure out what we should do. Then you guys showed up."

"What happened to Kevin?" She focused on the forest of gigantic firs while she spoke, as if she could pick him out amid the moss-encrusted trunks of the ancient trees.

"If he was one of those three, then he's probably headed east, towards Port Alberni."

He had her full attention now. "Why would he do that? He knew we'd be right back."

"I really don't know, Miss. They just seemed like they were in a big rush."

Jenne felt a little tug in her gut. Kevin surely wouldn't leave, knowing help was on the way. And what was back in the direction they had already traveled? She pulled her cell phone from her jeans pocket and hit his speed dial number before she remembered the cell hole they were in. It would have to wait until she got back to the hotel. What a complete shit of a day!

Jenne hung around the now-crowded crash scene for several hours, hoping somehow Kevin would show up. The police, rescue brigade, and, of course, the local newspeople had arrived in the meantime. She first relayed the details of the accident to the RCMP and then found herself milling around with the rest of the lookie-loos. The rescue brigade had been able to rappel down to the carnage and, as expected, both victims were dead.

She was still in a bit of shock. First the crash, then the ride to the inn and back to the wreck site. Kevin was gone and now two dead men. Going back to the inn seemed to make the most sense. At least Kevin would know where she was. Since any car headed north on this road was either headed to the inn or was a local from Tofino, it was relatively easy to catch a ride with the next vehicle.

"My God, Ms. O'Malley, I heard about the crash. I'm so thankful that you and your husband were not injured. Did he stay at the scene?" Mr. Bories was the first to greet her when she arrived at the inn. "Poor Tony. That man has been with me since I first got into the real estate business. I'm sorry, *had* been with me. He was a dear friend and a very trusted employee. That's why I had him meet you at the airport. I trusted him completely."

"Mr. Bories, I'm a little distracted right now. Kevin was supposed to stay at the wreck site until I came back. I don't know where he is. Some people said he took off with a couple guys. I'm very worried. And, please, call me Jenne."

"All right, Jenne, and please call me Howard. I realize you're exhausted and very upset, but there are some things I need to discuss with you. If you don't mind, will you join me in the bar? I think we could both use something to drink, and this will give me an opportunity to explain why I invited you and your husband to our grand opening."

"I'm afraid I had an ulterior motive in inviting you and Kevin up here. You'll recall when I chatted with you regarding your proposal… I think it was about eighteen months ago."

"Yes, you said you liked what we proposed but that you had chosen to go with Interiors by Martin." Jenne was nothing if not competitive and it always stung to lose out on a project.

"O'Malley and Associates was always my first choice. The logistics of getting materials here, the weather, everything was made just a bit more difficult because of the geography. And there was only a small window in which to complete this project. If you'll recall, you told me that you couldn't start on my refurbishment until you finished with that private golf club you were wrapping up. I just couldn't wait for you. An acquaintance recommended Marty, and we contracted with him. Something I'll regret until the day I die. Not only has he missed his completion date by three months but the furnishings that have been installed in no way are representative of those we approved of at the final presentation.

"So… he's late enough to have cost me over three quarters of a million in missed lodging fees, and he's destroyed a two-hundred-thousand-dollar grand piano. The balance of the furniture for the remaining suites is at the bottom of a ravine, and now my most valuable employee—and my best friend—is dead. I'm afraid… I'm afraid I don't know what to do."

Jenne felt bad for the old guy. Right now, he looked every bit his age. Problem was, she was in no position to offer any consolation. "Howard, I'm sorry you're in this pickle but that still doesn't explain why you wanted us here."

"I asked you to come because two weeks ago I told Marty I was executing the penalty clause in our contract. He's on the hook for several hundred thousand. The only reason his employees are here now is because I've also held back thirty percent of the furnishings cost. The inn is 95% complete, but I'd like O'Malley and Associates to inventory the furniture and artwork, the amenity package, and the quality of the floor coverings and all the surface treatments. I suspect Martin was dealing from the bottom of the deck from the beginning, and I'd like to see how deep a hole I'm in. I'll pay you your normal hourly fee plus another twenty-five percent, and I'd like you to supply any replacement furnishings. And I don't care how long it takes. I'm sorry to put it like this, but fuck Marty. He's made a complete cock-up of this place, and I'll be damned if I'll let him get away with it. Please say you'll help?"

"Geez, Howard, you really are in a mess aren't you? The only thing we know about Interiors by Martin is that the owner's a bit sketchy. The scuttlebutt is he promises one thing but delivers another. He's also been rumored to supply items that don't meet specifications. We've heard that many of the fabrics he uses won't even meet existing fire rating requirements, much less be of high enough quality for commercial use."

"So, will you take the job?"

"Kevin and I make these decisions together. Right now, my husband is missing. When we find him, we'll talk about this. I'm thinking there's a good chance we can help you, but, shit, Howard, help me find my goddam husband, then we'll worry about the mess you're in."

CHAPTER 5

While the pickup bumped and bounced over logging roads, game trails, and occasional footpaths, Kevin tried to put aside his fear. Two years as a junior officer, stateside, in the army had contributed only marginally in preparing him for an actual confrontation with real bad guys. The dialogue between his captors had dwindled from scarce to nothing, and the quiet had given O'Malley a chance to catch his breath.

It seemed that the guy with the bad skin, Donnie, was the one in charge. The fellow driving was too insecure and just a little bit scared, probably just taking orders. He apparently wasn't all that familiar with driving through the forests of the Pacific Northwest because the skin over the knuckles of his hands gripping the steering wheel was transparent. The furtive looks thrown Donnie's way convinced Kevin that he had only one person to worry about. As they negotiated a hairpin to avoid a fallen Doug fir, Jeff glanced at Donnie, perhaps for approval of his driving.

Because the two miscreants were looking at each other, neither saw the huge brown bear that had wandered into the center of the worn two-track that served as their road. Kevin had a half second to brace himself before the old truck plowed into the mid-section of the enormous animal. At seven miles per hour, the damage to both the truck and the bear was minimal. The shock at having annoyed such a fearsome creature, however, was significant. Along with polar bears, brown bears are the largest of all the bear species. The browns—grizzlies and Kodiaks—can exceed 1500 pounds and can stand nine feet tall on their hind legs. The one they had just hit looked like it weighed 1600 pounds, and it was pissed.

It bellowed a terrifying roar while slamming its front paws through the driver and passenger-side windows simultaneously. Donnie and Jeff were toast. A paw full of five-inch claws dismantled the right side of Donnie's head and throat. Blood spurted nonstop. No longer were the acne scars going to be a problem.

Jeff was a little luckier. The claws on the driver's side shattered the window and two of them continued directly into his left temple, breaking one off four inches into his temporal lobe. No screaming, just instant lights out.

Sitting cramped between two knuckleheads while being kidnapped wasn't his preferred position. In this case, though, it was the only thing that saved O'Malley's life. The bear effortlessly flipped the pickup on its side then shoved it over on its roof. His head slammed down onto the roof just as the bear clawed what remained of Donnie out through the passenger window. There were no longer any sounds coming from the body. Hopefully, he was gone. With a single chomp to the right shoulder, the brown grabbed Donnie and lumbered down the dirt road with him, perhaps to keep as a late-night snack.

Kevin was in shock. He was upside down in the truck, a dead man next to him, blood and gore everywhere. That residual putrid musky smell of bear was overwhelming.

Dazed and confused, but thrilled to still be alive, O'Malley crawled out through the passenger-side window. He stumbled away from the wreckage, not caring which way he was headed as long as it was away from his accidental savior.

After an hour of half running, half wandering, Kevin slowed to get his bearings which, of course, he couldn't. He did know he was somewhere within the vast Pacific Rim National Park.

This incredibly diverse territory extends from the west coast inland to the center of the island, and includes Port Alberni, Ucluelet, and Tofino. During this early fall season, the rugged coastal forests seemed to be rehearsing for the wet stormy winter that was around the corner. Fifty inches of rain, wind gusts exceeding 100 miles per hour, and thirty-eight-degree temperatures were commonplace during the November through January rainy season. It took these extreme weather conditions to shape and maintain this almost prehistoric forested region. Some of the trees were over 800 years old; they were over 200 years old when young Chris Columbus discovered the "New World." During one storm in the late nineties, over half the old growth trees were smashed by gusts over 120 miles per hour.

This time of year, the nighttime temperatures hovered in the low forties. That, combined with the dampness, sapped any reservoir of heat that remained in his body.

At another time, the raw beauty of the place would have been jaw dropping. Right now, it was just fucking freezing, and Kevin couldn't have cared less about how big the trees were. He had been slipping, sliding, climbing, and—rarely—walking through the mushy fir and cedar needles for twenty-four hours straight. All night long he had trudged, and the dawn finally arrived, overcast and dreary. He'd been certain there were more logging roads crisscrossing the entire forest. Not so. He had yet to find one that might be his ticket back to what passed as civilization here on this, the world's forty-second largest island.

The garb he was wearing did not equip him to combat the elements. His New Balance cross-trainers, with the rocker sole, were trashed, wet, and muddy. His Indigo Palms jeans had gotten ripped in blackberry brambles, and they were coated in mud from the knees down. His Façonnable Albert Goldberg–designed bomber was no longer stylish, just wet and torn.

The shock of seeing two men mauled by a mammoth bear had worn off. Nothing left but cold, hunger, and thirst. Every time he thought he saw something familiar, it turned out not to be. He figured he couldn't have been more than four or five miles from the main road when they ran into the bear. Problem was, if he had hoofed it in the wrong direction, after prying himself from the pickup, it might be double that now.

Was it only yesterday that he and Jenne had left Lake Union? For twelve years, the longest vacation he'd taken was a four-day weekend over the Fourth of July some three years ago. Now, since all the big projects were in the mopping-up stage, Kevin and his bride of six months had shut down the phones, boarded the dog, and given the employees some time off. Even though their destination was one of those jobs that the other guys got, the Tofino Inn and Spa had gotten enough press and publicity that his curiosity was piqued. His competitive nature along with just a touch of professional envy had gotten the better of him, and the opportunity to stay at the newly renovated hotel, gratis, when the fall weather was at its best, was too much to pass up.

He remembered Jenne hunkered down over the drawing table, putting some finishing touches on the stone pieces that would surround the centerpiece of the downtown Seattle hotel.

The sight of Jenne—pronounced "Jenny" but long ago changed because the "e" as the last letter was more symmetrical, after all— putting pencil to paper was always moving to Kevin. He'd met her when she'd headed up the interior design division of one of Seattle's leading architectural firms. His first conscious recollection of her was of her focused, frowning as she discovered some new little transition problem, smiling as she solved it, all the while drawing lines, erasing others, and brushing the rubber crumbs from the transparency to the floor. They had only been a couple for three and a half years, but he was sure it was to be for the rest of his life. The softness and yearning in his gut that almost buckled his knees when he glanced her way was but another subtle confirmation of this fact.

Kevin sat for a minute on a fallen cedar. God, he was exhausted! While he wasn't a gym rat, he still managed to work out several days a week. That combined with walking eighteen holes three times a week kept him in reasonably good shape for a guy in his early fifties. His status as a physical powerhouse was now being tested by extreme conditions.

He remembered an emergency responder on a talk radio show had said, "The first thing a person should do when faced with an emergency is nothing." Real easy, unless the emergency is a giant, stinking, pissed-off bear. The responder elaborated, "Take stock of the situation and the surroundings, assess and evaluate, make a plan and execute it."

Good advice. Maybe 24 hours late to recall it but still, good advice.

Okay. I'm lost in a forest on Vancouver Island, and my wife is probably coming unglued worrying. I'm cold, thirsty, and hungry, and I want to avoid really big fucking animals. Maybe something to drink first, food can wait. Then I can plan.

As part of the assessment process, O'Malley remembered that during his ride through the forest with the two kidnappers, they had traveled predominately uphill. During the last 24 hours he had been walking both up and downhill meaning he was probably walking parallel to the highway, not towards it. Downhill then, a plan! In the quiet solitude of his reevaluation, he realized that another sound intruded.

Maybe it was because he had stopped to assess things or perhaps he was just becoming more aware of his surroundings, but Kevin heard the faint gurgling of a stream. He lurched hurriedly through the woody debris, needles, and salal up over a small rise and then promptly tripped and tumbled fifteen feet or so down a gentle slope. He came to rest with one leg submerged in a rushing mountain stream, ten or twelve feet wide at most. The good news, it was fresh water to drink. The bad, it was absolutely freezing.

The stream was only three feet at its deepest, so drowning was not a concern. O'Malley knelt and gulped as much of the cold clear elixir as he could between breaths. After the deafening crash of branches during the fall, all was eerily still now, save for the rushing creek waters.

For no other reason than handy drinking water, Kevin thought it best to follow the stream for the time being. It was easy at first but occasionally a fallen snag blocked the way, requiring a detour for a spell.

It was at the end of one of these detours, while navigating back towards the creek, that he saw movement at the water's edge. Something was moving in the brush. It was not too big, but not small either. As he crept closer, he saw it. When he did, he realized his miscalculation. He had stayed close to the water because it gave him some direction but mostly so he had something to drink. Hmmmm, same reason the animals of the forest showed up here. A medium-sized bear—a black one this time—and her two cubs were clawing fish from the bank of the stream.

This mama bear was only a third of the size of the killer that had forced him on this journey. It was still a powerful creature though. Having lived in Washington for many years, he'd had some exposure to black bears. Hell, he'd even come across them on the golf course. They basically ignore humans. If they're not cornered or threatened or surprised, they were happy to be on their way, looking for food almost always. While the little family was busy fishing, Kevin managed to negotiate his way around the area, picking up the stream again several hundred yards away.

The late morning eased into early afternoon. He was exhausted and physically depleted. He was so used to hearing the rushing of the stream that he almost missed the faint crunch of gravel under tires. It sounded as though it was close by but the thick underbrush that ran along the banks made visibility difficult. It seemed it was coming from the other side of the stream. With renewed energy and whatever residual adrenaline his body could muster, he plowed through the icy water, up the opposite bank, through the brush and blackberries, and plowed into the front right fender of a white Chevy pickup. His initial shock and concern were assuaged when he saw "Parks Canada" stenciled on the passenger door.

"Whoa there, buddy, you ok?" The passenger riding with his window down looked shocked as well. "What are you doing out here dressed like that this time of year?"

"Would you mind terribly if I joined you inside. I've got a little story to tell you."

It took some time, but O'Malley managed to get the whole story out. The two rangers were on a routine pass through this section of the park when the intrepid explorer crashed into their truck. They were more than skeptical when told about the giant bear massacre. "We get a few grizzlies around here but 90% of the bears are black. The grizzlies sometimes swim over during the summer months. What you described almost sounds like a Kodiak, and I've never seen one in the park. For certain they're not native to the area."

"All I can tell you is it was brown and very fucking big. I'll show you where the truck is if you'll help me get my bearings."

After the rangers drove out to the highway, Kevin was able to direct them to the logging road that his two pals had taken. They went through the makeshift gate and after a dozen minutes or so they arrived at the scene of the carnage. The old Ford was still upside down. What was left of Jeff were just some bits and pieces. The creatures of the forest were very efficient at cleaning things up. The inside of the cab was splattered with blood, gore, and remnants of the fine meal had by the Pacific Rim Park dwellers.

"Holy shit! You weren't kidding."

"Told you."

"Jim, have you ever seen anything like this?" Jim was the ranger driving the truck. He was also the guy heaving on the other side of the truck. After a few coughs and a sleeve wipe, he was able to croak, "Nope, can't say that I have."

Joey, Jim's sidekick, was still a little stunned. "So how did you manage to escape?"

"The bear—the big one I mentioned—was preoccupied with Donnie. I kept quiet and was able to crawl out through the window. I made it a point to move very quickly in the opposite direction the bear took."

"Looks like we're gonna have to get some Mounties over here to button things up." Joey looked a little glassy-eyed himself. "How about we get you up to the inn, and we can radio the police on the way. Doesn't look like anything more is gonna happen here. Whatever kinda bear did this may want to come back for seconds, and I don't wanna be on the menu."

CHAPTER 6

Joey and Jim dropped O'Malley off at the porte cochere. He half fell, half tripped through the massive fir doors leading into the reception area of the inn.

"I need to find my wife" was all he could muster to the young receptionist on duty. If she was taken aback by his appearance, her training at some of the finest hotels in the States served her well.

"Welcome to the Tofino Inn, sir. If you'll give me your name and room number, I'll be happy to help."

"I don't know my room number, but my wife must have already checked in. Maybe early yesterday. I've had a bit of a mishap; my name is O'Malley."

"Oh, Mr. O'Malley, we're so happy to see you. We heard about the accident, then you disappeared and, oh geez, Mr. Bories will be very happy you're here. I'm pretty sure your wife is having coffee in the lounge; she was quite worried about you."

Kevin headed off through the ruggedly handsome lobby through the darkened entry to Chesterman's, the bar, named after the adjacent coastal beach.

It was late afternoon and the only lights in the place were small pendants over the booth tables. There were only two occupied booths in the bar. The closest one held a young couple speaking with either an English or Aussie accent. He never could tell the difference. The other patron was seated in the farthest corner of the room, slumped against the banquette on the back wall. She looked very worried—very beautiful but very worried. Her hazel eyes were glued to her smartphone. He remembered the first time they met. She had just come from a presentation and they were supposed to discuss the appropriate furnishings for her client. She was thirty feet away, but her smile was ten thousand watts. A tomboy who'd grown up with two older brothers, she was very comfortable with decision makers, whether they were women *or* men. If anyone were foolish enough to dismiss her empathetic smile for compliance, they were sadly mistaken. Her Croatian/Irish ancestry had been very kind to her. Her olive complexion, sparkling inquisitive eyes, and full lips always resulted in a few turned heads.

Great looks, better at most sports—not golf—than he was, a lesser person would be insecure. What the hell *was* she doing with him? Okay, not the time…

As he hurriedly crossed the room, bam, there was that smile again. It was always just a slight gut punch.

"Kevin, thank God. Where the hell have you been? You look awful, what happened?"

"Well, after you left the accident scene I thought I'd take a walk in the woods. You know, just to enjoy nature."

"Cut the crap, asshole. Tell me what happened." Apparently, no more sympathy would be forthcoming.

And so, he did. It took some time and two shots of Dalwhinnie with one ice cube, please. The deeper into the saga he got, the lower Jenne's jaw dropped.

"You're making this up, right?"

"The nature walk I made up. All the rest is true. The thing I can't figure out is why the hell these guys kidnapped me. I'm a freaking designer, not a spy or something."

"Could they have mistaken you for someone else? Maybe they wanted to just rob you."

"If it was just a robbery, they could have mugged me on the side of the road. This had to be something else. They were taking me somewhere for some reason but, for the life of me, I can't imagine what."

After another hour of batting ideas around and a couple of Wagyu cheeseburgers, for which the restaurant was famous, Kevin was toast. The glass of Turnbull Cab was still half-full, and he was fading fast.

"Kevin, let's get you back to the room and hit the sack. I think we should hook up with Bories first thing tomorrow. He's got some issues of his own to discuss, and he seems to know most of the locals around here, so maybe he can help us understand what happened."

"What a great idea, hon. I know you're going to be disappointed though. It's our first night here in this fancy new inn, and I'm too exhausted even for hotel sex."

"I'm crushed, Kevin, but somehow I think I'll manage to get over it. If you behave yourself, it's possible something can be arranged a little later in the week."

The next morning was Saturday. It arrived chilly, but crystal clear. The only sound they could hear was the ever-present pounding of the breakers out on Chesterman Beach. What was to be a leisurely breakfast with Bories was postponed by an early visit from one of the RCMP detectives, a Sergeant Preston. Apparently word had surfaced that Kevin was the only surviving member of a fatal bear attack two days prior.

Another opportunity to tell his story. This was getting tiresome. But the sergeant seemed less interested in the bear attack than why he'd ended up with the two bad guys in the first place.

"I have no earthly idea what they wanted," Kevin said. "All I can say is they seemed to know who I was, and they were taking me someplace for some reason."

"You should know that we've had these guys on our radar for a while. I'm sure you're aware Tofino is a very small town, and Ucluelet is even smaller. These two were seen at Jack's Pub a few times and, according to Jack, they didn't mix well with others. In fact, a week ago this Donnie character had to be escorted out after getting into a shoving match with one of the regulars. They showed up about a month ago. Nobody knows exactly where they live but that is understandable. I can't tell you how many cabins are sprinkled throughout this forest. They're all pretty much off the grid, so we wouldn't necessarily know how long they've been here. They've been seen at the local grocery a few times over the last month as well.

"We have a couple of guys following that logging road where the attack happened. If they come up with something or I can think of any other questions, I'll be in touch."

With that, Sergeant Preston was out the door. Ten minutes later Howard Bories arrived.

"It's such a relief to see you, Kevin. When I heard you'd gone missing I was very concerned."

"*Why* were you so concerned, Mr. Bories? We barely know each other?"

"Well, a lot has happened here over the last few months or so, only some of which I've shared with Jenne here. And please call me Howard. My reason for inviting you to our grand opening wasn't entirely altruistic, I'm afraid."

"What are you talking about?"

"I've told Jenne about my misgivings over Interiors by Martin and the mess they've made of things here. What I've yet to disclose are the other issues we have had to deal with ever since Marty's crew has been here on site."

"Go on…"

"Your wife can fill you in on the shoddy follow-through by Martin and what I'd like you to do to help. What I haven't told her is that I've had some past dealings with Martin Menucci."

"Then why would you ever do business with him again?" This was from Jenne.

"About six or seven years ago, I helped develop a small medical office building in Pacific Grove. It really wasn't up my alley, but a good friend was one of the landowners, and he asked for my assistance. We hired a reputable Bay Area architect, and they engaged the services of PG Associates, a local firm they tasked with the interior design duties. As it turned out, Menucci did all the purchasing for the firm. Since I was just consulting on the project, I had very little to do with the weekly construction meetings nor did I take part in any of the materials approval process.

"When I decided to take on this Tofino project, I was very pressed for time. I needed a company that could implement the design and handle the procurement. I was contacted by Martin, who had subsequently formed a new company, Interiors by Martin. He said they were available on short notice. All this, as you know, took place about a year and a half ago."

"Wait a minute," said Kevin. "I remember we were doing a remodel at a small inn in Carmel around that time. PG Associates was originally involved in the project, but the inn owner had some reservations about them handling the procurement phase. She told us she'd heard some pretty bad things about the person heading up their purchasing. Are you telling me that was Menucci?"

"It appears so. Even worse, my friend who owns the medical building was up to visit about three months ago. He complained that the five-year-old building in PG was a mess. The flooring was buckling, the lighting had to be replaced, and they've hired a new outfit to replace all the furniture and artwork. Naturally, after hearing this, I felt like a complete fool. That was when I invited you two up here. That was also when I put Martin on notice."

Many of the other guests were showing up for brunch. The activities here in Tofino were primarily beach walking and gallery visiting. The hotel even provided Wellies and umbrellas for those adventurous enough to brave the frequent rain and wind during a stroll up Chesterman Beach. The remoteness of the inn made it a perfect couples getaway. Now, with the refurbishment nearly complete, the full spreads in *Condé Nast* and *Travel and Leisure* were already generating phenomenal interest. The staff was doing an excellent job of keeping Howard's troubles under wraps.

Bories focused on what remained of his coffee. "What I haven't told you is very confidential. The only people who know this are my general manager and the local police."

Both O'Malleys looked at each other, then back at Howard. He looked as though he had reached some sort of crossroads.

"Over the last month, while Marty's crew has been installing the artwork and furnishings, we have been exposed to a number of unsavory characters. Martin has them under contract to complete this job."

"What's the big deal?" asked Jenne, "Moving furniture isn't exactly a job for Mensa candidates. There's always one or two rough characters on these crews."

"I've no quarrel with tradespeople or blue-collar workers. I have worked with all kinds of folks on my other endeavors. These people are just a little on the scary side."

"How so?" This from Kevin.

"I can't really define it. They seem nice enough, but they speak very quietly, and not very often. They dress appropriately and show up on time. Many of the local employees have complained about even being around them while they're here on site. They say these guys give them the creeps. Lots of staring but very little dialogue. Lately, several personal belongings have been reported missing by our staff. That's why I've contacted the police."

The O'Malleys gave each other a quick glance and an eyeroll. "Sorry, Howard, it seems like you're making a big deal out of nothing. Sure, Martin's an asshole. He's tried to rip you off, and we'll be happy to work with you to make things right, but this suspicion of his crew seems a bit paranoid. And we've still no idea why I was kidnapped."

Bories now looked every bit his age, and Jenne felt bad for the old guy. "Tell you what, Howard. We'll hang around for a couple of days. We'll check out the crew; I think they're still finishing up hanging the artwork. If we get bad vibes from these guys, we'll let you know. In the meantime, we'll keep in touch with the cops to see if they come up with anything. Also, just maybe we can take a little time to enjoy this place. It's been a very tough couple of days."

CHAPTER 7

Martin Menucci was currently enveloped by a buttery soft leather armchair imported from Italy. This iconic specimen was designed by the renowned Danish designer Jens Risom. With this quality of leather, one of these babies would ring the register at over eight thousand dollars. The lobby lounge here at the Valley Inn just off Carmel Valley Road sported thirty of these beauties. As comfortable as he was, he was still mildly pissed off that he hadn't been the purveyor who'd provided the furnishings. Still, though, the damn thing was incredibly comfortable.

Marty loved this place and the utter solitude here in the early afternoon. He loved the hand-scraped walnut floors, the zinc-topped bar, and the rustic knee-high mesquite coffee tables that were surrounded by these wonderful chairs. He especially loved the smell of the place. Today it was a sunny seventy degrees and the lounge was open to the magnificent gardens on the courtyard side of the property. The aroma of the blood-red bougainvillea, fifteen foot high birds-of-paradise, and pockets of star jasmine and lavender invaded the place. Mix that with leather, scotch, and whatever else was behind the bar and he'd be happy never to leave. If he stayed through the afternoon into the evening, the guests would start showing up and, later still, the jazz trio would arrive.

"Trent, bring me one more Bulleit Rye, neat. Then I gotta get going."

"Sure thing, Marty. I'll put it on the tab."

He'd been coming here for over three years, now. When the shit hit the fan, as it often did, he needed some alone time, somewhere to think. The Valley Inn was a little on the spendy side but that never bothered him. About eight miles east of Carmel, the inn was an island of tranquility in the heart of central California's wine country. Marty'd had nothing to do with the design or furnishing of the inn, and it showed. It was impeccably executed. Even though he was a con man and a shyster, he still understood and appreciated a quality product.

Menucci was rail thin, six feet tall, and leaning on fifty. He had the olive skin of his Tuscan ancestors, and his fondness for all foods Italian never seemed to put any weight on the man. He'd gotten his start in the design business as a "rag picker," a term of endearment given to those who sold, made, or represented textile manufacturers or jobbers to the design industry. After a dozen years in the business, moving from manufacturer to importer and then back again, he acquired the necessary contacts to strike out on his own. As an independent rep, he managed to pick up some mainstream lines as well as a few obscure offshore lines that were cheap knockoffs. It was the low cost for the latter that allowed him to more than triple the price to his customers. That none of these products met current fire codes or abrasion tests never concerned Marty. After all, by the time something terrible happened, he'd be on to another project.

He'd been successful enough to stash away a modest nest egg and then thought it prudent to expand his graft. But first he had to learn the ropes. It was easy talking himself into a job as a resource librarian with a small interior design firm in Pacific Grove. He knew the textile industry inside and out. He was a natural. The sheer number of products used on any given design scheme was immense. From furniture to artwork to fabrics to exercise equipment to audio visual equipment, not to mention window coverings and treatments, as well as floor coverings and signage and lighting and on and on. So while he had a good handle on the fabric aspects, there was still an awful lot to absorb. As a resource librarian, Marty was responsible for meeting with reps and keeping the design staff up to date on new and evolving trends in the industry. This position nationwide is filled over ninety-five percent by women, mostly fresh out of interior design school. Of the small percentage of men in the occupation, most were gay. Marty was neither. If anything, the man was asexual. His raison d'être was money. Everything else took a back seat. His dedication to learning his craft became legendary.

His singular focus on learning the business endeared him to the principals of PG Associates and their entire design team. His resource management contributed, in no small way, to the rapid growth of the company. Once a mom-and-pop operation, the firm now counted several high-profile hospitality clients, as well as a significant residential portfolio of the rich and famous. The design firm's fees had doubled over the two and a half years of Menucci's tenure. It was Martin's idea to expand the services of the firm from strictly design and consulting to include purchasing. He convinced Shelly and Vicky, the owners, that by offering procurement services, they could easily double or triple revenues. He also convinced them that they would be best served if he were to lead the parade. What could possibly go wrong?

At the outset Marty was indeed a star. A small hotel in Monterey, then a bistro in San Francisco, followed by a director's home in Montecito lent credence to his promises. The furnishings were first class, beautiful and durable, with a reasonable markup. Revenues were up. Both clients and PG Associates were very happy. It was Polly's Bistro in Santa Barbara that started things down the wrong path.

Marty felt that two hundred plus miles was far enough away to avoid any repercussions. Instead of shipping the specified dining chairs from Italy at a sell price of fifteen hundred per piece, he substituted a Chinese knock-off at the same sell price. The cost went from eleven hundred to five-fifty each. Forty chairs at five-fifty less cost meant twenty K in Old Marty's pocket. Since he was writing the checks and he had a pal at the importer, he just had the guy cut him back a personal check. Nice! And so, it began....

One under-the-table transaction led to another. In no time, Menucci had squirreled away nearly 100K. Also, in no time, word began to leak that some of the furnishings supplied by PG Associates were not up to spec. Twelve months after the grand opening of Polly's in Santa Barbara, a patron was injured. A rather rotund customer, a forty-something hedge-fund manager, had just bellied up to the bar, planting himself onto the nicely tanned leather swivel barstool.

Had this been the specified stool, the joints would have been doweled, blocked, and glued, the legs reinforced with steel rods. Unfortunately, these unseen fortifying embellishments would have added almost $550 to each piece.

It began as a tiny squeak. Then, as the gentleman leaned over to grasp his mojito, the squeak morphed into a crack, the same crack heard from "Boomstick" Nelson Cruz's bat as another baseball left the yard at 115 mph exit velocity. As the big fellow sprawled on the floor, head up against the footrail, it was obvious the man was accustomed to the tavern life. A small cut above his left ear, a mild sprain in his left wrist, and, yet, astonishingly, his right hand still managed to grip his mojito, only half-full now but still drinkable.

Polly—Polly really did own the place—was pissed. The customer was a kind-hearted soul and, with promises of free mojitos for the foreseeable future and paid medical copays for his injuries, he agreed not to sue. The stool in question was now kindling. The other twelve were removed immediately. Polly was on the phone to PG Associates the next day, and Martin Menucci was dismissed that afternoon. Shelly and Vicky agreed to replace the entire furniture package at Polly's. They then began the arduous task of researching every single purchase order ever written under Marty's watch.

"Trent, one more and, really, this is the last one." Marty, marginally inebriated at this point, was ruminating about the state of his business and how things had evolved to this point. The Tofino project had started out nicely. He'd managed to switch most of the specified furnishings to offshore knockoffs. Had there been no hiccups he would have pocketed a cool 100K. Now, with having to replace the piano, even if he got the money Bories was withholding, he'd barely break even.

Roger and Tiny had been with him for the better part of a year but the rest of the crew were Vancouver Island locals. Roger had managed to get a referral from his cousin in Nanaimo. One thing led to another and they recruited four able-bodied gentlemen from Port Alberni. He had only been on site a couple of times. He had left the management of the crew up to Roger, a decision for which he was paying dearly.

The four locals he'd hired seemed to be hard workers and they were well behaved. For some reason they generated a bit of unease with Marty. He was not unusually sensitive, nor did he have much awareness of other folks. Martin was genuinely narcissistic, perhaps only surpassed by a famous member of the Mar-a-Lago club in Palm Beach. So, for him to be even mildly aware of some sinister element of his local crew was remarkable.

The Tofino Inn was a setback. He'd lost out on the remodel of the Del in Coronado. He'd also missed out on the new Black Desert Resort in St George, Utah. It seemed the word on the street was that Interiors by Martin was a bad bet. Word had leaked about the Polly's mishap. He still had Magruder's in Scottsdale, though, an upscale 150-seat restaurant featuring steaks and chops. The only reason he had that job was because he was available on short notice and had the contacts to supply the furnishings with only a three-month lead time.

Still, the thought of peeling off a good chunk of cash from Magruder's and stuffing it in his Bermuda account was encouraging. The rye was dulling the pain. He'd make one more trip up to Vancouver Island, get rid of the crew up there and, screw it, he'd give Roger and that moron Tiny their walking papers as well. He'd hire some local talent in Phoenix to install the restaurant. Marty was content now that a plan was in place. Maybe he could even convince that prick Bories to release more of his money. He gulped the last of his drink, had the valet pull up his Tesla S, fully charged, and began the trek back to his condo in Carmel. Life was good.

CHAPTER 8

Jordan was upset. He'd never agreed with the kidnapping thing. He'd have been happy just getting paid for moving and installing the furniture. He told them it was a bad idea but, no, the pompous fucker always knew better. He and his mates couldn't wait to get away from this place, far away. They rarely came to the west side of the island. Nanaimo was home. Returning to DeCourcy Island was his obsession. He'd known his three colleagues most of his life and trusted them implicitly. The other two, Donnie and Jeff, were new to the Twelves, having just recently arrived. Jordy wasn't too sure about them, but he hadn't seen nor heard from them for a few days.

He'd seen Bories talking to O'Malley over brunch so either the two new recruits had fucked up the snatch or they'd never gotten around to it. Anyway, not his problem. They'd be done with the artwork in two more days. Hopefully that Marty jerk would show up, pay them, and they'd be outta here. They would have to report to Wilson and Daniel when they got to Nanaimo. The pricks would take half their earnings but that was okay as long as they could catch the next boat to DeCourcy. Then they would be among their own. Maybe they'd even be granted a visit with Brother XII.

The O'Malleys took the opportunity to stroll Chesterman Beach after their meeting with Bories. While they both felt there were certainly strange goings-on in Tofino, there was no doubt that Mother Nature had done some of her finest work here. Perhaps that was why many of the local artists chose landscapes and First Nation subjects to study. They stopped at the Roy Henry Vickers gallery. Roy was a world famous First Nations artist, and this spectacular habitat was the inspiration for much of his work. Roy's prints and paintings were unique. They were both spiritual and magical. Any exposure to his artistry remained tucked away in a small corner of the mind, easily accessed when most needed in times of stress, a truly special talent.

They returned to their suite in the late afternoon, took a nap, fooled around, and then returned to the bar for cocktails. Now, they could come up with a plan of action…they hoped.

"I think we should let the Mounties do their thing and not worry about why you were kidnapped. We can survey the furnishings, check out this mysterious crew, and come up with some sort of estimate to present to Howard." Jenne seemed to have organized her thoughts nicely.

"Makes sense to me. Although, I'm still a little uneasy about why those clowns decided to abduct me."

"Sergeant Preston told Bories he should have something to report by tomorrow morning. Maybe then we'll be able to rest a little easier."

"Okay. How about we take a stroll through the rest of the lobby and the first floor? We'll be able to get some idea what we're up against here."

It appeared most of the furnishings were well designed but that was only because they *were* knockoffs. In a commercial environment like this, they wouldn't last out the year. They'd have to be replaced. The artwork, on the other hand, was very well done.

"I bet he farmed out the art package to someone locally. There's no way Marty could have done this. It's too good. The giclées, the mats, the framing, all of it is professional. And those guys doing the hanging seem to be on top of things as well. The pieces are security mounted, well-spaced, and level. Go figure, they must know what they're doing." Kevin surmised that in this artist community, there was ample talent for delivering this product. Score one for Marty; apparently the man wasn't entirely without merit. "I'll bet he figured he wouldn't be able to fool the Tofino locals when it comes to artwork. Well, I agree, he was right."

"Let's call it a night, Kev. The crew will be finishing up in the morning. We can check up on them then, see if we can figure out what about them bugged Howard."

The next morning arrived drizzly and dark, not an uncommon occurrence during late October on Vancouver Island. When the O'Malleys strolled into the restaurant at eight o'clock, the sky had transformed from a flat black to a cold blue-gray, suggesting that sunglasses would not be required today. A breakfast of scrambled eggs, Canadian bacon (of course), and fresh-squeezed orange juice, polished off with an exquisite latte, fortified them for the day's challenges.

"Ya know, we're on the clock, Jenne, so we can write off some of these travel expenses."

"You've been kidnapped, escaped a bear attack that eviscerated two people, been lost in the woods, and seen two other people killed in an accident, and the first thought you have today is that we can save fifty bucks on our taxes? You are an amazing man, Kevin. You're probably from another planet but, still, truly amazing."

"Yes, darling, and that's why we make such a great team. I take care of the stupid trivial shit and you pretty much handle all the other stuff. It's perfect!"

With that, the designing duo began their probe into the strange crew hanging art in the Tofino Inn.

After inspecting the balance of the eighty-room inn and an occasional sly observation of the art crew, they proceeded to their two o'clock huddle with Bories.

"The crew seems to be doing a very acceptable job, Howard. Kev and I tried to engage them in a little conversation but other than a dismissive grunt they wanted nothing to do with us. Almost like they spoke a foreign language."

"Yes, that's the same feeling my staff has described. I'll be glad when they're gone. I told you that some of the guests have reported some missing items but nothing of any value, so after they finish up I think I'll just let sleeping dogs lie. I'll tell the police just to let it go."

"Probably for the best, Howard. Sorry we couldn't shed any more light on the subject. Jenne and I are getting one of your crew to take us down to Ucluelet in the morning. We'll catch the noon flight to Seattle. We have some other projects in the works, but we'll still be able to get right on with the replacement of your FF and E. Some of it will be fine, but we think about seventy to eighty percent of it should be replaced. At least that will get you over any inspection hurdles, and you'll be able to avoid any future lawsuits."

"That sounds like an excellent plan, Kevin. I can't thank you and Jenne enough for taking this on. I'll take care of all your expenses here at the inn, and your car and flight are on me as well."

"That's very generous, Howard, we really appreciate it. You'll hear something from us in the next couple of weeks. By the way, did you hear anything from Sergeant Preston? It's still got me wondering what that was all about."

Bories seemed to have just remembered something. "Of course. I meant to tell you straightaway. The Mounties followed the logging road another three miles to an abandoned hunting shack. They think there were provisions there for several people to last a week or so. By the time they got there, the bears had had a field day with things, garbage all over the place. If there was anything there to provide any clues as to who these guys were, it's long gone now. They're chalking the abduction up to a couple of rogue characters trying to score some sort of ransom."

"That doesn't seem to make much sense, Howard. They apparently knew who I was and, if that was the case, they'd have known we're not wealthy people."

"You'll get no argument from me, Kevin. Suffice it to say, those two unfortunates are no longer with us. Their motivations will probably remain a mystery now that there's no one left to question."

"Hey, Kev, maybe the bear knows something," Jenne added.

"Okay, Howard, looks like we're outta here. When my wife starts this crap, I know she's ready to close the cover on this chapter. We'll be in touch and, really, thanks for picking up the tab."

CHAPTER 9

After the O'Malleys departed, Bories retired to his two-thousand-square-foot owner's suite. Now that he was alone, he allowed himself to relax. At his age, with what was going on, his blood pressure medication was having difficulty keeping up. At least momentarily, he felt release from this pressure cooker of his own creation.

Howard's cover story of discovering the property by researching the Wiccans on Vancouver Island was accurate. What he'd also discovered while researching cults and strange groups in this corner of Canada was the history of the Aquarian Foundation.

Edward Wilson was a British mariner from Birmingham. During the mid-1920s, with the planet reeling from the dual catastrophes of World War One and the Spanish flu pandemic, Wilson embarked on a visit to France. While there he experienced a vision of a glowing Egyptian ankh, the hieroglyphic symbol meaning "life." Subsequently, he felt he was in contact with the "Great White Lodge," a panel of twelve mystical masters who controlled the human race. Wilson felt he was the disciple of this group and took the name Brother XII.

He traveled extensively, producing a manifesto and giving speeches. Soon wealthy patrons in Europe and the United States were attracted to this charismatic individual. After all, he promised a new race would rise from the detritus of the existing world. At its height, the Aquarian

Foundation counted eight thousand members among its flock. Most of these patrons were recruited from other groups with ties to the occult.

Brother XII wrote to his followers that a settlement was to be established in British Columbia. And so, it was. The small colony was established in Cedar by the Sea, an isolated area southeast of Nanaimo on the east coast of Vancouver Island. Several structures were built to house the members. A "House of Mystery" was also completed where Brother XII could commune with the panel of the "Great White Lodge."

Eventually, as often happens, the local Nanaimo inhabitants grew weary of the strange goings-on in the compound. Rampant sex and anti-Semitic and racist proclamations were the order of the day. Eventually, the Aquarian Foundation was forced to vacate their Cedar by the Sea settlement and moved just offshore to DeCourcy Island. This was no hindrance to the wealthy benefactors seeking redemption by following the teachings of Brother XII. As encouraged by the Prophet, these lost souls converted all their worldly possessions into gold, which immediately went into the coffers of the Foundation. More to the point, it was turned over to Brother XII.

Over time the Prophet became more and more paranoid, possibly aided by the substantial use of drugs. It is reported he became so paranoid he began burying caches of gold throughout the compound on DeCourcy.

A recently discovered tidbit about this restless mariner was his heretofore undocumented trips to Kodiak Island. About the time of their relocation to DeCourcy Island, Wilson made two trips to this wild, remote place, which displayed minimal evidence of human activity. As it was some seven hundred miles due west of Juneau and two hundred miles southwest of Anchorage, just getting to Kodiak was a treacherous proposition. The Gulf of Alaska is notorious for rough seas and is practically impassable after Labor Day. Brother XII made his voyages during early summer and early fall. He was entranced by the island.

Two thirds of Kodiak Island, the southwestern portion, is a protected wildlife refuge today. It's comprised of rugged mountains, tundra, magnificent spruce forests, rivers, and tidal flats. When the Prophet made his trips, the sheer numbers of birds, deer, bears, and fish seemed otherworldly. Truly, this was a spiritual place. It was on his second excursion that the idea of populating DeCourcy Island with some of the wildlife specimens crossed his mind, most likely another vision. His ship was one of the early diesel powered trawlers but still offered ample storage space midship, below deck. Wilson correctly surmised this would be his last trip across the gulf to Kodiak Island so what better time to round up a few specimens.

His crew managed to corral two Sitka deer. These were smaller than mule deer and very cute little guys. Plus, their space requirements were minimal. Days before they left for the return trip to British Columbia, they stumbled upon a very young bear cub struggling to extricate himself from the Karluk River. Today the river is still the home of one of the most heavily populated salmon runs in the world. In the 1920s it was virtually possible to cross the waterway on a bridge of these spectacular animals—bear heaven. The crew members were mariners, not zoologists. This cub was approximately three months old and resembled a wet twenty-five pound stuffed animal. They tugged him from the swiftly moving current loaded with sockeye salmon and loaded him into a caged area of the ship, adjacent to the deer. Had the cub been separated from his mother and not orphaned, it is likely several of the crew would not have been returning to DeCourcy.

Brother XII, while charming and charismatic, was not the fastest bunny in the forest. His scheme to populate the new settlement with the Sitka deer for food was legitimate. The idea of bringing a live Kodiak cub to a populated community was less so. But, the bear *was* adorable. Throughout their return journey the younger crew members took turns feeding the cub with an improvised baby bottle and scraps of fish accumulated from the galley. When they arrived back at DeCourcy Island, the entire village cheered the new additions to their neighborhood.

As time passed, the deer mated and populated the island. Karl, the Kodiak cub, now named after the river from which he was rescued, was a different story.

CHAPTER 10

Howard Bories shared many of the attributes of other well-to-do, self-made entrepreneurs. He was driven by one of the myriad reasons that motivate such people. In his case it was abject poverty and an abusive father that ignited the desire to rise above it all. He was an exceedingly persistent individual of above-average intellect. There was no deal too complicated for him. There was no negotiator he couldn't exhaust to the point of concession. The trappings of wealth weren't his objective. Winning was. The thought of someone or something besting him was repugnant. Sure, he'd been in the right place at the right time—Seattle in the nineties—but so had lots of people. The Bories Corporation had come out on top. Well, not the tippy top. That award went to Paul Allen's company, Vulcan Real Estate, but that hardly counted. That man had had more money than anybody, except his former partner.

Howard, resting in his suite, considered his predicament. Many of his developments had required difficult negotiations and miles of red tape. The Pacific Northwest's passion for the climate and the Earth required any new project go through an environmental impact study. This mandate inevitably added months to any construction schedule. If the study came back and necessitated mitigation, well, that could possibly mean years, not months, additionally. The cost of this extended timetable was tremendous. A hundred-million-dollar project was now one-twenty or more. Any such risk was to be avoided at all costs. If it took a hundred grand to avoid even the threat of mitigation, it was worth it. Twenty million was a lot of money.

The Puget Sound Planning Bureau was massive. Over five hundred employees saw to it that every project developed in the region was reviewed and inspected. Whether it was completed on time or lagged interminably was of no consequence to them. Their concern was the impact on the land, the wildlife, and the traffic. Because such a large number were employed by this bureaucracy, one or two, or maybe a few more, questionable hires were unavoidable. Howard's persistence was responsible for the Bories Corporation finding and exploiting these individuals. He rightly assumed that government employees in positions of consequence, not necessarily of importance, could always use additional income. Private investigators were hired to zero in on possible candidates working in Environmental Services.

After identifying two such candidates, it was a simple progression to intimidation, blackmail, and bribery. The first two to set the hook, the last to keep them there. It took only a rubber stamp on a civil engineering sheet to move any project along. Legitimate inspectors took this responsibility very seriously. Howard's recruits, not so much. Over the last fifteen years, the Bories Corporation had never once been held up on any construction project. Other developers were saddled with delays and mitigation costs while Bories profited by the millions.

Predictably, Howard's minions recognized that their efforts were not being compensated to the degree Mr. Bories was benefitting. He had increased their inducement twofold, but this only postponed the inevitable. In persons of questionable character, worthy human nature takes a detour.

After years of smooth sailing, the tables had turned. If Bories didn't come through with twenty million, Rob Bensen and David Jeppesen would spill the beans. This was their retirement plan. If they were found out, their pensions would disappear. They required one single payment, ten million each, to keep their mouths shut.

Howard Bories was a corner cutter in addition to his other character flaws. Many people have endured difficult events and circumstances in their lives without going afoul of the law. His overwhelming need to win, to best everyone, was paramount. He'd salted away a small fortune over the years but twenty million would make a serious dent in it. Money was his barometer for success. Thus, the more he had, the more exceptional he became. Howard was a devious, calculating, conniving individual. He was not above making payoffs or cheating the system. He was not, however, a completely evil human being. Things would have been so much simpler had he been. Then, instead of trying to figure out a way to satiate his conspirators, he could just have had them disappeared. As it stood now, he needed to come up with additional funds.

The Tofino Inn should have been a simple transaction. He had purchased the derelict property for a song. He had managed to skirt the very strict local Canadian building codes to reduce his construction costs. Menucci had offered a screamingly good deal on design and furnishings, the after-the-fact discovery of off-quality goods aside. His strategy to transform the inn into a world-class destination and then flip it to an international outfit was still promising. He had originally invited the O'Malleys to the grand opening to bolster his efforts at holding Menucci's feet to the fire. The idea of flipping the property only occurred to him recently when his two associates at the planning bureau suggested he pay them twenty million dollars.

With the O'Malleys coming to the inn, he'd had to make certain they were distracted. If any of the deficiencies were made known, his chances of a quick sale would be nil. He'd heard Marty talking about an outfit called VCS. Apparently these guys supplied contract labor to larger organizations. Obviously, if Marty was using them, they were shady characters.

After meeting with the principals at VCS, Daniel Phillips and Wilson Plante, Bories thought he might be able to arrange a diversion. At the first meeting Howard hadn't bothered to bring up anything nefarious. It was only after two subsequent get-togethers that he felt they were probably committing a little graft of their own. Seems it took one to know one. They were reluctant at first to provide anyone for the caper. It was when Will suggested that the two "new guys" might be open to it that they came around.

The notion of having a couple of cretins detain the husband for a few days seemed reasonable at the time. Howard mistakenly thought a distracted Jenne would be easier to manipulate. After all, it wasn't like the guy was going to get hurt.

In hindsight he should have had the woman taken. The husband would have been much easier to control. The dual tragedies of losing Tony and then the bear attack were devastating. Tony had been his only real friend. He never passed judgment and only occasionally offered advice. While money was his spouse, Tony had been his soul. Even now, the thought of cleaning up this mess without him seemed overwhelming.

The bear thing was surreal. At least he didn't have to worry about the VCS guys turning on him. He felt confident that he'd been successful stringing the O'Malleys along. Now that they were going to come up with a proposal to bring the property up to accepted luxury standards, they'd at least be out of his hair for a while. It was possible he could still right this ship.

CHAPTER 11

The skies had finally cleared, if only for a few hours. Bories had made the drive across the island shortly after noon and then headed south from Nanaimo to the small community of Yellow Tail. The Crow and Gate Pub had been a fixture in the community for over forty years. It was also where the two lieutenants from the Twelves, Daniel and Will—"don't call me Wilson"—invited Howard to meet them. The English pub was their favorite hangout. Famous for claiming to be the first neighborhood pub in British Columbia, the interior of the Tudor-styled structure was more reminiscent of the Lord of the Rings. Dark lighting, burnt umber walls and floors, and exposed brick on the bar served to make the low ceilings even more threatening. The food was excellent even if it was English. The duo favored the place because it was incumbent upon them to keep a low profile. That and the proximity to DeCourcy Island—it was less than two miles, directly across the Stuart Channel in the community's thirty-foot trawler—made the watering hole ideal.

After three and a half hours of driving under bright, sunny skies, it took Howard's seventy-five-year-old peepers several minutes to adjust to the duskiness of the pub. Locating his quarry in a dark corner, he hustled over, banging a replaced hip on only two of the row of four-tops along his route.

He had previously met with them in Port Alberni, several months ago. It was then that they'd arranged for the four Twelves to connect with the crew from Martin's. Only when he'd been threatened by his former accomplices was the idea of kidnapping O'Malley even considered.

Daniel, the shorter of the two, was of pale complexion and appeared to be mid-thirties. His curly black hair, striking blue eyes, dimpled chin, and trimmed, stylish week-old beard suggested a lady's man who never had to try to score. Will, on the other hand, was slightly older, well over six feet, and had a shaved head and a face only a mother could love. The nose was squashed to the side like he'd walked into a tree. The half-inch space between his two front teeth reminded Howard of Howdy Doody without the charm. His week-old scraggly stubble only reinforced his lack of commitment to presentation.

"So glad you chaps could meet with me. Lovely place you've picked as well." It was a simple thing for Bories to slide into the English vernacular. The venue, after all, dictated such. "I thought it made sense for us to get together to close the door on this affair. The four lads you hooked Martin up with worked out marvelously, as you indicated. I can't say the same for the clods that were supposed to hang on to O'Malley, though. How do you explain that cock-up?"

"We're very sorry about that, Mr. Bories. Those guys had only been with our group for a short while. We were reluctant to use them, but you required a more aggressive approach to the situation than we normally advise. They were the only ones willing to cross that line, so we felt they were our only choice." Daniel appeared to be the designated speaker for the two.

"That fuckin' bear took care of them, though, huh?" It was understandable, now, why Daniel took the lead in the conversation.

"Yes, Will, they are no longer with us. Daniel, I presume that Menucci will be paying your mover people. I'm also assuming that my deposit for the two kidnappers will be sufficient. I can't see paying further for services that weren't rendered."

"Well, I'm not sure that our boss will agree to that. He considered the bear attack sort of 'an act of God.' He's pretty adamant that we need to collect the additional eighteen grand you owe us. He says that guy they took was out of the way, lost for a few days anyway, so mission accomplished, correct?"

"Uh, no, I disagree. The RCMP's got involved, they still can't figure out why the guy was taken. It did not go down the way I expected so I won't be paying any more money."

"Shit, the head dude ain't gonna like this. I'm not tellin' him, Daniel, you're gonna hafta." Will's voice had risen above the hushed pub conversation in the background.

"Keep it down, Will. That's all we need is for the locals to notice us. I agree Brother Twelve is not going to be happy. I think, Mr. Bories, you're going to have to meet with our leader to explain why you're not willing to pay the balance of our contract."

"I'll be happy to explain my position to him to his face. Just have him meet with me at the inn."

"I don't think so, Mr. Bories. Brother Twelve doesn't like to leave the island anymore." Daniel's brows seemed a little tighter, his voice a little less friendly, his charm diminished. "You will have to visit him on DeCourcy to explain your concern. Either that or pay us the balance now."

"I will not pay you nor will I visit your little island. I'm leaving. If anyone wants an explanation they can come to me. I fail to see that you're in any position to dictate otherwise."

"Uh-oh, shit's gonna hit the fan now."

"Shut up, Will. *Mister* Bories, here is what is going to happen next. You will accompany us down to the harbor, where we will hop on the *Butterfly*."

"Yeah, that's our fuckin' boat."

"Will, last time. Shut the fuck up! If you don't accompany us, Mister Bories, here's what will happen. Jordan and his three pals will make life at the Inn at Tofino a living hell. They will harass the guests; they will steal things. They will do it quietly and without observation from the police. Your plan to sell the place will no longer be viable since no one will want to stay there. Does that sound like something you'd enjoy?"

Howard's demeanor had taken on a decidedly less assertive quality. His mind was balancing twenty thousand versus an entire truck full of crap. In hindsight perhaps engaging with these fellows was a poor choice.

"Okay, I give up. I'll pay you the balance, I just don't have it with me."

"Too late, Bories, we're taking a trip. If you make a scene or resist, we have other things we can offer. Perhaps Will can have a chat with you. You're going to have an opportunity that very few others have had. It'll take us just a few minutes to get to the harbor, then a half hour across the channel. We'll be there by seven. Our leader will be waiting."

Just over a mile from the English pub, Boat Harbour was the home of a small but very secure and well-equipped marina. The locals, it seems, were precise when naming indigenous attractions. This late in the season offered no challenge to parking, and very few vessels remained as the winter season approached. Will cast off the mooring lines and piloted them due east for DeCourcy.

The threesome onboard the *Butterfly* was treated to the vicious currents of the Stuart Channel. The thirty-foot Beneteau Swift Trawler was overkill for the short haul but anything smaller would have made this evening's crossing uncomfortable. The boat had been gifted to the commune by the great grandson of one of the original devotees of the cult and was worth more than all of their other possessions combined.

During a full moon, the change in tides, well over fifteen feet between the two, created a surge of over ten knots. Combine that with a northerly breeze of fifteen to twenty knots and the thirty-minute crossing doubled in duration. They finally reduced power as they approached Pirate's Cove, the only viable harbor on DeCourcy.

The stories he'd read of the Aquarian Foundation came back to him while Howard nervously contemplated what awaited. He mentally replayed the conversation with his abductors while they were in the pub. At the time he was distracted, more concerned with his eighteen K. When he thought back now, he remembered they referred to their boss as Brother Twelve. He'd always thought something about these guys was a little off, and so too the crew at the inn. Could they possibly have something to do with that old cult? The odds of anything that radical enduring for almost a hundred years was somewhat remote even up here in these sparsely populated islands. He'd know soon enough when he met the boss, but his anxiety meter was nearing redline.

As they glided quietly into the dimly lit dock, they dropped the side fenders. Will yelled out into the shadows. "Throw us a goddamn line, Joseph." Apparently his eyesight far surpassed his eloquence as a speaker.

Out of seemingly nowhere a line was tossed aboard, and Will secured the forward end. "Tie up that aft cleat, Joseph. We're off to see the boss."

They stepped down to the dock while Daniel took point.

DeCourcy Island is extremely bucolic and only accessible by float-plane or private watercraft. There are no services on the island, and power is supplied by generators or solar panels. There are no paved roads. Its privacy is its principal attraction.

A five-minute ride in a battered Vietnam-era army Jeep over rugged terrain brought the group to a large weather-beaten barn-like structure that appeared to have housed livestock at some earlier time. There were several other buildings of smaller construction that haphazardly ringed the barn. Although all appeared to have been built ages ago, they seemed to have endured the passing of the decades. The absence of generator noise suggested the sparse lighting came from oil lanterns, candles, and the occasional battery-powered lamp.

The twelve-foot-high sliding doors were wide open, revealing the dimly lit interior. A three-foot-high Egyptian ankh, seemingly illuminated from within, was centered on the facing of the second-story loft. The blue-green luminescence was incompatible with the otherwise rustic barn.

"Welcome. I'm told you have something you'd like to discuss with me. Some problem, a disagreement perhaps?" The voice was gentle, well-modulated, almost like Jim Nance at the Masters. Oddly, it appeared to be coming from a small, elderly figure, barely noticeable in the shadows, seated at a small desk adjacent to an Allis-Chalmers tractor. His plaid flannel shirt and Levi's fit seamlessly with his environment.

Bories, accompanied by his escorts, cautiously entered the opening, a sudden tightness in his chest. "Well, Daniel and Will here kindly explained the situation to me, and I've reconsidered. Now, I think I should pay the balance of our contract. Unfortunately, I've come unprepared and I'll need to return to the inn to get the money."

"Daniel, why don't you take Will and see if you can prepare the bunkhouse to accommodate Jordan and his crew when they return. Mister Bories and I would like to have a conversation."

After their dismissal, Howard was able to get a better look at the man. His Eminence or whatever they called him, he thought. The man had the wrinkled skin of an eighty-year old. White wisps of hair poked out from a John Deere baseball cap. His unshaven face sported at least a week's worth of stubble. Closer observation would have revealed tobacco stains leaking from the left corner of his pencil-thin lips, while his left hand held the requisite spit cup issued with every can of Copenhagen. His most striking feature was the shimmering blue eyes, almost opaline in their appearance, that rarely blinked. Mesmerizing, really.

"Howard—may I call you Howard? Yes, of course, I'm certain you'll want me to. You may call me Brother Fred."

This was getting odder by the moment. This tiny, old man, dip in his mouth, looking like Jed Clampett of Hillbilly fame, sounding like

Jim Nance, with eyes that could pierce the soul, was now meeting the Monopoly Man.

"We appreciate a quiet life here in our little community, Howard, and we would like to keep it that way. Daniel offered to assist in whatever little scheme you had planned to recover your investment from the Tofino project. I allow him some leeway when it comes to generating funds for our continued subsistence here at the Farm. We are able to grow our own food and raise our own chickens, the sound is abundant with fish, and the island is inundated with deer."

Bories wasn't sure exactly where this was going, but his concern was slowly being replaced by exhaustion. He was not a young man.

"That doesn't mean we can get by without additional income. We sell little trinkets and woven goods the sisters produce. We also take our excess eggs and produce to the market in Yellow Tail. Still, we sometimes contract out our services to make up for any shortfalls. Mostly, it's construction work or moving goods and equipment, hence the work we did for that Martin character. Kidnapping was not something we would have ever offered, nor would I have authorized it if I had known. Daniel explained that it meant we could go through the winter without having to leave the Farm. That is, once you paid us. The two gentlemen who took on the challenge were new to our little group. I had some reservations about them, and it turns out I was correct."

"Fred, I'm sorry, Brother Fred, I understand now why I need to fulfill my end of the contract, and I'll be happy to do so. I will need to go back to my property to get the funds, however."

"Do you have a credit card?"

"Of course, but seriously? I thought there was no contact with the outside world, no electricity?"

"We're not Luddites here, Howard. We have batteries and a satellite hookup, just for emergencies. We also have a chip reader. We use it when we take our goods to the market. What card would you like to use?"

Bories reached into his pocket and pulled out his platinum Amex card. "Here you are sir. There's no limit so the eighteen K won't be a concern."

"If it's not a problem, I'm going to add the two percent those mercenaries charged us. Good with you, right?"

"Of course. No reason four hundred dollars should come between us." He was secretly thrilled just to put this whole episode behind him. If he never saw these kooks again, it would be too soon.

With the transaction completed, Brother Fred struck a small triangle hanging on a nearby support column. "I've called for Daniel and Will. They'll take you back to Vancouver Island."

While they waited, Bories couldn't help himself. "So, have you and your people lived here on the farm for some time?"

Fred's eyes watered a bit as he recalled his life here in this idyllic place. "You could say that. I've lived here my entire life. I was born in that building across the way. It's now the bunkhouse. My father was very young when he died. His dad founded this farm almost a hundred years ago.

"We're all family here, you might say. There are a dozen men who do the manual labor—farming, hunting, and the sort. The women, there are seven of them now, take care of the young ones. They also weave rugs and create many of the craft items we sell at the market. They also provide comfort for the men."

Bories had heard enough. Sure, he was curious, but his gut was screaming, "No mas, get the fuck out of here." He was exhausted, too, and hungry. This place really did give him the creeps, as did this little gnome of a man.

Then he heard the magic words. "Well, Howard, I see the boys are here. They'll take you back to Boat Harbour, then drop you off at that pub where you parked your vehicle. Thank you for visiting. We probably won't be seeing each other again."

The sendoff seemed more odd than ominous but, either way, he was thrilled to be back on the *Butterfly.*

"So, did you enjoy your meeting with Brother Twelve?" Apparently Daniel was less threatening, more respectful to Bories now that his conflict with the family was resolved.

"That's not exactly the word I would use, Daniel, and I thought his name was Fred?"

"Sorry, that's what he goes by when he interacts with outsiders. We know him as Brother Twelve. His grandfather was a great man and the founder of our group. At one time over eight thousand members were faithful to our way of life. They espoused the teachings of the original Brother Twelve and contributed considerably to support him and his followers."

The tidal currents had subsided, and the channel crossing was far easier than earlier. Will was on the bridge, allowing for more intelligent conversation here in the cabin. Even he was less confrontational than on the way over.

"So, you're saying that Fred, number twelve, whatever, is now the Grand Poohbah, and he decides the fate of the world? And where have all the past contributions gone. Are they invested or something?" Somehow it was always money with Howard.

"It isn't becoming of you to insult Brother Twelve. Even though our group has dwindled, he has seen us through some difficult times. He no longer encourages others to see things our way, the only way possible to repopulate the Earth after the apocalypse. He directs us to live a quiet, private existence on the Farm. We only interact with outsiders when it helps fund our community. That's why it was so important to persuade you to remit the balance of your contract with us.

"The tithing we received in the early days went to purchase the land we currently call home. The first Brother Twelve, as prescient as he was, was not without controversy. Towards the end of his life, some of his decisions were questionable. He wasted some of our contributions on loose women and useless travel to far-flung islands. He also encouraged the donations be made in the form of gold. His thinking at the time was that even without investing it in anything else, the value would remain constant or increase.

"If we still had any, I think he would have been proven accurate. Our present leader has told stories of the early years, how chaotic those times were. There were rumors of the remaining gold being buried somewhere on DeCourcy. We were chatting among ourselves, and we all feel strongly that if Brother Twelve knew anything about that, he would have used it for our continued existence. Living hand to mouth as we do, depending on outsiders to buy our produce and trinkets, is demeaning. We have confidence in our leader, though. He's seen us through the past fifty years successfully, and we know he'll continue to do so."

Whew, Howard was *really* happy they were pulling into the slip. These folks belonged on an island. They were certifiable. He did wonder about the gold though.

After dropping Bories at the Crow and Gate, the duo headed back to the *Butterfly*. The ten-year-old Outback they kept here in Yellow Tail was perfect for transporting them around when they were on the bigger island. "So, did you say anything about that bear story that the old guy tells all the time?"

"That's not something we should share with outsiders," said Daniel.

"Who cares, it's probably just bullshit anyway. Who's gonna believe that the Original brought a bear back from Kodiak Island? That after four or five years he grew to over a thousand pounds? That he stood over nine feet on his hind legs? That before Fred was born he swam off to Vancouver Island cuz he was in love with a grizzly? I'm tellin' ya, that Fred spins some wacky shit sometimes."

"Will, this is the last time I'm going to tell you. Please don't call him Fred, and never say he's wacky. He's our leader. Sure, every once in a while he comes up with a story that's hard to believe but that's for us, his followers. It's DeCourcy lore, if you will. It's not to be shared with others. Am I clear on this?"

Will was a little less fervent in his dedication to Brother XII than Daniel. He'd joined the community because he was tired of living with his brother, who was a stupid man, on Whidbey Island. There was a roof over his head, very little was demanded of him, and there were seven women to choose from. It's true they were like the Stepford Wives without the good looks, but still. It's not like he had to go searching for a booty call.

"Yes, Daniel, it's clear. I promise not to divulge any more DeCourcy lore." If Daniel detected the sarcasm, he ignored it. He seemed stunned that Will had used "divulge" in a sentence. Must have been something he'd overheard from Bories over their travels today. "Like I said, nobody's gonna believe that bear story anyway. Bears falling for bears from different races, swimming and stuff. It's bullshit, like I said."

Daniel was finished talking to this dullard. Will actually believed that bears were racist and there were different *races* of bears. This was starting to remind him of that real estate phony turned president. Rhymes with dump. Hah, he thought, his first smile since hanging out with this simpleton.

CHAPTER 12

The O'Malleys were elated to be back in their studio. The Vancouver Island fiasco had left them mentally and physically drained, and the return to normalcy was indeed welcome. The two-story former fire house on Old Main street in Bellevue had been converted into a showroom/office combination with an upstairs loft that served as their living quarters. This former Seattle bedroom community had been transformed over the past two decades into one of the wealthiest cities in the country. Medina, Clyde Hill, and Hunts Point, all adjacent towns, were home to the Nordstrom family, the Gates family, and Jeff Bezos, just to drop a few names.

Kevin had purchased their building for three hundred thousand back in the late eighties when he first moved to the Northwest. At the time it felt like a fortune, but he thought it might be a decent investment and the loft provided comfortable living quarters with a killer view of Lake Washington. Over the last couple of years he'd been offered eight times that. The thought of someone tearing it down just to throw up ten stories of condos with retail below was revolting. They loved living in the old part of town, even if it was morphing into the Land of Oz. This had been their workplace for the last two years. They'd converted it after the startup IT company leasing it had outgrown the space.

"So whatcha thinking we should do about Tofino?" Jenne said, apparently she couldn't wait to get back there.

"Since your experiences there were nowhere near as much fun as mine, why don't you tell me what *you're* thinking."

"Well, we said we'd get back to Bories with a proposal. I took copious notes while I was there, so why don't we put something together. I've started an outline. We can plug in some numbers for the FF and E and figure out how many hours it'll eat up. We should be able to put it together by the end of the week. You can email Howard and ask him when we should go back up there to meet with him."

"I'll set it up with him. I have to tell you though, whenever I think of that place I get a little loose in the lower intestines. I'm still having nightmares of bears and body parts."

"That's okay, hon. Another five or ten years and you'll forget all about it. Look at it this way—we'll make a full markup on the goods. That place is in trouble. If they get any kind of occupancy at all, that crap in there will fall apart. You touch base with Howard, and I'll get going on the rest."

Kevin had a sudden thought. "You do realize that's not the only project we have up there in that neck of the woods, right?"

"Huh?"

"We were supposed to get that art package installed at the Brentwood Inn before the end of the month. It's expected to ship later this week, and we need to tell them who's going to receive it."

"Shit, with all the excitement I totally spaced on that job. Maybe we can ship it straight to the client and get some locals to do the install." Jenne appeared more comfortable having challenges for which to find solutions than she was when they were solved.

"Good luck with that. Sure, we can ship it there but it's still another country, and we don't have folks up there that we've worked with before. It'll take a few days to get through customs. Maybe that will give us time to come up with a crew. If I can set up a meeting with Howard next week we might be able to take the ferries through the

San Juans over to Sydney. We can stop by the Brentwood, work out the details with Marie, and then head up to Tofino. It'll be a long haul, but we can kill two birds with one stone."

"How about we spend the night in Tofino after we meet with Bories. We can see what they've done with the place, how they've dealt with the loss of that final load of furnishings. Maybe we can talk to those guys who hung the art package there. They seemed to know what they were doing."

Kevin looked mildly concerned. "Remember how standoffish they were? Remember Howard said some things had gone missing? I'm not all that comfortable with that scenario."

"Okay. How about we at least talk to them, that can't hurt. If we feel better after that, we can hire them. If not we'll come back and go to plan B. If it works out, we can meet them at the Brentwood on the way back to layout the package. It should be there by then."

"Okay, if it doesn't work out, what's plan B?"

"Don't know yet."

"Perfect."

Marty dreaded the idea of heading back to Tofino. Carmel was beautiful this time of year. Temperatures were in the sixties and seventies when the fog lifted. There was the occasional rainstorm, of course, but they were infrequent. The weather on Vancouver Island, on the other hand, positively sucked in the late fall. Cold, cloudy, and rainy was a certainty.

He *had* to go up there, though. That prick, Bories, still had three hundred grand of his money. He was supposed to pay off the local crew as well but, fuck them, he had planned to stiff them anyway. What could they do? They were local yokels and once he left that place he was never coming back. It *was* another country after all.

He arranged to fly to Seattle next week and then take Kenmore Air to Nanaimo. God, what a pain in the ass this place was to get to. He'd make certain the future projects, if there were any, were in warmer parts of the country, *this* country.

He told Bories that he was replacing the destroyed truckload of furnishings. Let him think that. After he left the Tofino Inn and Spa next week he was never going to return. If Bories released his retainage then great. If he didn't, he'd tell Bories to pound sand, he was never getting the final shipment anyway. What a shit show this turned out to be!

Howard Bories was a worried man. He *could* cover the twenty million to shut his conspirators up if he absolutely had to. But he'd rather not.

Apogee Properties, based in Sweden, had already shown an interest in the Tofino Inn. They were well known in Europe and the Far East and were anxious to move into the lucrative North American market. A boutique destination resort in British Columbia could be just the entrée they needed to begin their assault on the U.S. and Canadian pleasure seekers. Their first visit had been just prior to substantial completion of the inn remodel and before any furnishings were installed. They'd been suitably impressed and planned another visit after completion and the grand opening. They always visited prospective acquisitions anonymously, as paying guests. If they were spending a hundred fifty million on a property, they wanted to be certain it was as advertised. Bories expected they'd be sending someone in the next week or two. If all was as expected, the deal could be consummated within a month or two.

It would take a few months to replace the truckload of furnishings that had been destroyed in the crash. Bories didn't trust Menucci to follow through so he'd made the decision to shutter four of the largest suites on the property. He would relocate the case goods and artwork to the empty lobby areas and the smaller suites so that the property looked fully furnished if, by chance, a prospective buyer were to visit.

If and when he managed to flip this property, he would find a nice quiet place in a sunny destination where he could while away what was left of his life. He enjoyed the challenges of development, but he *really* was getting too old for this shit.

CHAPTER 13

When Karl arrived on DeCourcy, he was sick and confused. He'd spent the first few months of his life with his mother. Milk whenever he was hungry, warm hugs whenever he was cold. She taught him how to find food. The fish were good, the berries were better, and the honey was the best. He never had the chance to get it for himself but when his mom managed to battle the bees for the delicacy, it was a happy time for him and his brother.

And then the happy times went away. They were crossing the meadow, looking for bees and the marvelous honey. There was an unnaturally loud boom. Then another, and another. His mom had allowed him to lead the family that day. He was frightened. He looked to his mom for help, but she was on the ground, still. So was his brother. Three creatures with big sticks came running towards him. He ran and hid in the forest.

He watched the creatures from his hiding place. They did awful things to his mom and his brother. Then they took them away. He was alone, and he was hungry. He didn't care about the honey anymore. He just wanted food. He remembered where his mom took them to catch the fish. They were in the cold roaring river and there were lots of them. It took him most of the afternoon, but he found the place. His claws were nowhere near as big as his mom's, but he thought he could catch one. When he reached into the frigid water from the bank, he stumbled and fell. He was still young and hadn't developed much of a coat or an insular layer of fat beneath. The water was freezing. He bounced off the submerged boulders. The fish were everywhere. He felt something pulling him from the river. More creatures with white faces. He was afraid but after battling the current, he had no strength left.

They took him to the place of the really big water. They put him in a cage in a foul-smelling cave that floated on the big water. He was in there for a week and some other creatures came and gave him milk and some fish. They weren't like his mom, but they were kind to him. He was still weak from the river, but the milk and food helped. After a while they took his cage out into the sun. It was very bright, and it was much warmer than the home he had known. They took him to a large building that smelled of other animals. He stayed in his cage until the creatures built a larger one inside the building. Then they moved him to it. He saw two of the creatures frequently. They brought him water and fish and some other food he had never tasted before. As the months went by he grew, and he grew. The creatures seemed surprised at his size. The cage was cramped. He was bored. The only time he saw the creatures was when they fed him. During the six months he had spent on DeCourcy Island, he had gained over two hundred pounds. The creatures were not as nice anymore. They weren't prepared for how much food a Kodiak cub could eat. They just threw the fish into the cage and sometimes he didn't have enough water.

One night, when he was very thirsty, he began scratching at the thick wood slats of the cage. His claws were now over three inches long and were very sharp. He scratched so hard that he cracked the board. He swatted it and it came loose. He swatted the next one and *it* came loose. His thick paws were able to pull the remainder of the slats apart. He scampered to the opening in the building and saw the moon for the first time in six months. He ran for the forest.

It took Karl some time to determine the landscape of his new habitat. He discovered he was surrounded by the big water. But it wasn't as big as where he was born. He could see other land across the water. He spent the next two years on DeCourcy foraging for food and sleeping when he could. He had grown to over eight hundred pounds, and he would add an additional four hundred over the next few years. He would see the creatures occasionally, but he made sure they couldn't see him. There were lots of small deer on the island that provided nourishment. There were lots of berries too, even more than when he was little.

Karl was lonely. There were no other bears on the island. He also discovered a new feeling. He was horny. He had easily roamed the width of the island and lately he had traveled the length. He discovered that when the tide was low he could travel to two connecting islands. Sometimes he did it when the tide wasn't low. He discovered he could swim. In the two and a half years of his freedom, he had not seen another bear. One afternoon he traveled as far north and west as he could go, even swimming through short stretches of salty froth.

Although he had no knowledge of geography, he was the beneficiary of over a million years of genetic selection. A million years of finely tuned instinct. He was driven by forces he did not understand. No creature sustains such longevity without an overwhelming desire to reproduce. He was now on the far western edge of Mudge Island. He sat on the steep, rocky cliff and contemplated the severe tidal flow between his location and Vancouver Island. He sat there for hours, until the flow subsided. It was only a hundred yards or so across, but this was a greater distance than he'd ever swum before. He climbed down from his perch, waded into the water, and began paddling. It was a ten-minute swim before he made the far shore. As he climbed up the bank of his new world, he sniffed the air, using his incredible olfactory prowess. Something good was gonna happen here, he just knew it.

Brown bears have been known to range over three hundred miles. Karl was a brown bear, more specifically, a Kodiak. There were no Kodiak bears on Vancouver Island. There were grizzlies from time to time, however. They would swim over from the mainland to forage and, yes, to hook up. In time Karl managed to navigate his way to Strathcona Provincial Park in central Vancouver Island. This rugged wilderness is comprised of snow-covered mountain peaks and isolated alpine lakes. Karl eventually hooked up with a cute, if a little on the heavy side, girl grizzly. They had three cubs, all very large. In time the cubs grew and matured and found families of their own.

At maturity, Karl stood nine feet tall and weighed in at twelve hundred pounds. His claws were over six inches long. His progeny, probably due to their attraction to the full-figured gals, evolved to exceed even Karl's size. There has never been a documented mating of a Kodiak and a grizzly. Of course, no one had ever thought it was a good idea to snatch a cub from an Alaskan island either. The Kodiak genes, while severely diluted through three generations, were assertive little fuckers. These, combined with extraordinarily large grizzlies, made for fifteen hundred pounds of very nasty bear. Until recently the generations following Karl were content to live out their lives in the safety and comfort of Strathcona. Some, though, managed to wander to other parts of the rugged island. They favored the solitude, safety, and abundant food supply of the most isolated provincial parks. They did their very best to avoid human contact. Occasionally, though, it was unavoidable.

CHAPTER 14

After ensuring that three pallets of art would be shipped directly to the Brentwood Inn, the O'Malleys pulled the proposal together for Howard and set off Monday morning for Anacortes. Itself an island connected by bridge, this quaint little town was the point of departure for the fleet of Washington State Ferries, serving the San Juan Islands, as well as international service to Sydney on Vancouver Island.

The weather was sunny and cold, a welcome diversion from the usual dark drizzly skies of fall in this, the farthest northwest corner of the U.S. This time of year, the offseason for most boating enthusiasts, there was no reservation needed to drive aboard the *Tillikum*, one of the several ferries serving the archipelago. This route was a little longer than one of the direct boats from Seattle, but both Jenne and Kevin enjoyed the leisurely pace and spectacular scenery. The *Tillikum* would stop at Lopez, Shaw, and Orcas Islands before it headed across Haro Strait to Sydney. The journey through the islands took almost three hours but it sure beat driving up I-5 to Vancouver (the *city*, not the island). The wait at the border alone could take that long. Also, the customs stop in Sydney was a mere formality.

After landing in Sydney on Vancouver Island and going through the brief customs inspection, they headed for the Brentwood Inn on Brentwood Bay. It was a short twenty-minute ride, and Marie Houser welcomed them upon their arrival. Marie was a longtime client and the owner of the boutique luxury hotel. The sheltered bay was a wonderful place to visit and relax. The O'Malleys had stayed here only twice but the service, food, and hospitality were such that they were looking forward to spending the night. They didn't have to be in Tofino until tomorrow evening to meet with Bories.

"Marie, great to see you. Kevin and I wanted to get a chance to review the art package with you. It should be here by the end of the week."

Marie was attractive for an octogenarian. She had owned the place for thirty years with her husband. He had passed away ten years before, and running this place was what gave her life meaning. She was only five feet tall but her perfect makeup and daily coiffed hair made it obvious she was in the business of hospitality.

"Wonderful to see you two again, Jenne. I'm looking forward to replacing all the tired room artwork as well as seeing those special pieces you've selected for the lobby areas. We have cleared out an area down by the spa where we can store the pallets until you and the crew get here. Who will be doing the hanging this time?"

Kevin tried to convey an air of confidence. "Our normal guys are off to Montana to hunt moose or some silly thing. We've discussed it with the crew that did the work up in Tofino. We were impressed with the quality of the work they did there. We'll firm it up with them when we get there."

"As long as they're competent and can get it done quickly, they should be fine. You two have always come through for me, and I trust you will this time."

The O'Malleys made it to their suite overlooking beautiful Brentwood Bay. Just north of the world-famous Butchart Gardens, the idyllic harbor was situated on the east side of Saanich Inlet. This body of water separated the cities of Victoria and Sydney from the other ninety-eight percent of Vancouver Island.

"I thought you were against hiring the guys that did the work in Tofino."

With a sheepish grin, Kevin tried to save some face here. "Well, you seem convinced of their dependability. And, besides, who else are we gonna use? I defer to you, dear, when it comes to judging character."

"Bullshit. Marie just put you on the spot, and you had to pull something out of your butt, right?"

"Yup. I figure if they turn out to be slugs, I can always blame you. We'll be here to lay out the pieces so even if the guys are a little sketchy, we should be able to control things. Let's just hope they're available."

"I'm sure with that silver tongue of yours, you'll be able to convince them. Let's go get some dinner."

The next morning broke overcast and blustery. They had the option of taking the Mill Bay ferry directly from the dock outside the inn or driving completely around the inlet. Five miles on a teeny tiny ferry—fifteen cars only—or almost fifty miles through Victoria traffic. Easy decision.

The gusting wind and low temperatures made the trip across the bay mildly uncomfortable. After two unsuccessful attempts to dock, the northerly winds blowing the forward end of the ferry away from the dock, the pilot finally backed the boat up to the pier and the smattering of vehicles backed off the ship.

"Kind of an inauspicious start, wouldn't you say?"

"Kind of a big word for you, Kevin. You've been cheating at 'Words with Friends' again, haven't you?"

"Nah, I just like to surprise you every once in a while. It should only take an hour or so to get to Nanaimo. Then we begin the trek across the spine of the island, over to Tofino." Their Ford Explorer came with every conceivable option, so the ride was comfy. Jenne assumed the navigational duties while fiddling with the touch screen, the satellite radio, the heating and cooling, and the massage levels in the bucket seats. Kevin just drove, sort of. With the adaptive cruise and lane-centering features, what he really did was occasionally steer. After a coffee stop in Nanaimo, they would continue west for four hours until they reached the Tofino Inn and Spa.

Howard Bories was not looking forward to meeting with the O'Malleys this evening. Perhaps he could forgo dinner with them and substitute cocktails only. He was going to shoot down their proposal anyway. What difference did it make?

He was fairly certain Apogee would send their people to check things out over the next few weeks so there was no reason to spiff up the place with legitimate commercial furnishings. If he was successful in spinning this sucker, his worries would be over. He was very confident in the staff and the chef. He was less confident the damn dog, Burton, would behave, but the guests liked having him around. The cannibalized suites would be an issue but they were scattered around the property so he was certain they could be avoided. His main concern was controlling the access of the property evaluators while they were guests here at the inn.

Marty had just landed at SeaTac airport. He had to hoof it to the international terminal in forty minutes to make his Air Canada flight to Nanaimo. He hated the dark winter skies in Seattle and dreaded the choppy flight to Vancouver Island. The last time he visited was in the summer. The mild temperatures, late sunsets, and almost no rain made that time of year almost tolerable. He actually enjoyed the floatplane trip to Nanaimo. Unfortunately, after September the only option was through SeaTac.

Bories knew he'd be arriving. Marty couldn't wait to be finished with the cocky little twerp. He'd arranged a breakfast meeting to wrap things up. He would assure Howard that the replacement furniture was ordered and on the way. He'd pretend that he was following up on his claim with the trucking company, although he really didn't give a shit. One way or another he was done with this country. If Bories didn't fork over the balance of his retainer, he would threaten to lien the place or whatever they call it in Canada. If that didn't work, fuck it, maybe he'd just steal some towels and a couple of robes. He would tell the local crew that the check was in the mail. Right, the local yokels would probably believe him. He just hoped the goddam car rental was still open when he landed. He fucking hated this.

Jordy and his crew had finished the balance of the artwork. Bories had had them move some pieces from several of the suites to other places in the hotel. Three hundred pieces seemed like a big job but once the items were located and measured it became more Zen-like. Measure, level, drill, screw, hang, lock, measure, level, drill, screw, hang, lock, always the same, only the size of the artwork changed. He got lost in it, sort of liked it. It took his mind off DeCourcy.

The manager of the inn had allowed them to use two adjoining rooms while finishing up the installation. This would be their last night here, then off to report to Daniel and that clod, Will. Martin was supposed to pay them in the morning. They should be in Nanaimo by early afternoon and with any luck the *Butterfly* would get them to DeCourcy by nightfall. Brother XII would be happy for their contribution to their community.

Both Mike Fox and Rick Pike were looking forward to checking into the Tofino Inn and Spa. They were seasoned appraisers with Apogee and were responsible for evaluating the viability of purchasing the property. While most of the guests at the inn were couples—it was a romantic getaway after all—the two were posing as birders. Clayoquot Sound is internationally famous for bird watching. Now that the inn had reopened, it was expected that fully twenty percent of the future guests would be naturalists. At least that was Apogee's hope, and their representatives were there to make sure the accommodations were suitable.

In the past the diminutive, professorial looking partners were mistaken for a couple, but both were happily married, to women. They showed up at the front desk in appropriate birding attire and immediately inquired about the best trails and hikes for observing the indigenous fowl. They had reserved adjoining junior suites and were thankful that the perquisites of their profession included luxury lodging. Apogee had rigorous grading criteria for prospective acquisitions and both men were sticklers when it came to making their reports. They were serious about their jobs and intended to keep them. If a property were acquired by the home office and proved to be unprofitable or too costly to maintain, their tenure would be short-lived.

It was essential, too, that their evaluation include the food, the wine list, the service, the physical condition of the property, and the concierge service. It was a tough job, but someone had to do it.

After settling into their rooms, they headed off to Chesterman's. The bar also needed to be appraised, after all. After perusing the drink offerings and the wine-by-the-glass selections, they made their choices. Pike selected a glass of sauvignon blanc from one of his favorite Sonoma wineries, Rochioli. It was rare that an establishment offered this by the glass. It was in short supply and it was expensive. Impressive so far, thought Rick. Mike opted for a seventeen year old Hibiki by Suntory, also a rare find. It was an elegant scotch-like whiskey, incredibly finely distilled. Again, so far so good.

The couple decided to dine in the bar area. It was warm here by the ledgestone fireplace and, hell, why get up and relocate. With a balsamic glazed tenderloin and grilled Alaskan salmon on the way, a Leonetti merlot from Walla Walla was selected to accompany the entrees.

The service was amazingly attentive without being overbearing. The food was prepared exactly as requested and the Leonetti, well, really tough to screw that up. Mike and Rick headed back to their suites satisfied that, at least so far, this approval process should be an easy call.

Burton was a mutt. A six-year-old Old English sheepdog and German shepherd mix. The general manager, Trish, had rescued the dog from a shelter when she had relocated to Tofino. She was forty-two, single, and her reputation at operating a five-star resort was legendary. As a former Seattle native, she'd agreed to take the job in this remote location because it was closer to Seattle than her previous posting in San Diego. She had been contacted by a headhunter out of L.A. and had accepted the position after visiting the Tofino property several times.

She had enjoyed the San Diego posting and the many social activities it presented. Her roots were in the Northwest, however. Her parents and two sisters still lived there, and the prospect of living closer—even if it was three hundred miles away—was attractive. After making the move, she realized she'd been unprepared for how small the town was. If she was going to stick this out, she at least needed some company.

She made a trip to the local shelter, looking for a small- to medium-sized companion. She always felt sad at these places. The lonely frightened faces, all just looking for a little love and all of them more than happy to return it twofold. She imagined it had the same feel as a prison—lots of cages, noise, and foul smells. Most of the dogs were youngish and terrified. The mixed herding dog surprised her. He was much more curious than afraid. Trish stopped in front of his cell. He walked unafraid up to the gate and looked her straight in the eye. He sat on his haunches still holding her gaze, then bolted up on his hind legs and attempted a high five.

She immediately grabbed one of the volunteers. Can I visit with this guy? What's his story? Where's he from?

The attendant told her what she knew, which wasn't much. "He was found wandering outside the provincial park a couple of weeks ago. We think he's about six years old. As you can imagine most folks want younger or smaller dogs. This big boy hasn't had much interest, and we probably won't be able to keep him much longer."

"Is he friendly?"

"The volunteers love him. It'll really upset them if we have to euthanize him. They would adopt him themselves, but most folks here can't afford to feed a large animal like this." While the conversation continued they headed to one of the "get acquainted" cages. As soon as Trish was seated, the attendant disconnected the leash. The dog walked up to her, sat down facing her, and gently put his right paw on her knee.

"Does he have a name?" The dog held her eyes while he still rested his paw on her knee.

"The park ranger that brought him in was Bert O'Neal, so everyone's been calling him Burton. I'm sure he won't know the difference if you'd like to change it, though.

"Well, Burton, it looks like you're coming with me." Trish settled up with the folks at the shelter, hooked the dog's leash up, and headed out to her Toyota Ridgeline pickup. The large animal had the black and tan coloring of a GSD and the floppy ears and longer hair of a sheepdog. He was thirty-three inches high on all fours and weighed at least one thirty. He had both hair and fur and newly defined the term shedding. She opened the rear left door while Burton sat by her feet. After she folded up the rear seats, the dog dutifully hopped up without need of encouragement. She loved this dog already.

At first Howard balked at her bringing her dog to work. She assured him of two things: First, she'd make certain there would be no problems with the dog interacting with the guests. Second, she would quit if he didn't agree.

Howard seemed to know when his back was against the wall. Trish's people management skills were legendary and at this stage of operation he couldn't afford to lose her. Since he was not a dog person, his awareness of such things was unevolved and, as it turned out, the guests loved the dog. He reluctantly acquiesced. Burton, the mascot!

CHAPTER 15

"Got a text from Bories. He says he'd like to meet at five-thirty for cocktails to go over our proposal. Will we be there by then?"

The cell service heading west past Port Alberni tended to be sketchy at best. Jenne saw the time on the text was over an hour ago.

"I thought we were meeting him for dinner?" Jenne knew Kevin was looking forward to Howard picking up the tab.

"I guess he's had something come up. It's four now and it looks like we're about an hour out. Correct? I can text him back."

"Yup. We're also getting closer to the crash site and the place where the monster bear had lunch with my kidnappers. Just thinking of it makes me a little queasy."

"I'm really sorry you had to go through that, Kevin. I'm sure it was awful for you. When you disappeared I was lost. I was frightened and I don't want to think about what might have happened. I really do love you, you know?" She reached across the console to squeeze his arm. "Don't ever do that shit again. I mean it."

"Um, okay, I promise. Does this mean we can have sex tonight?" The squeeze turned into a punch. So much for tender moments.

The O'Malleys had time to check in and dump their bags at their room before heading off to Chesterman's. There they found Bories sitting at a table for four, just to the side of the fireplace. He looked every bit of his seventy-five years, almost like the experiences of late had taken their toll on the man. He had a tumbler of clear liquid in front of him, most likely not water.

He stood up to greet his guests. "Wonderful to see you two again. Let's hope your stay here will be far less exciting than last time. Please, have a seat, let me get you something to drink." Howard motioned to a waitress, who immediately appeared at his side. "Marjorie, please bring the O'Malleys something."

They both ordered one of the exquisite chardonnay selections, then settled in to share their plan with Bories.

When their wine arrived, they shared the obligatory clinking to "cheers" and prepared to go over the numbers. "Before you begin, I have some difficult news to tell you." Howard radiated discomfort with his delivery.

"I've decided not to go forward with any replacement of the furnishings at this time." Jenne and Kevin glanced across the table at each other, trying to come to grips with what they had heard.

"I realize I told you to come up with this proposal, but some things have happened, and I need to make adjustments for the near term. Of course, I'm sure it's taken considerable time for you to pull this together, and I'll certainly reimburse you for your efforts and expenses."

Jenne was the first to voice her thoughts. "I guess you know what's best for your situation, Howard. But what about all this crappy stuff you have in here? You know it won't hold up, and if the fire marshal ever gets around to checking flame spread issues on the fabrics, he'll close you down. I thought you told us you were going ahead with the replacement."

"I know what I told you, and I'm sorry for the inconvenience. I'm not at liberty to explain my decision, nor will I. Just be assured that you will be paid, and any discussion of going forward with this, at this time, is closed."

The sudden turn of events left a quiet discomfort at the table. Kevin turned to Jenne, had that silly, quirky smile on his face, and said, "So, honey, how about those M's?" It was his go-to line when things got too quiet or too serious. The sudden reference to the perennially futile efforts of the Seattle baseball team either broke the tension and the pressure was released or, as in this case, left people thinking Kevin was possibly mentally challenged.

"Sooo, Jenne, what do you say we head over to the bar, grab a burger, then hit the sack. Howard, I don't know what brought about the change in plans but, hey, you're the boss. Thanks for the opportunity." The last bit, a touch of sarcasm. They both stood, shook hands with the old guy, and took their drinks with them as they headed over to the bar.

Chesterman's was only half-full this early in the evening. The intimate lighting at the bar combined with the subtle backlighting encouraged a casually relaxed atmosphere. Just moving across the room helped their attitudes.

"Nice one on the M's, Kev. Now the guy thinks you're nuts."

"Hey, I no longer give a shit. Sure, we spent the better part of a week pulling this together, but we're going to bill him for every second of our time. The longer we're around this place the less I like it. We should have considered the last trip an omen and not returned."

"I hate to say it, but I agree. After tomorrow we're outta here and we're not coming back. Damn, I almost forgot, we have to connect with that crew that did the artwork and the moving here."

"Okay, wait here a minute, his Highness is still over by the fire." Kevin ambled over to chat with Bories once again.

"Howard, is the crew that did the moving and art installations still here?"

"Yes, I think so. Why?"

"We thought we'd talk to them about a job we have coming up south of here."

"I think I told you they're a little odd."

"Yes, you did, but we'd still like to talk to them."

"Well, okay. Just call them from one of the house phones. The front desk will connect you. The head guy is Jordan."

"Okay, thanks. See you around."

They were able to get the hotel operator to connect them to Jordan's room. "Hello?" he answered on the first ring.

"My name is Kevin O'Malley. We got your name from the owner of this hotel. We own an interior design firm, and we're installing some artwork at an inn south of here. We wondered if we could talk to you about doing the installation."

"Ahh, well we just finished here, and we were headed back home tomorrow. I don't think we want to do any more work for a while."

For a while? What the hell did that mean, Kevin thought. "Well, if you change your mind before tomorrow morning is over, give us a call. We're checking out late morning."

"Okay, bye. Oh, and thanks for asking us."

Well, they *were* odd. Kevin's sense was that they were just shy and possibly a little naïve about life. If he heard from them, okay. If not then, plan B, whatever that was.

"Well, you got the gist of that, Jenne. So we're going to have to find another crew. Maybe we can hire some of the local gallery folks from Victoria. They must have someone who can hang art." "I guess, but it'll have to wait until morning. They're all closed for the day now."

"Okay, so do we head back to the room and have a sex fest, or did you have something else in mind?" These blatant calls for frolicking in the sack never ended well.

"Actually, great idea. Let's go. And close your mouth, you look like a doofus."

His mouth was hanging open because he was stunned by her response. He dutifully closed his mouth, avoided saying any more stupid stuff, and followed her back to the room with a spring in his step.

Marty's breakfast meeting with Bories did not go well. He would not release any of the retained money until the replacement furniture was received and installed. Even after explaining that what was being withheld far exceeded the replacement goods, the hotel owner wouldn't budge. "Howard, I think you're being a prick." Marty figured insults were going to work where reasoning had failed.

"Your thoughts really don't concern me. When and if we get the balance of what you have promised, I will release your funds. Now, if you don't mind, I've other issues requiring my attention."

Howard left the restaurant in a huff. Marty's gaze followed him as he left through the lobby and lighted upon Jordan and his crew, just now entering the restaurant. Jordan was the tallest of the four at six three and, now in his mid-thirties, still looked like the prototypical high school quarterback.

"Hi, Jordy, I was going to call you after my meeting with Bories."

"I'm glad we ran into you, Marty. You promised payment, in cash, when the job was complete. Now it is."

"I know our agreement was seven grand cash, but I'll have to write you a check."

"That wasn't our agreement, and I'm pretty sure Daniel won't approve. He was adamant that we collect what you owe us and that it be in cash."

"Well, I don't know what to tell you. I don't have the funds with me, and there's no way for me to get cash here in Canada. You'll just have to take my check." Marty was an idiot when it came to money. The amount he owed these guys was a drop in the bucket, yet he still felt the need to screw these guys. Just because he could.

"We need the cash. Daniel said no checks."

"I don't give a shit what Daniel said. I'm leaving for California now. Tell Daniel I'll send him the check." With that Menucci rose and walked briskly to the front desk to settle up. It had been an unforgettably shitty visit to the Tofino Inn and Spa, and he was finally through with this place. He'd text Tiny and Roger and give them their walking papers as well.

Jordan sat with his three mates, all picking distractedly at the sumptuous breakfast buffet. "Daniel is gonna be pissed. He was planning on taking his cut when we met up in Nanaimo. What are we gonna do?"

Eric was the first to respond. "What can we do if Marty only sends a check and now he's sending it to Daniel?"

Jordan responded as if he were talking to a fifth grader. "Eric, there is no check in the mail. Marty's gonna fuck us. We're not gonna get paid."

Eric looked as though he'd been slapped in the face. The other two, Warren and Eddie, wore vacuous expressions. Jordan had been friends with these three since high school. He was the smartest of the three and it fell to him, reluctantly, to guide them through the gauntlet of life.

They'd been born and raised on Whidbey Island, the longest, skinniest island of the San Juan Archipelago. Whidbey was a lovely, pastoral place. Its inhabitants were artists, writers, and craftsmen. It was also a bedroom community for the Boeing employees working at the Everett Manufacturing Facility. Halfway up the island was the city of Oak Harbor, the home of Naval Air Station Whidbey Island. The four friends had enlisted in the navy directly upon graduation from South Whidbey High School. They had signed together with the proviso they be stationed together in Oak Harbor.

The men had been raised cautiously by well-meaning conservative parents. Whidbey has its share of both liberal and conservative individuals.

Thing is, on Whidbey, as in many small communities, sometimes these preferences migrate towards the extremes rather than the center line. The four families didn't just lean to the right, they were card-carrying Fox News subscribers and anything else was blasphemy. As teenagers, the boys possessed relatively appropriate interpretations of right and wrong. Their views on women, brown people, gay people, immigrants, the homeless, and the poor tended to be less informed. The navy has a way, as do all of the armed forces, of altering preconceptions and misconceptions.

The four reported to the Great Lakes Naval Training Center on the western shore of Lake Michigan for basic training. The base is halfway between Chicago and Milwaukee. Like all recruits, they were thrown together with poor people, gay people, brown folks, and women.

It was a numbing two weeks getting acclimated to things. Then, strangely enough, people they had always been leery of just became sailors going through the same shit they had to endure. They learned that a woman could save your life just as easily as a man. They learned that brown people, folks with accents, and even gay people all had the same goal. "Please, God, just help us get through this nightmare." After a sheltered upbringing on a small island in the Puget Sound, being tossed into the all-inclusive flavors of the U.S. Navy was eye-opening.

Upon graduation, after eight weeks of training, the four friends reported to the Naval Air Station on Whidbey Island. They were glad to be home. Their appreciation and tolerance for others, though, had grown exponentially. Now, at family gatherings and visits, the opinions and viewpoints of their relatives were considered misinformed rantings. Any futile effort to convince them otherwise was dismissed. Their relatives were tolerated, but the visits became few and far between.

After their four-year commitment was complete, they moved off the island, relocating to the thriving Seattle metro area. The foursome rented a small two-bedroom apartment in Issaquah, a growing community but still a half-hour drive to the big city. It was the only thing they could afford in this area of rapidly rising housing costs. Construction skills learned during their tenure on the navy base were a perfect fit for the booming building frenzy in the Northwest. It afforded them ample opportunity to pick and choose their projects.

Jordan and the others saved as much as they could. The trappings of big city life were nice but, at heart, they were still small-town folks. One of the contractors they had done work for had landed a hotel project in Victoria, B. C. He asked if they'd mind joining his crew there to assist in completing the job. They were happy to. After being on the job for six months, they grew to like the smaller community. They gave up their Issaquah hovel and rented a small cabin on Cowichan Bay, just south of the city of Duncan.

Two years passed and the construction jobs on southern Vancouver Island dwindled. More of their work was coming from Nanaimo, to the north, which was undergoing a growth spurt. The next decade was spent doing pickup construction work, furniture moving, and any other odd jobs that came along. The four friends hung together. They had occasional dalliances with members of the opposite sex but nothing of any permanence. It was rare that four buddies could hang together for so long. Their experiences growing up and serving in the navy only reinforced their friendship.

Coming back from a small moving job in Nanaimo, the boys stopped for happy hour at the Crow and Gate Pub. They ended up sitting next to two men lamenting their inability to pull together enough of a crew to complete a furniture installation for the Coast Hotel. Jordan noticed that the good-looking guy seemed to be directing the conversation.

"Excuse me. I'm sorry, I couldn't help overhearing. The four of us have extensive construction experience. We're pretty handy when it comes to furniture moving too. If you're looking for manpower, we're your guys. I can give you plenty of references."

Daniel appeared pleasantly surprised. "Tell you what. Give me a list of references and your phone numbers. We're tight for time on this job, so if they check out and we can agree on wages, you can start next week."

"Yeah, maybe you can work for us." The rough-looking dude was less inspiring, thought Jordan.

One project led to another through Daniel. Jordan's team was paid by the job. They learned how to install artwork. At ten bucks a frame, the team's efficiency translated to over fifty dollars an hour. The money was excellent. As the months passed, Daniel took on more the role of a broker. He would find the projects, Jordan and his guys would do the work, and then they'd pay a commission to Daniel and Will.

During a particularly inactive period, Daniel asked Jordan if he'd like to do some work for some friends. "They live on DeCourcy Island and keep to themselves. The property they own is a little rundown, and it needs some updating. They can't pay your normal rate but they're wonderful folks, and they really could use the help."

"Well, there's not much going on here so, sure, why not."

Looking back, that was the day Jordan began the journey that changed him. The next day the *Butterfly* took Jordan, Eric, Warren, and Eddie to Pirate's Cove on the east side of DeCourcy Island. They drove up the dusty gravel road to the Farm. Jordan could still remember his first exposure to the place. The weather-beaten barn and adjacent buildings contrasted exquisitely with the robin's-egg-blue sky and the soft celery-green background of the neighboring meadows. It was the most peaceful place he'd ever seen. His three friends seemed to be experiencing similar feelings. They drove up to the barn. A little old man in a plaid shirt and jeans came outside, a spit cup in his left hand.

"Hi, you can call me Fred. This is our home, but Daniel seems to think it needs a little work here and there." His outstretched right hand was boney yet delicate. Jordan took it and clasped it gently. It sent a strange warmth through his body. He let go.

"Um, we've been working with Daniel for a few months, and he said you could use some help so here we are."

"We can't thank you enough. Daniel and I guess Will, here, will show you around. Again, thank you." With that, the little old guy ambled back to the barn.

For the next few weeks, Jordy and his men worked shoring up sagging roofs, reinforcing termite damaged walls, and repairing many of the rusted metal roofs. The evenings were spent gathered around a firepit, sharing dinner with the rest of the community. Daniel and Will were there frequently, Fred seemed to eat alone in his barn. A ramshackle bunkhouse that itself needed some work served as their sleeping quarters. The bedding was worn but comfortable, and the women and young girls treated them like royalty.

They learned some of the antiquity of the island by listening to snippets of conversation from the men who did the bulk of the farming. The residents referred to Fred as Brother XII. Eventually the crew engendered enough trust from the members so that they freely shared their experiences. There were few older people, and no one came within two decades of Fred. Many inhabitants of the compound were disenchanted with life on the outside. Most had led sheltered lives in small towns, and having an authority figure in Brother XII served to give them direction. There were no mandatory services or requirements. If one of the citizens was feeling poorly or needed cheering up, they were free to call on Fred. All that was needed was a knock on the barn door. He would sit at his desk, and they would talk. After a time they would leave feeling like a weight had been lifted.

That the community lived frugally was clear. The commissions generated by Daniel were tithed to Brother XII, who saw to it that food and clothing were provided. Medical services were limited. One of the women had been a nurse, so she was called upon from time to time to stitch up a wound or diagnose a cold or the flu. She dispensed medicine when she was able to get it. She was always after Daniel to bring more supplies. He complained he never had enough money. There were approximately thirty-five souls on the Farm. They were poor but they had a leader who loved them and didn't judge them. They returned that love. The men shared the women. The women didn't seem to mind; they almost seemed to feel it was their duty. The infrequent disagreements were met with a stern look from Brother

XII and they melted away. There were whispers of long-ago-buried gold, but enough time had passed, and enough holes dug, to put those rumors to rest. If Fred knew anything, he wasn't sharing, and the truth would die with him. The entire commune would surely die with him as well. He had shepherded this flock through some difficult times, and most of the sand was out of the hourglass.

It appeared to Jordan that the only money coming in, other than produce and craft sales, was what Daniel contributed through his commissions. These were kind and gentle people, although school was still out on Will and maybe even Daniel. Eric, Warren, Eddie, and Jordan felt at home on DeCourcy. It had the peacefulness of Whidbey without the judgment and the familial complications. Although they were told they'd be paid, they forgave the debt. Brother XII was so moved that he invited them to stay as long as they wished.

That had been six months ago. The sharing-of-the-women matter was a little out of their comfort zone. Other than that, they were content. They'd see Fred, usually at mealtime, but mostly he kept to himself. He told them if they ever needed to chat or "unburden" themselves—that's the word he used—his door was open. Jordan was still not sure what to make of the guy, but he had to acknowledge that there *was* something extraordinary about him.

Daniel Roger Phillips had been a techie with Google. He joined the company after three years of college at the University of Washington. He had grown up in Wenatchee, a small town east of the Cascade Mountains. As a very bright kid, school studies were not a challenge for him. Upon graduation from the local high school, at the top of his class, he received an academic scholarship to the premier school in the state. As an only child, an unfortunate accident by a couple already in their forties, Phillips was allowed to forge his own way, overlooked by his disinterested parents. With no siderails to limit his fierce curiosity, his computer time exceeded ten hours a day. When he wasn't immersed in MMORPG, massively multiplayer online role-playing games, he was researching alternative religions and cults. He was an odd, introverted kid whose forays into sites more suited to those destined for prison helped mold his future, yet his keyboard skills were unparalleled. A natural evolution of these talents was his study of computer science.

Google signed him after his third year at UDub. He had been on their radar—the company had headhunters and spies at all the leading schools—since his high school days. One summer at their computer school camp had exposed his genius. With a healthy signing bonus and a salary that would make a second-round baseball recruit jealous, he began his coding career.

He hated everything but the money. For five years his life was nothing but writing code, and he couldn't have cared less. The wages and stock options were appreciated but the idea of working for someone else was no longer attractive. He considered the managers to whom he reported to be morons. While the nightlife and social opportunities in Seattle for a handsome, wealthy millennial were limitless, regrettably, Daniel grew bored. Instead of clubbing on Capitol Hill or hitting the pubs in Fremont, he retreated to his juvenile research topics. It was while he was studying the Wiccans of Vancouver Island that he stumbled across the Aquarian Foundation. While analyzing the original donors to the foundation, he realized that most of the contributions were in gold. He became obsessed with determining if Edward Wilson had squirreled the treasure away or had just pissed it away.

There was scant material available online detailing the activities of the current and past members of the group. Daniel eventually stumbled across the writings of John Oliphant, the acknowledged expert on the life and times of Edward Wilson and his infamous faction. It was in these texts that he discovered Wilson had amassed half a million dollars in gold from unwitting donors. Oliphant's extensive research on Brother XII, while enlightening and informative, shed little light on what had become of the treasure. Continuing his research, Phillips came across an article on page twelve, below the fold, of the *Nanaimo Daily News*. It was dated from the early nineteen fifties and noted the exploits of one Ferdinand Wilson, who had won a lawsuit awarding him a large parcel of land on DeCourcy Island. Armed with this discovery, Daniel sold his belongings, cashed in his stock options, and moved to Vancouver Island. This mystery was going to be best solved in person.

Daniel Roger Phillips moved to Nanaimo. It wasn't higher math to calculate that a half million in gold from the twenties translated to many millions today. It would most likely be a wild goose chase, but the idea of tracking a fortune in gold piqued his interest. Writing code for Google was awfully fucking boring. At least this was something he could sink his teeth into. It wouldn't happen overnight, but it just might be worth the journey.

CHAPTER 16

Daniel managed to convince the manager of the Yellow Point Lodge to lease one of the rustic cabins on a month-to-month basis. It was the offseason and some income was better than none at all. The cabin was directly across the channel from DeCourcy and, until he could figure out a way to ingratiate himself to this Wilson character, he could at least be visually connected to the place.

Over the next few weeks, Daniel tried to mix with the locals as much as possible. It was a very small community, and the Crow and Gate seemed to be where the natives gathered. The bartender at the pub, Leonard, was an affable sort, and Phillips leaned upon their blossoming friendship to gather intel about the DeCourcy Farm.

"They keep to themselves except for the second Tuesday of the month. There's a farmer's market in that open field over by Boat Harbour. They bring fruits and vegetables they've grown, and some trinkets—bracelets and stuff—that the women make. Bunch of people that live around here bring things to sell too."

"Do they always show up? Do just the women come?"

"Mostly it's just the women and girls. But when they have lots of things to sell, sometimes they bring that old guy with them."

"The old guy?"

"Yeah. He's supposed to be some mystical soothsayer or something. To me, though, he just looks like some little old farmer. The women treat him like he's some sorta saint. If you ask me, I think it's a little weird."

"Sounds a little odd to me too, Lenny. Maybe I'll stop by there next week. I could use some fresh fruit."

And so Daniel made certain to visit the fruit stand operated by the DeCourcy group the following week. Two women, who appeared to be in their thirties, were arranging and polishing apples and pears. They were dressed in jeans and sandals and protected from the chill in Carhartt jackets that were two sizes too big. Knitted hats covered their shortish hair, giving them the appearance of adolescent males. The boxes of produce, off to the side, were piled chest high. He approached the women, intending to strike up a conversation, try to get to know them. Only when he stepped up to the front of the stand was he aware that a tiny elderly gent was sitting on one of the upturned crates, mostly hidden by the fruit cartons.

"I'd like a dozen apples and about six of those pears." It was the best he could do. He was distracted by the old man. He had smiled at the guy, and his overture had been acknowledged by a slight nod and a gaze by the most intense eyes Daniel had ever come across.

"So did you grow these here locally?"

The women were bagging his purchases. "Yes. We have a farm on DeCourcy. Lots of fruit orchards, and we grow vegetables too, when the weather gets a little warmer."

"Well, I've recently moved here from Seattle. It's nice to know where I can get fresh fruits and vegetables. My name is Daniel." He reached to shake their hands.

"Pleased to meet you. I'm Molly and this is Anne."

As they exchanged introductions, the old fellow stood up and slowly but deliberately extended his hand. "Hi, Daniel, I'm Fred. Nice to meet you." His voice belied his appearance. As they touched, a warmish tingle radiated up to Daniel's shoulder and then to his chest. The man's friendly smile was countered by his inquiring crystal-clear blue eyes. "Welcome to our part of this world. Perhaps we'll see you again."

It took the better part of that first year for Daniel to ingratiate himself to the DeCourcy folks. It was usually Molly and Anne that came to the market. Sometimes Emma joined them and every second or third trip Fred came along. He noticed the ladies didn't call him Fred. Once or twice he overheard them using Brother something or other to address him. He suspected it was *twelve*.

He often helped them carry their supplies to and from their car. He always purchased more than he could use, and he made certain to generously tip them. One Tuesday that following summer, he was chatting with Anne and Molly while they were packing up the car to drive back to the harbor. As Anne turned to take the remaining tomatoes from Daniel, she twisted her ankle and tumbled to the ground. "Shit, look at me. Sprained an ankle and squashed the tomatoes. Just great."

It was the first time he'd ever heard an off-color word from her. "Let's get you in the car. I'll ride to the harbor and help you load the boat."

Despite their protestations, he insisted. After loading the *Butterfly*, he realized that Anne was the boat pilot, and she couldn't stand on the bridge. Daniel's summers in Seattle weren't without time on the lakes and the sound, and he was proficient at navigating both powerboats and sailboats. "Looks like I'll be taking you over to your island." Both women shared a look of concern but seemed resigned to the fact that they were out of choices.

"We really appreciate this, Daniel. Brother, um, I mean, Fred will be grateful, as are we. Will is one of the farmhands. He can manage the boat enough to take you back."

Molly had radioed ahead to let Fred know what was going on. The VHF receiver was the one concession to the outside world that was Fred approved. Well, that and his chip reader. Shepherding his flock was paramount. If it was necessary to communicate with the outside world for safety sake, then so be it. They arrived thirty minutes later to a gaggle of ten or so men and women lined up on the dock. Fred led the parade and nimbly tossed a line so Molly could tie off the boat.

Daniel was eagerly received by the congregation. After they assisted Anne to her quarters, Fred insisted he stay for dinner. "It's getting a little late for Will to take you back tonight. We have a spare bed and plenty of food. Will that work for you?"

Daniel couldn't believe his good fortune. He actually felt a pang of guilt, but it quickly passed. "That sounds good, Fred. I don't have anything pressing tonight, nor do I in the morning."

One night turned into two and then a week. Most of the men on DeCourcy were not overachievers. They were happy to be left alone and Fred, Brother XII, was there for support if it was needed. They had a warm bed, food, and occasional female companionship, and all that was required of them was intermittent manual labor.

Over that first week, Fred spent a considerable amount of time with Daniel and apparently enjoyed conversing with someone of intelligence superior to the members of his flock. Fred did not come across as brilliant, but he seemed charismatic and incredibly intuitive. Nursing this small community for decades had instilled a deep sense of obligation in the little guy.

He shared with Daniel the difficulty of their hand-to-mouth existence. Daniel wondered whether this guy really did know anything about the gold. Surely, if he did, he would use it to augment the groups' living standards. On the other hand, maybe he just preferred to use their meager existence as a distraction to keep diversions and temptations from them.

Daniel was a patient man. He rightly assumed the solution to this mystery was not going to happen overnight. Yet, he was committed to his scheme. Towards the end of that first week, he developed a proposal that he thought could support the little community and further develop his relationship with Brother XII, as he now referred to him.

"Sir, as you know, I worked in the computer field before I left

Seattle, and I'm aware that there's a construction spike in the local economy. I'm convinced I can develop a website that would encourage independent construction workers to subscribe. It will be a simple matter to lobby the larger general contractors to use the service to fill their inevitable manpower shortage. I'll then charge a fee to the workers for them to use the site. We can start out here in Nanaimo and then expand things all the way to Victoria."

"It sounds interesting, Daniel, but I don't think we want to avail ourselves of any charity here."

"Look at it this way. I'd really like to spend some time here on DeCourcy. Think of it as remuneration for you providing food and a place for me to sleep when I'm here. It seems like such a tranquil place, and I would dearly like to know it and you better."

It would have been easy to assume Brother XII was gullible, but Daniel felt that would be a mistake. He also knew that the income from the community's meager sales of late just wasn't sufficient.

"Tell you what. How about we give it a try for a while and see how things work out." It was still difficult for Daniel to assign the timbre of the voice he was hearing to this skinny old man.

Over the next several months, he launched and promoted the website. Well-placed ads on Facebook and, of course, Google generated considerable interest by the unaffiliated tradespeople. It was a simple matter to contact the local job superintendents and offer his services. Daniel was in his element and soon the DeCourcy settlement was the beneficiary of several thousand dollars a month courtesy of Vancouver Contracting Services LLC.

Soon Daniel was spending three or four days a week on the island. He'd grown closer to Brother XII and felt assured Fred felt the same. The women were overly solicitous, and it took a conscious effort to maintain his chaste approach to them. Especially Anne. When she lost the knitted hat and cleaned up some, she was a looker. He was still amazed that these people stayed here. It *was* a paltry existence even with his contributions.

One of the more recent arrivals, a guy named Wilson, seemed to show up whenever Daniel was present. Will was capable of piloting the *Butterfly*, and it was he who ferried Daniel back and forth from Boat Harbour. That he was somewhat of a reprobate was obvious to the majority of the residents, save for Brother XII. The old guy was benevolent and tremendously tolerant of flawed people. He *was* a wonder. Daniel wasn't fond of Will, but he managed to tolerate him when his presence was unavoidable.

As the enterprise continued, VCS became the favored outfit for contract workers on Vancouver Island. From time to time Daniel would act as the go-between when the GCs compensated the contract workers. This afforded him ample opportunity to scrape a slice off the top. Cash always came in handy. For Will, the graft was like a Bacon Bit to a bulldog. The man lived in the present. Booze was his friend, off-island women were his comfort. He avoided the DeCourcy women, thankfully, and always found an excuse to travel to Nanaimo to see what turned up. Daniel had told Jordan that if the man hadn't been in the DeCourcy community, he'd be in the slammer.

The VCS website had been on Marty's radar when he secured the contract for the Tofino project. When it came time to install the inn, he'd contacted Daniel. By that time, Jordan and his crew were full-time residents at the Farm and whenever a job fit their specialties, it was offered. They were used to the drill now. Get paid, let Daniel take his piece, head back to DeCourcy. It was difficult to see what Brother XII saw in the man, other than his financial contributions to the community. But they had complete faith in their mentor. He must know something they didn't.

As soon as Jordan got the bad news from Marty, he got Daniel on the phone. Both he and Will were in Nanaimo visiting with some construction outfits. "Marty stiffed us. He said he didn't have the cash with him, and he'd send you a check. It's bullshit, right?"

"That guy really is a prick. When did he leave, and what's he driving? Will and I will have a chat with him. In the meantime, I don't think the folks on the island will be happy if you return empty-handed."

Jordan was not comfortable with any part of this conversation. "He just left about fifteen minutes ago. He's driving a bright red Mustang; I think there was an Avis sticker on it.

"We ran into those Seattle designers this morning, and they offered us a job down in Brentwood Bay. It's only a few hundred pieces but it's something. Maybe we should take them up on it."

"Maybe you should, Jordy. I'm sure Brother Twelve will be appreciative of your help. Make sure you call me when you're finished so we can pick you up in the *Butterfly*. You can leave the Outback at the harbor."

Will and Daniel were using a rental, a new Ford F-150, since Jordan's crew was using the Outback. "Good thing there's only one way back from Tofino, huh?" Will was nothing if not observant.

"Yes. It should take him some time to get through Port Alberni. If we leave now we should get there in plenty of time to intercept him, maybe near Loon Lake. We can talk about what to do with him on the way." Daniel had always been arbitrary when it came to the law.

CHAPTER 17

"Honey, did I tell you how wonderful you were last night?" Kevin still had the look of a teenager after his first encounter with the opposite sex.

"Yes, dear, only three times. You'd think we'd never had sex before."

"Well, with you, darling, every time seems like the first time."

"Good one, Kev. God knows I appreciate the compliment, but you're still not getting me back in the sack this morning. How about putting the rest of those things in the car so we can get going. We've still gotta figure out something for Brentwood."

As Kevin was reliving last night's escapades, his cell phone started doing a jig on the nightstand. "This is Kevin."

"Mr. O'Malley, this is Jordan. You talked to us yesterday about some work in Brentwood Bay. We have more time over here than we thought, so if you still need a crew, I think we can accommodate you."

"That's great news, Jordan. We'll pay ten bucks a frame and we'll do all the placement and the measurements. Does that sound okay?"

"That sounds great, sir. When should we meet you there?"

"If you don't mind working Friday and the weekend, we should be able to get the pieces placed by Thursday evening. Will that work?"

"No problem for us, we'll be there Friday morning. Do you think we can get a couple of rooms there?"

During the offseason, occupancy rates were wanting in this part of the northern hemisphere. Marie was a good sport, and she would be happy to cut the rack rate in half for their crew. "I'll set it up, Jordan. They'll be expecting you."

"Whew, problem solved, Jenne. Looks like those guys can help us after all."

"That's great news. Let's just hope the stuff gets there by Thursday. We can head down that way and chill out for a day. That way we'll be able to start the layout as soon as the artwork arrives."

Brother XII was wearying of his lot in life. For eighty-five years he had lived on DeCourcy Island. The inhabitants of his little commune had been transient at best. Fred did not peg the needle at the top end of the IQ scale. What he lacked in formal intelligence, however, was more than compensated for by his perception, his sensitivity, and his intuition.

His knowledge of the history of this place far exceeded other living souls. Still, it was riddled with holes and inconsistencies. While Fred was yet in his early teens, his father had passed away. Many of the stories passed on by his dad he remembered vividly. Some, especially the early ones, were a tad hazy. He knew all about the original founder of the Farm and its odd buildings. That his grandfather was charismatic and brilliant, there was no doubt. There was also no doubt about his philandering, his selfishness, and his ability to take advantage of those ill-equipped to deal with the vagaries life tossed their way.

His father somehow managed to sidestep the negative character flaws of the commune's founder. Over his short life he'd been determined to convert the Farm from a haven for wealthy sycophants to one of refuge for the downtrodden and the forgotten. He was well on his way to achieving his goal when fate intervened. During a routine trip across the channel for supplies, he lost power in his small boat. The normally calm waters were hit by a severe southerly squall and the boat was swamped. Fred Sr. was not a swimmer and did not survive. His body was never recovered. Several of the women living on the island took the responsibility of raising Fred through his teenage and early adult years.

Whether charisma can be inherited or not is an open question. There are certain physical qualities that may assist in generating this magnetic personality trait. It might have been the strange quality of his eyes, his unearthly godlike baritone, or his ability to convey a feeling of warmth and well-being. Or, perhaps there *was* some mystical quality that had been passed on. In any case, Fred had it, and he knew it even if he couldn't understand it.

He had done his best to carry on in the tradition instilled in him by his father. The old buildings still were serviceable, and the soil still produced ample crops to sustain them. The only holdover from the early religious days was the Egyptian ankh that his grandfather had mounted on the face of the loft in his barn. Brother XII was happy to let his flock practice whatever form of religion made them happy. If they were agnostics, fine; pagans, fine; Jews, Hindus, Muslims, Catholics, all were welcome. His only stipulation was his absolute prohibition of proselytization. To Fred, that was a deal breaker. Anyone could choose any direction they so desired, but they had to decide for themselves.

The only rules he enforced were designed for compatible coexistence. It was rare that folks needed any reminders. His door was always open, and his kindness and wisdom seemed to infect the others.

The constant struggle to keep things afloat was getting to him. Yes, Daniel had helped a great deal with his contributions. Somehow, though, Brother XII nursed a slight discomfort when he considered the windfall. Daniel was very intelligent but still, his essence seemed at odds with the congeniality of the Farm. The stories of buried gold on the island were among those early hazy ones passed on from his father. He was pretty sure if there had been gold buried somewhere, it was long gone by now. Still, those rumors somehow persisted. If there was gold, it sure would come in handy now.

The addition of Will to the community was also disturbing. Fred never questioned where his people had come from, but Will too, seemed a poor fit. Daniel would stay for a few days and then leave. Sometimes Will would join him. All of the other residents were content to stay on the island, at least until they chose to leave permanently.

Jordan, Warren, Eric, and Eddie had been with him for the better part of a year now. They were terrific guys. They seemingly could assimilate anywhere but maybe it was just more comfortable here on DeCourcy. They were his kind of people, though, and he'd feel much more at ease if Daniel and Will were more like them. "Everyone's different," he recalled his dad saying. "Some are just more different than others. Like you."

Fred had met with that Bories guy to placate Daniel. He would have preferred to let the matter drop, but Daniel had insisted and Bories *had* paid, so he figured things worked out okay. Fred was not big on confrontations; he would rather just let things work out on their own. They usually seemed to, mostly.

Will and Daniel jumped into the F-150 and took off towards Port Alberni. Marty had been on the road for a short time, but they would still get to the east side of that town before Marty would show up. Daniel figured a red Mustang would be a slam dunk to spot even if they were parked off to the side on Loon Lake Road. There was still some uncertainty about what to do with the guy if he didn't cough up the cash, but they weren't letting him go. No way would they take his word about a check.

After an hour or so they found a spot on Loon Lake Road where they could see the Alberni Highway clearly. There were enough curves in the road at this juncture that Marty's speed wouldn't prohibit them from seeing him.

Forty-five minutes later a cherry-red Mustang cruised through their sightline. "Let's go, that's gotta be him. Where do ya think he got a rental like that?" Will could be depended upon for inane banter.

"I'm pretty certain you can get one at the rental agency, Will. How about you shut up and follow him while I check the map on the nav system here and figure out where we can intercept him." Insulting Will was futile at best so Daniel gave up and studied the road ahead on the nav system.

"There aren't many opportunities to run him off the road. Most of this highway is only two lanes and traffic seems awfully steady coming the other way. Let's just follow him for a while. Maybe he'll stop to take a leak or get some coffee."

The closer they got to Nanaimo the more difficult it would be. Too many people. They followed him past Loon Lake and past Cameron Lake. It was no problem staying close. Marty wouldn't know who they were, and it was difficult to pass anyway. Daniel was getting concerned they might lose their chance at catching him when he pulled into a solitary 7-Eleven gas station combo just a mile and a half past Cameron Lake.

They drove up to the front of the convenience store and parked to the left of the Mustang while Marty went inside. "Stay in the truck, Will, and get out when I raise my hand, but stay behind the door." As Martin exited the shop, Daniel sidled over to him. "Excuse me, are you Martin Menucci of Interiors by Martin?"

"Yeah, who wants to know?"

"My name is Daniel Phillips. You *do* remember our phone conversation when VCS provided a crew for your installation out in Tofino? I think you owe us and our associates some money."

"I don't give two shits what you think. Get outta my way, I'm leaving." Daniel, while of shorter stature, was younger and in great physical shape. Marty, older and skinnier, was easily cut off from his rental. Daniel raised his hand. Will opened the driver's side door and stood behind it.

"Marty, you see that guy on the other side of this truck? Do you know why he's standing there? You probably don't, right? I'll tell you why. Firstly, his name is Wilson, but call him Will, he likes that better. Secondly, he's very big and strong and, yes, not too bright and not too good-looking either, but that's not his fault. What he usually does is just what I tell him to do. Oh, and he's also holding a twelve gauge pump behind the door, waiting for me to give him instructions."

Marty's complexion seemed to whiten considerably. "I don't know what you're talking about. Get out of my way."

Daniel crowded his space even more, while Will pasted a terrifying smile over his misshapen teeth, seeming to intuitively understand the situation, strangely enough. "Marty, I think it's best if you get into the truck."

"Okay, I'll get in the truck, but I bet there's CCTV cameras here, so they'll know who you guys are."

Right, who cared about cameras, Daniel thought. They didn't have a gun and this clown got in their truck on his own. Sheesh!

As soon as Marty got in the back seat of the crew cab, Will slapped a zip tie over his wrists. "Where'd that come from?" asked Daniel.

"I always keep 'em with me. Sometimes my women friends like a more exciting experience."

He knew he shouldn't have asked; this fellow was just a treat to have around.

"So where are we takin' this guy?" Will had pulled back onto the highway and was headed east, towards Nanaimo.

"I thought you guys just wanted to talk. I can't leave the car there; the rental outfit will charge me an arm and a leg to come pick it up." Marty appeared more nervous now.

"We do want to talk to you, but I think it's best if we take you to the island."

"What island and why do we need to go there to talk? If it's about the money, maybe I can come up with it."

"The way I see it you owe us seven thousand bucks, and it was to be in cash, correct?"

"Yes, but I don't have it with me. Let me stop at a bank, and I can see what I can work out."

"Marty, here's the deal. You have an extremely shitty reputation, so we don't trust you very much. We're taking you to DeCourcy Island where we'll convince you not to fuck with us anymore. I can't imagine anyone will be missing you."

"It's only seven grand, it's not like it's a fortune. C'mon, just let me go. I'll get it for you."

Will was looking like he'd rather be done with this clown but for some reason Daniel had taken a disliking to the man. "Marty, shut up, and stop whining. Think of this as an adventure. You'll thank us later. I'm sure of it." Will looked as though he wasn't convinced Marty was gonna thank them.

Boat Harbour was deserted so it was a simple chore to get Marty on board the *Butterfly* with little fanfare. His wrists, still clasped in front of him, were raw and bleeding. They cast off and began the short journey to DeCourcy. Marty was shoved below deck, while Will and Daniel huddled on the bridge. "Daniel, let's just let this guy go. Why are we hanging on to him?"

"I just don't like him, Will. I really hate it when some guy fucks people over just for the fun of it. I don't think he ever intended to pay Jordy and his crew."

"How about we take the zip ties off him?"

Daniel was used to Will obediently taking directions, but he looked concerned at the moment for Marty's well-being.

"Okay. You can go down and cut him loose. You'd better tell him that he needs to behave when he's on the island, though, because we're his only ticket back."

The trip across the channel was brief and the three of them, especially Marty, were exhausted after the tensions of the day. "I think there's still some kind of cage in the very back of the barn. Let's put him in there until I can come up with a plan." The ancient enclosure was not in the best of condition, but if it could contain eight hundred pounds of bear then Marty wouldn't be going anywhere.

When they arrived at the dock, Brother XII greeted them. He saw the surprise on Daniel's face at his presence.

"Who is this gentleman, Daniel? I wasn't told you were bringing a guest here."

"This *gentleman* was going to screw over Jordan and his crew. We brought him here to convince him that it wasn't his best course of action. I'm sorry I didn't radio ahead but he won't be here for long. I thought we could keep him in that old cage in the back of the barn for a couple of days."

Fred was growing increasingly uncomfortable at Daniel's belief that he knew what was best for the people here at the Farm. The little guy was a gentle soul and any hint of disharmony caused him distress. He was not inclined to deal with conflict directly; however, he felt he had no choice in this instance. "Daniel, I don't like you bringing your problems here. I realize that you contribute significantly to our community but that gives you no right to upset our friends. You're already here so we can't do anything about this right now. This man can't go anywhere on the island anyway so just let him sleep in the bunkhouse. Jordan won't be returning for another day or two."

While this exchange was unfolding, Will helped Marty onto the dock. The con man stared at Fred, seemingly perplexed at what was happening. Fred was used to being stared at. His appearance, his voice, and his eerily calm demeanor in the face of challenging situations always unnerved people. He wasn't certain what plans Daniel had for this fellow, and it was the first time he had felt any sort of threat from any of the folks on this little island.

"I'm sorry, Fred, but I have to disagree. We're putting him in the barn." Brother XII looked stunned. Will stood with his mouth agape, and Marty just chewed away at the inside of his cheeks. It was the first time anyone had disagreed with Brother XII and to address him by his first name here at the Farm was a direct insult.

Daniel grabbed Marty by his arm, shouldered his way past Fred, and made his way to the Jeep to head up to the barn. He left Will and Brother XII at the dock, both looking stunned.

"I'm sorry, sir, I don't know what's gotten into Daniel. Should I go after him and see what his plans are?"

"Tell you what, Will, you walk back up to the compound and keep an eye on things. Make sure that no harm comes to that fellow. If Daniel puts him in the cage, just make sure he has enough food and water. He should be safe in there. I'm going to hang out here for a bit and try to think some things over."

CHAPTER 18

Fred sat on the deck of the *Butterfly*. He had been there for over an hour and the darkness was absolute. With the overcast sky, even the stingy light cast by the stars and the moon wasn't offered. The tiny night-light in the cabin of the trawler cast a dull glow but that was it. He felt every one of his eighty-five years. He had nursed this little community along for over sixty years and he was tired. He had done his best to nurture and offer support to the lost souls who found their way here. Many of them left with kindness in their hearts and renewed vigor for their futures. Some were still here and some just wandered off, no worse or no better for their tenure on DeCourcy. Fred was especially proud that he had carried on with the wishes of his father. That the community was a haven for those disenfranchised folks on the margins of society had been his dad's ultimate goal. His grandfather may have not been the most altruistic of souls, but the eventual product of his efforts did a better job of assisting those in real need than the original had.

Because of his peaceful nature, anger and reprisal were strangers to his personality. Fred was slightly pissed though. Not so much because Daniel had insulted and disobeyed him, but because his flock was in danger of being exposed to the elements that had led them here in the first place. To slam the door in the face of those finally finding their way was repugnant to him. Brother XII needed some assistance.

If Jordan, Eric, Warren, and Eddie were here, he could go to them. Anne had mentioned something about the crew being down south in Brentwood Bay on a job. If he could get them back here, maybe he could resolve the situation.

It had been years since he'd been on the water. Taking the *Butterfly* over to Boat Harbour by himself was laughable. Anne was an excellent captain, even in the dark. That GPS thingy he'd heard about might just be the ticket. Fred was old but he was still in good shape from his physical labor at the Farm. He hiked back up the hill a mile or so and knocked on the door of the women's quarters. Molly's eyes widened at the sight of him. "Hi, Molly, would you ask Anne to put some warm clothes on and come out here?"

Molly did as was asked of her and, shortly, Anne appeared, Carhartt jacket in tow. "Brother Twelve, what a surprise. What can I do for you?"

"I know this is unusual, Anne, but I need you to take me across the channel. I need to reach Jordan and his crew."

"They're down at the Brentwood Inn. Can't Daniel just call them on his cell?"

"No cell service here on the island, and Daniel is the reason I need to talk to them. I need to do this in person."

"We'll still need a ride when we cross over. What about that?"

"Will and Daniel had a pickup they were renting. If you can get Will alone, maybe you can get the keys." This was the longest conversation she'd ever had with Brother XII, and she appeared a little stunned at the direction it was taking.

"I think I can handle that. Why don't you head down to the boat, and I'll meet you there."

Fred turned back down to the dock, and Anne went after Will. Within ten minutes Fred heard the Jeep coming down the hill. This wasn't in the plan, and he worried that Daniel had learned of his departure. The car lights blinded Fred, adding to his fears.

"Thanks, Will. Remember, this is between us, right?"

"Yup, sure. See ya."

"Will insisted on driving me down here. Daniel was still in the barn with some other guy and wasn't aware of what we were doing. That Will is not as much of a punk as I thought. I got the feeling he wasn't thrilled about his pal's actions."

"I'll fill you in on things when we're under way. I'm just not comfortable with the turn things have taken. I hate to bother you, but do you think you can drive me to Brentwood Bay?"

"Of course, Brother Twelve. You've done more for me than I can ever repay. I'll always be in your debt."

"Anne, how about you call me Fred. I'm kinda tired of that Brother Twelve title. It's ok on the island, especially with new arrivals, but it just seems a little pretentious."

Anne seemed at a loss for words at this much different side of Brother XII. She had known him only as the leader of the commune, the spiritual compass. "Sure thing, Fred."

The entire artwork package arrived promptly on Thursday morning, and the O'Malleys arrived just as the semi was offloading the pallets. Marie had provided an unoccupied banquet room for them to unwrap and stage the pieces. Though they had gone through this routine numerous times, they were still amazed at how much packaging was involved in the process. Soon, after the final pallet had been emptied, fully half the room was piled with Styrofoam, cardboard, and tape. At least the cardboard could be recycled.

Next came the arduous task of carting the pieces to the various floors of the hotel, lifting each one to measure, center, and space it, and then noting the specifics on the corner wrappers. They were done and exhausted by midnight. Good thing the inn was only partially filled, and nobody objected to them roaming the halls. They crashed as soon as they got to their room and made sure to leave a call for seven in the morning.

Jordan, Eric, Warren, and Eddie arrived promptly at eight and met the O'Malleys in the restaurant. "Hi, guys, glad to see you made it here on time. Would you like some breakfast before you get to work?" Jenne was impressed by their punctuality.

"If it's all the same with you, ma'am, we'd like to get started. We can start with the vacant floors and then finish up the rest after everyone checks out for the day." Both Kevin and Jenne were impressed that this crew didn't have to be told about the nuances of working in an occupied hotel. They seemed much friendlier than when they first met in Tofino, and any reservations the O'Malleys harbored were slowly dissipating.

"Sounds excellent, Jordan. There's four of you so do you think you'll be done by tomorrow?"

"Mr. O'Malley, unless one of us breaks a leg, we'll be done by five o'clock today. We've got a very good system, and you've done most of the hard work by laying everything out. We'd still like to stay the night here, though. It'll be easier to drive back in the morning."

"Two things, Jordan: first, call me Kevin, and this partner of mine is Jenne; second, if you guys finish by five today, dinner's on us here in the restaurant. Deal?"

"You bet, Kevin, and it's Jordy. The others are Eric, Eddie, and Warren. We'd better get to work; we'll see you back here at six, so we'll have time to freshen up."

As the crew left to begin their assigned tasks, the O'Malleys stared nonplussed at each other. "If these guys are as good as it appears, we've struck gold. They seem very professional and capable. I'm still a little confused, though, about the negative impressions we got from Bories."

Jenne, too, offered her sense of the men. "From what I can see, we shouldn't have any problems. I sorta like them. Let's finish our coffee and go up and check on them in a couple of hours, see if they have any questions."

A bit later the couple took the elevator to the third floor where Jordy et al. had started. They exited the car and were shocked to see the entire floor completed. "Holy shit. Not only are they done on this floor, but it looks like everything is straight, security mounted, and spaced perfectly. Maybe we can use them on all our projects."

Jenne was impressed but not totally convinced. "They're done here but let's check on them downstairs, while they're working."

Taking the stairs down to the second floor, they bumped into Eric after entering the hallway. "Eric, we were surprised that you already completed the third floor."

"That was the easy one, Jenne. All the guest rooms were empty. We have to be more careful and a little quieter here because there are still some folks that haven't checked out. It'll take us a little longer but, hopefully, we won't get any complaints from the noise. Pretty sure you'll still be buying us dinner though. Jordy's planning on it."

"Eric, it looks as though we're having dinner with you. See you tonight." When they retreated to the elevator and the door eased shut, Kevin looked at his wife. "Well, what do you think now?"

"Geez, they're good. How they ended up with that Marty douche-bag is a mystery." Jenne was prone to colorful language among con-tractors; she said it put them at ease.

"Yes, it is. We've got the afternoon free to meet with Marie and see if she really wants to redo the lobby next year. She'll be thrilled with the new pieces and even happier that we'll be completed by the end of the day."

Kevin had reserved a table for six in the dining room at the Brent-wood Inn. The room was a two-story affair with spacious views of the picturesque bay and marina and displayed gobs of exposed fir and pine. It was an informal setting blessed with a spectacular view. The table was located in a small alcove that overlooked the bay, yet it was sheltered from the cacophony of the rest of the diners. Even though the hotel was lacking occupants, the restaurant was locally famous, and seating was always at a premium.

"Congrats, Jordy. You and your crew did an admirable job today. Even Jenne couldn't find fault with your work."

If Kevin thought he was getting lucky tonight, these kinds of comments weren't going to help, Jenne thought.

"Don't pay any attention to Kevin. He wouldn't know good work from bad. Thanks for your professionalism and your courtesy. Marie was very happy with your efforts." Jenne could give as well as she could take.

"It was a pleasure working for you both. In the past, our relationships with our agents haven't been as enjoyable." Jordan looked as though he wanted to offer more but was reluctant to do so.

After cocktails were ordered, the small talk that always seems to happen between people of different ages and socioeconomic levels eventually petered out. "Jordy, you and your friends here are very professional, and we really enjoyed your work. I hope you don't mind me asking, but how did you ever get hooked up with Interiors by Martin?" Jenne was determined to turn over a few stones.

"That was arranged for us through VCS. It's a referral outfit for contractors and subs. We have a relationship with the owners of the site."

After cocktails and a few glasses of wine, the crew opened up a little. "Jordy, why can't we just work for legit businesses like the O'Malleys here? Daniel is starting to get under my skin." Warren addressed the question to Jordan but, clearly, the intent was for all to hear.

"I don't think these folks want to hear any of our problems, Warren. We'll figure things out."

"Maybe there's something we can do to help. We know lots of firms in the industry. We sure would hate to share you but, if it would help out, we'd be happy to," Jenne told them.

Maybe it was the offer of help from Jenne or maybe it was just hanging out with fair-minded business owners that was the tipping point for Jordan. Whatever it was that turned the tide appeared to energize him. "You know we live on DeCourcy Island, right?"

"Yes, we know that. Seems like a very small place. How did you decide to move there?" Kevin peeled the onion back a little.

Jordan started with their upbringing on Whidbey. How the four of them grew up together, served in the navy together, and eventually ended up working together. He shared their experiences with Daniel and Will. He spoke fondly of Brother XII and the community on DeCourcy and the utter peace of the place. From time to time the other three would chip in with their feelings and what their take on island life was. The names of the women and farmhands were tossed about in their tale of life on the Farm.

Kevin and Jenne were so engrossed in the outrageous story that they only picked at their food. They could understand people from a small town wanting to rekindle their youthful experiences. When they mentioned this Brother character, though, their eyebrows raised at each other. There may have been a kick in the shin as well.

As often happens with alcohol consumption, some names that probably shouldn't have been shared, escaped. "Remember those guys that were with us for only a month or so, Jeff and Donnie? What a couple of losers, huh!" Eddie had had one or two more than the others.

Kevin's eyes expanded to twice their normal size. Jenne could see something very significant had been said, but she hadn't yet made the connection. Jordy had, though. If looks could kill, Eddie would now be a casualty. Warren and Eric began studying the ceiling. The table grew unearthly still. Jenne had finally grasped the gravity of the moment. Kevin was the first to break the silence. "So, Jordy, why don't you tell me about those Jeff and Donnie fellas? Do you know where they are now? Because I do."

Jordan knew when it was time to go all in. He admitted the two kidnappers were from the island, but no one knew very much about them. Brother XII let anyone who wanted to join the community do so. Just as long as they carried their own weight. They had only been there a few weeks and they seemed a little rough around the edges.

He acknowledged that Daniel had come up with the scheme at the request of Howard Bories, and that the abduction was to confuse the quality issues at the inn. He also confirmed that Bories only wanted a proposal from O'Malley and Associates so he could distract them and then decline to go through with it. He explained that the reason they agreed to do the job here at Brentwood was because Marty had screwed them, and they couldn't go back to Daniel empty-handed.

Neither Kevin nor Jenne could find their voice. They were still trying to grasp the scope of this thing. Finally Jenne said, "So all these shenanigans going on were just so Bories could conceal Marty's fuckups at the Tofino Inn?" She tended towards the profane when she was pissed, and she *was* pissed. She hated to think they were just being used.

To Jordan's credit, he didn't try to duck any of the issues. "We only knew about it from Daniel, and we tried to talk him out of it. He said it was just a temporary diversion and no one would get hurt, so I guess we just looked the other way. I'm really sorry. Daniel seems to be close to Brother XII, and he brings a substantial amount of money to us, so I guess we cut him a little slack. He told us Bories was going to sell the place as soon as he could and didn't want anything mucking up the deal."

After all the air had been let out of the balloon, the six dinner guests sat there looking at each other. Finally, Jenne said, "I think it's going to take us some time to absorb everything. We don't hold you responsible, Jordan, but you should have been more forthcoming. We'll have your check ready in the morning and, if you need to cash it at some bank, we'll go with you to vouch for the account. Why don't we meet here at nine o'clock. Kevin, let's call it a night." With that, the two designers left the table. The other four occupants were still toying with food, looking like scolded dogs.

By the time Anne and Fred got to Boat Harbour and found the pickup, it was already nine o'clock. The drive to Brentwood Bay would take a couple of hours, so they planned on spending the night there. "Fred, did you bring any money with you? I sure didn't."

"I've got the cash from our last Tuesday market. I'm pretty sure it'll be enough for a room for you. I can sleep in the truck."

"No offense, Fred, but you're too old to sleep in the truck. You take the room."

"Tell you what, let's decide when we get there." Fred shut the door on that discussion.

The drive south offered Anne and Fred an opportunity to get to know each other a little better; rather Fred got to know Anne a little better. Like many of the itinerants that came to DeCourcy, she had grown up in a small community. She'd married her Montesano High School sweetheart and worked as a teller in the local bank. She became pregnant at the ripe old age of nineteen. Unfortunately, due to complications during her third month, she lost the child. Her high school sweetheart, while a terrific tight end for the Bulldogs, was a less-than-stellar life partner. He left the small town, divorced his wife while she was recovering, and moved to L.A. to pursue an acting career.

Broke, disillusioned, and depressed, she moved to Seattle with her best friend, Molly. The tech boom, the traffic, and the big city were overwhelming. The small-town gals moved farther north to find a more hospitable environment. They lived in the small town of Langley, on Whidbey Island, for a few years before moving to Vancouver, B. C., in protest after Trump was shockingly elected. They had donned their pink pussy hats and marched in the protests shortly after His Highness assumed office, but finally they just moved out of the country.

Vancouver was just like Seattle, but with more non-English-speaking people. They liked the idea of living in a foreign country, especially one with a great-looking, young prime minister. They still longed for a smaller venue though. They had been working in the food service industry since their escape from Montesano. They waitressed when they could, then graduated to barista after the mandatory servitude in a Seattle Starbucks. Regardless of the country, the Northwest was always in need of capable baristas.

While doing their thing in a coffee shop just south of Stanley

Park, they overheard one of the regulars talking about a commune on a small island just off the coast of Vancouver Island. They packed up their meager belongings that weekend and took a ferry over to Nanaimo. It took them two more days to find someone to take them to DeCourcy Island. That was three years ago. They had found the peace they were searching for and, with the benevolent Brother XII, a mentor they respected and admired. Recently, though, Anne had felt restless, almost as though she was looking forward to another chapter in her life. There was the occasional sex with the men on DeCourcy but that's all it was, just the physical act without the intimacy. They were gentle and kind but did nothing to fill her heart. Maybe somewhere down the road, she thought. This would have to do for now.

Shortly after eleven, Anne, unused to any drive longer than five minutes, finally turned the pickup into the Brentwood Inn. "Here's the deal, Anne. Go get a room, go to bed, and I'll meet you for breakfast. Park us over in that corner of the lot." When Fred looked at her with those eyes, and spoke with that voice of his, there was to be no further comment. "Just leave me that big coat of yours and I'll be fine. This way we'll have enough for breakfast too."

CHAPTER 19

After Daniel's encounter with Brother XII, he slipped another zip tie on Marty's wrists and shoved him into Fred's barn. In the furthest corner sat what was left of the bear cage from long ago. Daniel still wasn't sure what to make of those stories, but whatever had been in this thing had been very large and very strong. Someone had repaired a significant portion of the enclosure with two-inch-thick vertical-grain fir slats, similar to the original construction. Over the years it had been used to store old furniture and lumber to be used for repair of the structures.

Marty seemed to have surrendered his efforts at any resistance but that didn't stop him from complaining. "I can't believe you're going to leave me in this thing. I told you I'd give you the money. What the fuck more do you want?"

Truth was that Daniel wasn't sure what he wanted. He'd gotten so wrapped up in the abduction that he'd lost sight of his original intentions. Maybe all those hours in front of a screen had messed with his head. And what the hell was that altercation with Fred? It was as if some other being had entered his body. Now he had this Marty fuckhead stored in a bear cage in Fred's barn, and he wasn't even sure why. Will had gone off by himself. Maybe he had stopped by the women's quarters.

He paused to gather himself for a moment. It was the first time he'd been in this place, alone, without Brother XII. He looked the interior over with a tighter focus. There in the corner was the old guy's little desk. Directly opposite, in the west corner, was his bed and an armoire for storing what few items of clothing he owned. Daniel felt, for a moment, as though he were doing something irreverent, unfaithful. The Egyptian ankh from long ago was above his head, still mounted on the face of the loft. And still with that slight luminescence from within.

His consuming pursuit for the gold was never far from his consciousness. There would never be a better time to look for any papers, maps, or clues that could lead him to the treasure than the present. No one else on the Farm would dare come in here, and Marty wasn't going anywhere. He'd figure out what to do with him later.

Starting in the loft, he began his quest. The loft offered nothing but old hay bales, some twine, and lots and lots of rat shit. He walked carefully with only an oil lamp for illumination. He doubted anyone had been up there in decades. Next he turned to Fred's so-called living quarters. The armoire held two pairs of jeans, socks, underwear, and three plaid shirts. The man was not a frequent shopper at Neiman Marcus. He rifled through the little desk drawers. Nothing.

Marty was observing the hunt curiously. "Looking for something, asshole?" Daniel had to hand it to the guy. He was tied up and stuck in an ancient bear jail, and the skinny fucker still had an attitude.

"I am and it's none of your business. Shut up!"

"You don't seem to be having much luck. Maybe I can help if you tell me what you're looking for."

Just what he needed, some con man helping him look for a treasure map. On the other hand, the guy was locked up, what could he do? "Okay, here's the deal. I'm looking for either notes or a map or maybe some clue to some gold that was here a long time ago." The only place he hadn't searched was inside the cage. "I'll cut those zip ties off and you can look around in there."

Daniel snipped them off with his Swiss Army knife. Marty was almost amused at the turn of events. "Whatever gave you the idea that there's gold here? Do you think these people would live like this if they had money? I thought you were supposed to be intelligent. Sheesh!" Marty, again with the smart-ass shit. The guy was amazing.

"If there's gold somewhere on this island, either they don't know it or the old guy isn't sharing. If you want to get off this island just look around in there and, please, just shut the fuck up. You're really fucking annoying." Marty kept quiet for a while and began to turn over buckets and boxes, all full of straw, dust, dirt, and more rat shit. Shortly after he began his search, he pronounced, "Sorry, buddy, no gold in here with me. No maps or clues either. You ever stop to think maybe it doesn't exist?"

Just then the large sliding door opened, and Will entered carrying water and some sandwiches for Marty. "Daniel, goddamn, what are you doing in here? I don't think you should be going through Brother Twelve's stuff like this."

"Remember we talked about the buried gold here on the island, Will? We won't have a better time to look for it. I even let numbnuts here help by letting him search the cage. You going to give us a hand?"

Will had apparently sprouted a seedling of a conscience. Even *he* seemed uncertain what conflicts he might encounter because of it. "I'm not comfortable snooping through his stuff. He's always been good to me, and he's let me stay here even when he probably should have asked me to leave. You can do whatever you want, but I'm gonna go hang with the others."

Daniel was a little bit surprised by Will's conversion, but only considered it for a moment. Now that the possibility of locating the gold was just around the corner, nothing else mattered. As soon as the door rolled shut, he resumed his hunt for some scrap, some hint of a clue that would lead him to the rumored cache. He had done the math and was shocked at what the value of five hundred thousand dollars in gold from the nineteen twenties would be worth today. The conservative estimate, based upon the current price for gold, was between thirty-five and forty million.

"What happened to your buddy? I thought you guys were pals." Marty was nothing if not an opportunist. "Looks like he developed some morals. Good thing that hasn't stopped you, huh?"

Man this guy was a fucking pest. "Marty, would you please just shut the fuck up. I need to think here."

Even caged up like he was, Marty couldn't resist a comeback when he was teed up this well. "You know what they say, first time's the hardest. Good one, right?"

"Yeah, Marty, good one. How about eating your food there. Maybe with your mouth full you won't be able to talk, or you'll choke. Both are excellent outcomes."

Daniel was on his third inspection of Fred's desk, but nothing had materialized. All the while Marty watched the hunt for clues. Even without the constant nagging, his presence was annoying. Daniel was regretting bringing him over here. What *was* he thinking. Sure the guy stiffed him for a pile of money, but didn't he finally agree to pay? He had committed to solving this ninety-year-old mystery, but he was thinking that his proximity to Brother XII and the rest of these escapees from reality was leading him away from rational thoughts and actions. Maybe he'd haul Marty's ass back across the channel in the morning, take him to the bank, get his money, and get rid of the asshole. Well, not *that* kind of get rid, just take him back to his car.

"Have you looked through the other buildings here on this property?" Apparently, while being cooped up with nothing to do, Marty had suddenly developed an interest in Daniel's quest.

"Of course I have. Now be quiet and mind your own business." At this point in time Marty's only business was trying to get back to Carmel.

"If you found this treasure, what would you do with it?"

Daniel paused for a moment, almost as though he was considering the question. He really hadn't gotten further along in his thought process than just discovering if the gold existed and then locating it.

He hated like hell answering Menucci, but just the act of doing so helped formulate his plans. "I guess I hadn't gotten that far along. I'd probably cash it in and go somewhere warm to live. I'm already sick of this place anyway."

"So, what, you'd just walk into a bank and say, 'Hey I found all this gold somewhere. Please give me some cash for it.' That about right?"

Daniel was beginning to feel like Marty was guiding him rather than provoking him now. "Well, I think they'd get suspicious if I did something that stupid."

"Okay, so you'd just hide it and cash in a little at a time? If it exists, how much do you think there is?" Marty was wheedling his way into Daniel's consciousness now.

He guessed it couldn't hurt to share his research with his new pal here. He was still locked up, what could he do? "Based upon the information I've found, if it's here somewhere, there's almost fifteen hundred pounds of gold. It was tithed to the original Brother Twelve who started this community. Obviously, he was very persuasive with those who followed his teachings."

Marty sat up a little straighter, did away with his smirk, and started to get more serious. "Yikes, that's a shitload of moolah. Did you figure out what it's worth today?" Marty and money were always friends, even under these circumstances.

"I think it's around twenty million or so." No sense in giving this guy too much information.

"Okay, got another question for you. You're looking for almost a ton of gold. You think you can do this by yourself? You think you can find a couple of kids or maybe some homeless folks to give you a hand moving it?" Marty was gearing up, ready to close another deal.

Daniel actually felt like the grammar school student who hadn't read his homework assignment and now was being singled out in front of the class. Rather than get all defensive—the guy was still caged, in any case—he fessed up. "To be honest, I hadn't thought that far ahead. I guess moving that much weight would bring its own challenges. I was thinking Will could help, but the sap seems to have developed some principles. Anyway, the task at hand is to figure out if and where."

"I have a couple of thoughts."

"Of course you do. You never shut up."

"I have an account in a small bank in Bermuda. I've dealt with them for many years, they're very confidential. Also, they are used to handling precious metals, diamonds, and several other forms of currency. If one were to present them with a considerable sum of money, in the form of gold, they would be happy to exchange it for the currency of any country in which you would like to reside. That is, *if* there really is any. Of course they would charge a ten percent fee for their service."

Daniel looked as though he was considering this new development. "Seems like a possibility, but somehow, I think you'd like something in return for this little tip."

Marty was happy to solve problems for people, particularly if there was something in it for him. "Since you're kinda on your own now, it looks like you could use a little help. I do have connections that will help down the road, but there's still the question of where is it and how do we move it? You've done all the upfront work on this, so how about me getting forty percent to help you finish this?"

Since Marty thought the value was twenty million, forty percent was eight million. Even with the ten percent service fee, he'd still end up with twenty-eight million bucks in pesos, yen, or Benjamins. Normally he would negotiate harder, but time was running out, and he'd overheard Molly and Will saying that Fred would be back in the morning. He felt bad about scaring the little old guy off but, screw him, he had gold to find. "I'm not certain you're going to be worth it, but okay. Any idea how to find it?"

"Actually, I do. How about letting me out of here?" Now that they were quasi accomplices, there looked to be no reason to keep him locked up.

Marty walked out of the pen, stretched a bit, then stood in the middle of the barn. "You said that if it was really hidden, it would have been from the late twenties or early thirties, right?"

"Yes."

"And all these buildings were here then?"

"Yes."

"It seems that, although the building is very old, most of this stuff—the desk, the bed, the armoire—looks to be only twenty or thirty years old."

"So?"

"So if there was a clue or note or map or something, and if the old guy doesn't know about it, then it would have to have something to do with those early years. The founder would have done something with it, kept it somewhere, that was durable and timeless so he could recover it. Make sense?"

"So far so good."

"Okay, you looked through everything in here, right?"

"Yes, you saw me doing it, three times." Daniel was becoming annoyed; it was as if Marty knew something and was taking his time in sharing.

"You're right. I saw you look throughout the entire barn, and I searched the cage. There *was* one place you missed, though."

"Stop fucking with me, Marty. If you know something, tell me."

"Well, I don't know for certain, but I do know that you missed something, and it looks very old."

"And that would be?"

"That would be that funny-looking thing on the face of the loft. Looks like it's been there forever; also looks like there's a little light behind it or something."

Daniel looked to where Marty was pointing. The three-foot-high ankh, the Egyptian hieroglyphic meaning "life," was still mounted where the first Brother XII had put it. "Holy shit, I never even thought of that. It's always seemed just part of the barn. Let's take a look. I'll go up to the loft and pry it off the beam."

Daniel climbed the rickety stairs to the loft, cleared away most of the rat shit, and lay down with his head extended over the edge where the ankh was attached. The oval loop at the top appeared to be hung over a one-inch-thick spike that was driven into the beam. He started to lift it off, over the bulbous head of the spike, and was astonished at the weight of the thing. "Goddamn, this thing is heavy. I'm trying to get it off the head of this nail, but I can barely lift it." He grunted and lifted, and finally cleared the top of the spike. As it was freed from the beam, it slipped from Daniel's hands and fell the twelve feet to the concrete floor of the barn.

The ankh hit the floor face-first and smashed into hundreds of pieces. Some of these looked to be either glass or some sort of mineral and emitted a soft glow. Daniel hustled back down the stairs and caught up with Marty, who was surveying the damage. "Look at that slimy shit on the back of those chunks." He picked up a smallish fragment and, when he rubbed at the gel-like substance, it stuck to his finger. He looked like an adult version of ET.

"What is this stuff?"

"I don't know, Daniel, but they must have coated the thing with it when it was made. I guess that's the stuff that makes it glow.

"The old man is really gonna be pissed. That thing was from his grandfather. He apparently brought it here from France."

"Well, he may be upset but evidently there aren't any clues to any gold in or on this thing. It was a couple inches thick and made completely of that material. It certainly wasn't hollow."

Daniel was quiet for a moment. Something he'd seen didn't make sense. He bolted back up the stairs, lay down at the edge of the loft, and once again hung his head over. "Marty, throw me that big chunk of glass or whatever it is." He dutifully tossed up the heavy shard.

"I couldn't figure out why I had such a hard time lifting that thing over the head of this spike. It's because it's not like any piece of rod or steel I've ever seen. The head of it is almost two inches thick, and it's round. It was hard to see before because the ankh covered it." With that he proceeded to whack the end of the spike with the remnant from the ankh.

After two or three hard hits, the round portion began to dent, almost as though it was made of something soft, like aluminum. Finally it popped off and fell to the floor where Marty stood, fixated on the operation.

"That's interesting, I guess, but there's nothing in here," he offered as he picked it up to investigate.

"That's because it's not in there, it's in here. The spike is hollow." He reached inside with his glowing finger and pulled out a rolled up piece of paper. "Let me get down there so we can look at this in the light." The oil lamps weren't particularly bright, but anything was better than the dark loft.

As the two conspirators huddled next to the brightest of the lamps, Daniel slowly unfurled the brittle brown paper. Because it had been tightly rolled, many cracks and splits appeared as the process was completed. They held the corners down with small pieces of the ankh until, finally, they could see what message had survived from the days of the founding father.

CHAPTER 20

Saturday morning arrived under unusually sunny skies. During the fall rainy season, these days were rare and were to be appreciated. Sunrise was shortly before seven so when the O'Malleys arrived at the restaurant, an hour or so later, the light was streaming through the clerestory windows.

Jordan, Warren, Eric, and Eddie were seated at the same table as the previous evening. This time of year the hotel was sparsely populated and Saturday morning breakfast even less so. They were the only patrons in the place. Seated with them was a young woman, probably in her late twenties. She was smallish with very short auburn hair tucked under a ball cap, a wisp of a ponytail sticking out the back. Her fair complexion, bright eyes, and very bright smile brought to mind a young Tea Leoni. She seemed right at home with the crew and, even in passing, her frequent looks at Jordy were hard to miss.

When Jenne and Kevin sat at a two-top adjacent to the group, Jordan walked over and invited them to join their table. "This is Anne, a very good friend of ours, from DeCourcy," he said as they moved over to the larger table. "Anne, these are the folks we were just talking about, Kevin and Jenne. They've been very kind to us, and last night we had a sort of clearing of the air regarding some of the unsavory aspects of Daniel's activities." Anne stood up, looked them directly in the eyes, and with a firm handshake offered, "Very pleased to meet you. During the last ten minutes Jordy's told me a lot about you. Thank you for allowing them to explain things."

It was hard to understand why such a self-assured woman would be tucked away on a tiny island, frittering away her life. Of course, that was easy to assume when there was little appreciation for the journey she had traveled to get there. "It was nothing, Anne. Jordy and his crew do excellent work. We're just sorry we didn't come across them sooner. As for the rest, well, let's just leave it in the past." Jenne could afford to be gracious since she'd most likely never see these people again.

"So what brings you here?" Just as the words left Kevin's lips, a tiny elderly gent in wrinkled jeans, a plaid shirt, and an open Carhartt fleece-lined jacket ambled across the room. He carried a spit cup, and his dirty John Deere cap was tilted jauntily to the side.

"Mornin', folks. I'm with her. These people are my friends, from DeCourcy Island. My name is Fred."

The O'Malleys weren't sure what to expect when they saw the little guy from across the room. At the moment, though, they were still in shock at the power and timbre of the man's voice. When they stood up to shake his hand, the quality and color of his eyes actually left them speechless. Kevin was the first to find his voice. "Uh, hi, I'm Kevin and this is my wife, Jenne."

While the O'Malleys were still coming to grips with the incongruities this fellow presented, the rest of the table was totally at ease with his presence. "Fred and I drove down last night from the harbor." When Anne referred to her companion as Fred, the entire crew's heads swiveled in her direction. "It's okay, you guys, he told me when he's off island he's Fred, right?" she asked, looking in his direction.

"Fred's good. I told Anne the other title was archaic and too formal. Fred suits me better too." The O'Malleys felt like outsiders at a family reunion.

"So, um, Fred, Anne didn't get around to telling us why you drove all the way here. And where did you sleep?" Jordy was trying to get a handle on the situation.

"I slept in the truck. Plenty of room for a little fellow like me. Hell, I've slept in a barn my whole life. That Ford pickup has more comforts than I'm used to."

This undiscovered side of Brother XII looked to be a little unnerving even to Jordan. The guy had actually said "hell."

"I'll tell you why we came, but I hate to expose our dirty laundry in front of our guests here."

"If you don't mind, Fred, Kevin, and Jenne know all about Daniel and the Bories thing. Last night over dinner we had a long discussion about our present situation. They know everything and, unless they'd rather not sit in, I would like them to. Their perspective is much appreciated and, as you know, when most of your life experiences are from a tiny island, sometimes a more worldly viewpoint is helpful." Jordan, too, seemed a bit more assertive. "Kevin, Jenne? It's your choice but I'd really like you to stay." Jordan seemed to want their input.

"Sure, let's hear what you have to say." Jenne loved intrigue.

"Welcome aboard, then." Fred's voice was unnerving. He turned to Jordan. "I asked Anne to take me across the channel, then drive me here so I could ask for your help. You know that Daniel has been acting somewhat oddly as of late. Last night he returned to DeCourcy with Will, and they brought a guy named Marty with them."

Jordy replied, "He's the one who wouldn't pay us for the installation we did at the Tofino project. I knew Daniel was angry with him and wanted to make him pay up, but I don't see what bringing him to the Farm would accomplish."

"I thought it was odd when he brought Bories to see me, but that issue seemed to resolve itself. This time I told Daniel to just let Marty sleep in the bunkhouse and return him in the morning. He ignored me and locked him in *my* barn, in the old bear cage. I may be on in years, but I can take care of myself. What disturbs me is the level of disquiet this brings to our community. Daniel likes to come and go as he pleases, and he has never really been committed to our lifestyle. I'm very worried for the rest of our family on DeCourcy. Those people are dealing with their own problems and conflicts and will do so in their own time. The strife and conflict Daniel has brought can no longer be tolerated. I came here with Anne to ask you to come back with me and help us remove Daniel from DeCourcy. I'll not allow him there anymore."

If the O'Malleys thought they were going to be innocent bystanders, the tide looked to be turning.

Fred continued. "It's not like there are any weapons there or anything, and I can't imagine there could be any violence. I just think with a show of force we can safely get him to leave."

Eric spoke up. "We should be able to take care of this with Jordan, Warren, Eddie, and myself. Involving outsiders, no offense you two, won't be any help."

"I'm not so sure of that." This from Anne. "All of us live on the island. Daniel does not. If Kevin and Jenne wouldn't mind terribly, I think them being there as outsiders would erase any doubts that Daniel might have of resisting us. I know it's an awful lot to ask, but it's such a nice day and all, maybe you'd like to go for a short cruise." This was said with an exaggerated lift of an eyebrow and a slight grin.

"Gosh, that sounds really exciting, and here we are with a free Saturday because Jordy and his crew were so efficient. Almost like it was meant to be."

"No, really we would like to help, and my wonderful husband was being deadly serious, weren't you?"

"Of course, Sweetums, I'm behind you all the way."

Anne again, "There's one thing I haven't mentioned. When I talked to Will, he told me that all along Daniel has wondered about buried gold on the island. He said that has been his main objective from the beginning. Is that possible?"

Fred let out a deep sigh. "I told Daniel that those are old wives' tales. Back when my grandfather started the settlement, many of his followers were wealthy. He asked that all contributions be in the form of gold. Guess he was worried about paper money. Anyway, rumor has it that he buried it somewhere on the island. Every once in a while someone sneaks over and digs a few holes, but nothing has ever been discovered. I believe he spent it all. Towards the end of his life he was into drugs and he traveled constantly. Nobody knows what really happened to it, but I can't imagine it's still on DeCourcy." Fred certainly had a way of captivating his audience.

The more the O'Malleys heard about this place, the stranger the tales became. Now, even if they had been on the fence about going, their curiosity was so piqued there was no holding back.

Fred continued. "So I guess all that stuff about Daniel wanting to contribute to the health and well-being of the community was bullshit. Uh, sorry, seems like I leave home and I turn into a heathen, but that young man is definitely starting to piss me off. Uh, sorry, again."

Kevin and Jenne had met many people in their lives but to say this specimen was unique was putting it mildly. It was impossible not to really, really like the man. If his grandfather's charisma was anything like Fred's, it was no wonder he attracted followers willing to tithe generously.

"Well, gang, and Fred, like it or not we're coming with you. We are very interested in seeing this little paradise of yours," Jenne said, barely concealing a grin.

Howard Bories was content for the moment. He had dispensed with Martin and avoided paying him. He had turned the O'Malleys away and gotten them out of his hair. And now, at least according to Trish, two of the appraisers from Apogee were staying here at the inn.

Normally it was difficult to discern the investigators from the paying guests. But Trish was a savvy operator. She had noticed the two birders were considerably more observant than the other guests. The way they treated the staff, the degree to which they evaluated the menu, even the junior suites they chose all contributed to her suspicion. Birders just didn't rent seven-hundred-dollar-a-night rooms. That and their halfhearted discussion about where to see the yellow-breasted whatever was a tell.

According to his general manager, things had gone swimmingly so far for the Apogee employees. Now that they had been identified, it would be easier to make certain their stay was perfect in every way. The only issue to be concerned about was the work Marty had done and the items he had provided.

Rick and Mike had awakened the next morning having slept deliciously. The nine-hundred-thread-count sheets covered by the eight-inch-thick down comforter made for comfort in the extreme. The woven wool carpet felt wonderful underfoot. The heated towel bars, heated tile floors, and subtle but effective LED lighting turned the bathroom into an executive spa experience. The bean counters back in Sweden were going to be delighted with their reporting.

Mike dressed in his "birder" disguise and prepared to meet Rick for breakfast. His outfit was completed by a nicely organized Burberry backpack given to him as an early birthday present by his wife. As he exited his room, he placed the pack behind him while he made sure to affix the "Do Not Disturb" sign on his door. He preferred to have no one enter his room regardless of whether the bed was made or not.

The thunder of hooves could be heard echoing through the hallway before he turned. When he finally faced away from the door, what he could recall later was "a huge black and tan furry animal, almost bearlike." The beast quickly chomped on the lovely plaid backpack and bolted towards the corner suites. Obviously, just the hint of the aroma from the peanut butter Clif bar was plenty to draw Burton from Trish's office. The dog's nose was legend. Unknown to the folks at the rescue shelter, in his previous years he provided law enforcement with hundreds of drug busts. Had there been peanut butter Clif bars in adjacent vehicles, perhaps that number would have been much smaller. Burton was a chowhound, there was no getting around it.

Mike chased the galloping thief down the hallway, ordering him to stop. Burton was relatively intelligent. He knew basic commands—no, down, sit, shake, walk, bath, heel, and good dog. He wasn't familiar with "stop." No matter, though, the promise of a Clif bar was far more attractive than paying attention to any of the commands he did know.

Once the big fella made it to the far end of the hall, away from the lobby, he executed a hard right and found himself in front of one of the executive suites. This section of corridor was only about a dozen feet long and when Mr. Fox turned the corner, he was face to face with a hundred and thirty pounds of hungry dog. Burton had been around the hotel guests for a few weeks now, so he was used to people, suitcases, and the normal hustle and bustle of hotel life. He wasn't that used to an angry guest chasing him, trying to separate him from a delicious treat.

Burton was a sweetheart of an animal. His basic training and interaction with disciplined officers had taught him well. Sometimes, though, under stress, he reverted to what he thought pleased people the most. The high five.

Mike was startled to see the dog sitting there with his backpack, soaked in drool, hanging from his choppers. When he screamed, Burton immediately went into high-five mode. He bolted up on his hind legs and reached high over Mike's head, looking for a reciprocal slap in the paw. The counterfeit birder mistakenly took the action for a deadly attack on his life. Screaming even louder, he twisted out of the way, tripped, and fell forward through the unlatched door of the suite.

Fortunately, he was able to brace himself before he smashed his face into the expensive carpet. He was half in and half out of the door and, for the moment, there was no animal chewing on his person. As he turned to see where the large canine had gone, he was met with a face full of dog slobber. Apparently, Burton, seeing that the high-five maneuver had failed to produce the desired results, had fallen back to the tried and true friendship display—the face lick.

Mike Fox was beginning to realize that this giant dog was a big teddy bear. A hungry teddy bear who liked Clif bars, but nonetheless a friend, not an enemy. He did, then, what the dog was expecting, a rub behind the ears and an "Atta boy." From that point on, they were best buds. Mike expelled a giant sigh of relief.

As he picked himself off the floor, with Burton's assistance of course, he noticed this, the largest of the suites, was devoid of furnishings. Not a stick of it in the place.

While Burton was busy tearing through the paper wrapper on the peanut butter treat, Mike picked up his birthday present and began to roam through the empty suite.

The hotel was supposed to have been complete, so this was undeniably odd. Empty rooms tend to look much larger than when they're fully furnished. They also expose any warts or shortcomings that would otherwise be hidden by the beds, night tables, and sofas. Where the carpets were seamed, normally under the bed, there were small separations in the woven material. Upon closer inspection, this time with a flashlight and magnifying glass—Mike was always prepared—he found elements of backing material.

Often, carpets are tufted or woven into a polypropylene scrim called a "backing." In this instance the carpet appeared tufted rather than woven. A tufted product can be significantly cheaper and may not hold up as well. It was still a wool fiber but when he rubbed it briskly, the fiber broke apart. Mike knew that wool quality varied considerably, and this carpet looked substandard.

He next turned to the bathroom. At the transition, where the carpet met the tile floor, there were tiny chips on the edge of the porcelain tile. Fox knew that this happened occasionally, but usually with inferior products, almost always imported from countries with inexpensive labor costs. His suspicions about the rest of the finishes were aroused.

The lighting looked to be fine but, since the discovery of the flooring deficiencies, he thought it prudent to take a closer look. He unscrewed the faceplate from the vanity light over the quartz countertop. What he didn't see was more disturbing than what he did see. There was no UL label. Underwriters Laboratories offers the most widely used certification for electrical fixtures in North America. No legitimate commercial, or for that matter residential, contractor would install a fixture without this certification. If the fixtures in the hotel were imported from overseas, from a manufacturer that didn't submit them for testing, then they would be half the cost of approved ones.

Mike Fox was now seriously concerned. Burton had finished his purloined treat and was comfortably stretched out on the carpet. The Burberry backpack was soiled with slobber but otherwise intact. Maybe that stuff would wash off. Hell, his wife probably paid enough for it.

"C'mon, Cujo, let's go find Rick. We can stop by the manager's office on the way." He needed to hook up with his partner to discuss what he'd found.

After parking Burton at Trish's office, Mike went to the restaurant to find Rick. His associate was hunched over a stack of pancakes smothered in butter and Vermont maple syrup. He did have to inspect the breakfast buffet, after all.

"Rick, I think we may have a problem." This immediately stopped a forkful of breakfast goodies on its journey to Pike's mouth.

"What do you mean? These pancakes are fabulous."

"Yeah, it's not the pancakes that I'm concerned about."

"What, you didn't sleep well, no hot water?"

Fox proceeded to relate his findings from the empty executive suite. He mentioned how the dog led him to the room but left out the part about him screaming in terror. The look on Rick's face went from questioning to concern to determination. "If what you've found is any indication about the rest of this place, we may have a problem. How do you want to proceed?"

"We may have to talk to the general manager, but first I'd like to take a closer look at some of the furnishings. The artwork appears to be first class, as it should be—it's the first thing you see. I'm a little more concerned about the upholstered goods and the casework. At first glance they look fine, but let's go to the lobby and take a more thorough look."

Rick left his sumptuous breakfast behind, no longer interested. They walked the short distance to the lobby. As expected, it was empty on this Saturday morning. They each chose a separate seating group and proceeded to turn cushions, tip over chairs and open the drawers of the side tables. They tore off tags and gathered lot numbers.

"I think we've got enough info from here. We can also go through the stuff in our rooms. We're going to have to tell the manager who we are and then ask to see the specification manuals from the architect and the interior design team."

As they approached Trish's office, Mike's buddy from before noticed his arrival. This was the purveyor of fine treats who would surely offer another as a reward for a show of affection. Upon opening the door, Burton launched into high-five mode, scaring the shit out of Rick.

With a childish screech, he ducked away, leaving Mike to reciprocate the dog's greeting. "Afraid of a little hug, Pike?" Easy for Mike to say. He'd been afforded some privacy during his embarrassing scream.

"Burton, get down!" Trish was out of her chair quickly, attempting to discipline the beast. She knew nothing of their previous bonding experience.

"No problem. So it's Burton, is it? We're old friends. We met earlier in the day, and I was the one who dropped him off here a little while ago." Burton was now snuggling up against Fox's leg as the man scratched behind his large, floppy, hairy ears.

"I'm really sorry. My name's Trish, and I see you've met Burton. Sometimes he gets out and wanders the property but he's harmless. Well, except for that high five thing. I'd like to throttle whoever taught him that."

Mike took the lead. "I gotta admit, he did give me a scare at first, but he really is a great dog. I'm afraid we are here under false pretenses, we're not really birders. We work for Apogee, and we were sent to evaluate this property and report back to the home office."

"Yes, I suspected as much. You two pay way too much attention to things. Also, you really don't come across as the outdoorsy types."

"Well, thanks for the tips. We'll work on those things," Rick responded, not unkindly. "Mike was chasing Burton here and inadvertently fell into one of the executive suites. It was empty. Can you tell us why that would be?"

"A few weeks ago, just before the grand opening, a terrible accident occurred on the highway. There were two deaths and the last truckload of furniture was lost. Howard's longtime associate was killed in the crash. We had to cannibalize the larger suites to make sure the public areas were complete. I'm told the replacement pieces will be here in a few months."

"I'm really sorry about the accident, and I can see where moving those pieces around would make sense." Rick had a few additional questions. "Did the architect and the spec writer leave the project manuals with you? And, if so, could we take a look at them? I'm sure you're aware that Mr. Bories is trying to sell this place, and it will help our appraisal process."

"I do have the manuals here, and you're welcome to them as long as they don't leave the inn. I came on board just a month or so before the remodel was wrapped up or else I would have more knowledge of the design process. The procurement was handled by Interiors by Martin, and I think the original specifications were done by a Seattle firm."

"We should be here a couple more days, so if we could just look them over during that time it would certainly help. We'll make sure to get them back to you before we check out."

"Here they are. Just make sure you get them back to me, or I'll send Burton after you." Mike appreciated her sense of humor, secure in the knowledge that the big brute was a pushover. Rick nervously cracked a smile, but he wasn't so sure.

CHAPTER 21

The drawing was very faint on the discolored ninety-year-old paper. Whatever development there had been on DeCourcy was minimal compared to many of the Gulf Islands. The presence of "the Farm" and the desire of others to be left alone was enough of a deterrent to discourage those more socially motivated from seeking refuge there. As such, the geography had changed little in the intervening years.

Marty, naturally, was the first to comment. "Looks like there's a road drawn up to the far northeast corner of the island. You can see here where it stops and there's a circle drawn."

"I can see that, but so what, it could mean anything."

"Yeah, it could. But then why take the time to hide it up there? Just for fun, ya think? There's some other stuff on the back side of this, but I can't read it in this light."

Daniel was becoming impatient. "These fucking oil lamps suck. We need someplace brighter to figure this out."

"Wait, I've got my cell flashlight. Phone's not worth a shit here on this island but the light still works." The Samsung Galaxy flashlight wasn't much, but the LED was considerably brighter that the century-old oil lamp.

Under brighter illumination Marty could read the scrawling on the reverse side of the paper. "I guess there's an old barn on the property where the circle is. It says something about a cistern. What the hell's a cistern?"

"Since there's no public water on this island, the only water source is from wells," Daniel explained. "Back in the early years, they would supplement very shallow wells with collected rainwater that they would store in a cistern. They used to be made from bricks or even wood, but after nineteen hundred they started using concrete. Some of them are still in use today." Daniel's research of DeCourcy Island had detailed some of the challenges of the early settlers.

"Does this mean there's gold stuck in some old storage tank here?" Marty jabbed a finger at the document.

"As you so sarcastically pointed out earlier, why bother to hide something that talks about an old barn and a cistern? I'm pretty sure we're looking at the resting place for a ton and a half of gold."

"Motherfucker! Holy shit! What now? Let's get going."

"Hold on there, Marty. Let's think about this. We need to come up with a plan. If it's there, we've got to move it. Then we have to figure out a way off this island. We've got to get it done fast too because in the morning Fred and the others will be here, and they'll know that something's going on. After we get off the island, then we need to figure out how to get it to Bermuda. Geez, this doesn't sound very hard, does it? It's midnight now. Whatever we do we'll need to get going first thing in the morning. We use that old Jeep to get back and forth to the dock, but I think we can use it to get up to that old barn. It's only about a mile and a half from here."

Marty was coming to grips with their logistical nightmare. "That shit's gonna be heavy. Can the Jeep handle it?"

"And take it to where? We can't come back and steal the boat, idiot."

"Okay, how about this." Marty was brainstorming. "We go up there in the Jeep, see if we can find it. We leave it there because nobody else knows, right? Then we come back here before the troops return, and we get a ride back to Boat Harbour in the *Butterfly*. Will or Anne can take us back. Make sense?"

Daniel hated to admit it, but Marty's approach had a semblance of logic to it. "There's gotta be something wrong with it because *you* thought of it but, right now, it seems to make sense."

"Don't be such a dick. It'll give us time to get some equipment together and rent a boat. Is there another way to get to that part of the island with a boat?"

"There's a small inlet between DeCourcy and Link Island. People anchor there in the summer, but we shouldn't have any trouble this time of year. Only thing is, there are some rocky stretches in that area, so we'll need to be careful."

"Sounds okay. We'll probably need to improvise a little anyway."

With a plan of action agreed upon, both men began the task of cleaning up the mess they had made when the ankh had been destroyed upon hitting the concrete floor. They would need to be off the island before Fred returned to his barn but cleaning it up might prevent Fred from glancing up at the loft when he entered the barn.

After Will had dropped off Marty's sandwiches and spoken with Daniel, he became concerned that something terrible was going to happen. He'd been at Daniel's side often during his short tenure here at the Farm. It buoyed his insecurity to feel that someone much smarter than he would be his friend. His need for acceptance had obscured the mercenary tilt to Daniel's character, but now he saw him for what he was.

Will had bounced from job to job and town to town. His early days of street fights had produced the squashed nose, and he owed the rest of his physical attributes to his unfortunate gene pool. He *had* liked hanging with Daniel but some of the calmness of Brother XII and the rest of the peace-loving folks here had begun to rub off. He perceived that Daniel posed some threat to this community, and he was determined not to let that happen.

The vibe he felt when dropping off Marty's food was disturbing. So much so that when he left the building, he took an immediate left and stood to the side of the small square window that was, from the interior, positioned to the right side of Brother XII's desk. He could hear clearly the exchanges between Marty and Daniel. He gasped out loud when the ankh crashed to the floor, but the noise inside covered the sound.

When Daniel and Marty hunched over the desk, he could clearly hear their discussion of the found message. Marty's "motherfucker" even caused him to jump. He knew Daniel had a thing for some lost treasure, but he never considered the rumor had any truth to it. After the two conspirators committed to their plan, Will headed back to the bunkhouse. He needed to share what he'd learned with someone, but Brother XII was gone, and Anne and Jordan were gone. He supposed he could confide in Molly, but it was just too late. He'd wait until he saw her in the morning.

Just after sunrise the next day, Daniel and his new best friend took the Jeep up to the northeast end of DeCourcy. It was a short hop, but the rutted dirt road made for slow driving. The road narrowed and continued down a tiny finger of land where it started a downhill stretch, finally dumping into a small inlet.

"We must have missed something. There's only about three hundred yards of land to our right before it slopes down to the water," Daniel said with a frown. He backed the Jeep up to where he could turn it around. "Keep your eyes open. See if there's a path or an opening on my side. It should be between this road and the cliffs."

They traveled back the way they had come for only a few hundred feet before Marty shouted, "There, back there. Back up a little." The Doug firs and the cedars were a solid canopy here, and the rising sun highlighted what could have been a road long ago. The fallen branches and cedar droppings were over a foot thick, but there was still a slight raised area bordered by two linear depressions.

"Let's park it here and see if that goes anywhere." Marty was already hopping out of the old surplus vehicle. They walked along the depressions, stopping frequently to step over fallen fir boughs. The waves crashing on the rocky shore could be heard the deeper they went. The farther from the road they got, the more difficult the walking, almost as if they were wading through deep snow. It was still early, and the towering trees created a cave-like effect. The low angle of the sun precluded it from penetrating the forest.

Shortly after they lost sight of their vehicle, they came upon a clearing that was encompassed by a broken and tired split-rail fence. There were no buildings, no barn. "Guess we struck out, no barn, no cistern." Marty was easily discouraged. Of course, he hadn't spent years researching this thing.

"Let's look around. What's that pile of wood and shit over there?" Daniel was a persistent son of a bitch. "It's got years of branches and crap piled on it, but it could have been some kind of building." They trudged over to what looked like a collapsed building from years ago.

"Coulda been a barn, I guess," was Marty's speculation.

"I suppose, but if it was, would it have a cistern, and where would it be? Usually they ran the downspouts into them, so they weren't far from the building itself."

They spent some time lifting branches and old, weather-beaten barn siding and tossing it aside. "I don't know, Daniel, this isn't getting us anywhere."

"Look, we know that the directions we found led us here. We also know that, other than this spot, there's not much else around here. Ninety years have gone by since the guy hid this gold, so let's give it a little more time."

They spent the better part of two hours lifting the heavy siding and timbers and moving them aside. Eventually they uncovered a concrete slab. "If this was part of the barn then we should be able to see the edge of the foundation." Daniel, at least, seemed to know the rudiments of construction.

A half hour later they used one of the pieces of siding to uncover the perimeter clay tile lines. From there, by digging down every ten feet or so, they traced it to its termination. It was a circular concrete cover, about three feet in diameter. Both men stopped to catch their breath. They looked at each other expectantly. "Help me get rid of this cover. We're gonna need something to pry it off. It looks heavy." Daniel, ever the director.

"There's an iron bar over there that looks like it's part of an old door. If we can poke it through these two rusted handles, maybe we can lift it together." Marty climbed over several piles of old barn detritus, tugged loose the bar, and shoved it through the inverted U-shaped handles.

The years had provided an airtight seal and the cover proved stubborn. With copious grunting and swearing, they finally lifted it free. The resulting stench of mildewed water and dead organisms was foul. "Let's see that phone. We need some light down there."

Filthy water filled the old concrete basin to about four feet from the top. "Marty, hand me that branch over there." Daniel took the six-foot-long fir bough and stuck it into the cistern as far as he could. It stopped about a foot below the level of the water where it seemed to bottom out. "These things are usually six feet or more deep. We're hitting something at five feet. It's gotta be the gold."

Marty wasn't so sure. "One of us needs to get in there and reach down to see what's there." His look at Daniel conveyed the intent that Marty wasn't stepping into that stinky mess.

"All right, get outta the way."

Daniel braced himself and eased down into the brown slimy stew. He gingerly slid into the mess, halfway up his calves. "It feels really uneven underneath this mess. I'm gonna see if I can feel what's down here." He reached beneath his feet and felt some sort of brick building material.

"I think they piled a bunch of bricks in here, but the fuckers are really heavy." He reached beneath the water with two hands and lifted up the masonry unit. Only that's not what it was. They got the thirty-pound loaf-shaped item up and out of the cistern before some of the sludge oozed away. Underneath was a dull yellow gold bar, stained brownish by the years of sediment in the concrete tank.

"Fuckin ay, we found it." Marty was beside himself. "Let's take some back with us."

"Marty, don't be a dipshit. Let's stick to the plan. We'll put it back, replace the cistern cover, and come back when we organize what we'll need to get this stuff off the island. No one knows anything about this place, so it'll be safe until we return. Don't get crazy on me now."

Marty appeared to sober up a little. "Okay. Let's cover this up and get back to the Farm. The boat should be getting back around noon or so, and it's best if we meet it before that Fred guy gets up to the barn."

They replaced the cover, spread branches and cedar droppings over the location, and took the Jeep back to the southern end of the island.

With Jordan and crew leading the convoy in the old Outback, the O'Malleys followed. Anne and Fred brought up the rear in the pickup. After settling up at the Brentwood, they took their time driving to Boat Harbour. They arrived at noon and parked each vehicle in the mostly deserted lot.

The *Butterfly* was in her slip, waiting for them to board. The O'Malleys were going through the motions, still uncertain of what awaited them on DeCourcy Island. They were by themselves on the aft deck. "Hey, Kev, I bet you never saw this coming when we were finishing up at the Brentwood."

"You got that right. One minute we're replacing artwork, the next we're on a boat with members of a commune and their strange little leader. To tell you the truth, though, I kinda like these people. They may want to live a little differently than we do, but they have a peacefulness about them that I admire."

"I agree, but after listening to them about this Daniel character, maybe we'll run into something not so peaceful." They rounded the south end of the island and headed into Pirate's Cove.

As they eased into the slip—Anne knew her stuff when it came to handling this boat—they became aware of several individuals on the dock, waiting for them to arrive.

Jordan was the first to speak up. "Uh-oh, looks like Daniel's at the dock, and he's got Marty with him. What the hell's going on?" The rest of the occupants on the *Butterfly* looked on apprehensively as Will, also there, threw them a line. With fenders in place and both ends cleated off, the eight sailors disembarked with Fred leading the way.

"Brother Twelve, I want to apologize for yesterday. I was so upset with Marty not paying Jordan and his crew that I kinda lost my mind. I've been under some stress lately, and I let it get to me. I was very rude and disrespectful. After you left and I put Marty in the barn, I settled down and came to my senses. I talked at length with him, and he agreed to come up with the money he owes. We were waiting for you to return with the *Butterfly* so we could get back to Nanaimo so Marty can get to a bank." Daniel rushed his delivery some, but he thought he hit all the right notes.

Fred's eyes glazed over a bit with this onslaught of surprising information. "Daniel, please meet our guests, the O'Malleys. This is Kevin and Jenne." Regardless of the situation, Fred was a stickler for propriety. "They decided to come with us to see our little community here."

"Nice to meet you. I'd really like to visit with you but Will promised to take Marty and me back so he can get us paid." Daniel was doing his best to vacate the gathering. Will cast furtive glances at both Brother XII and Daniel and was understandably uncomfortable.

Fred, as always, seemed to sense there was more here than just small talk. "Will, why don't you take these two back to Boat Harbour. Then when you return you can pick up the O'Malleys, after we've had a chance to show them around."

The immediate call to action had a way of dialing back the tension on the dock. Will jumped aboard followed by Marty and Daniel, and they commenced the short journey to Vancouver Island.

After their departure Fred, Jordan and crew, Anne, and the O'Malleys huddled up. Molly suddenly appeared out of nowhere, almost as if she were waiting for Daniel's departure.

"Thank God you guys are here."

"Why, Molly, what's been going on?" Anne was the first to question her good friend.

"I don't know everything, but Will overheard those two in the barn last night. He told me they had found a clue to some old stash of gold. I didn't get the whole story because Marty and Daniel showed up, and he didn't want them to hear."

"I told him those were just rumors and there was no gold." Fred looked a little annoyed.

"Well, according to Will, you might be mistaken. Let's wait until he gets back, and he can fill you in." Molly headed back to her quarters, leaving the rest of them on the dock.

"Jordan, I'm going to show our guests around. Why don't you and your crew go get some rest. I have a feeling you're going to need it. Anne, you may as well visit with Molly, see if you can learn anything else."

When Fred headed over to the Jeep, Anne jumped behind the wheel to drive them up to the barn. The rest of the convoy hoofed it up the hill. Anne left Fred and the O'Malleys at the barn and went to catch up with Molly.

Will was uneasy ferrying the treasure hunters over to Boat Harbour. Anne had slipped him the keys to the truck, and he in turn gave them to Daniel. He felt a sense of loyalty to Brother XII and, if there was gold somewhere, he would feel terrible if it fell into someone else's hands. The old man had been really good to him, and he'd be damned if he'd let these two get away with something. He had heard their plans but wasn't certain how to make sure that didn't happen. Marty and

Daniel had left the Farm at sunrise and hadn't returned until almost noon. They looked as though they had been slopping pigs when they got back. They smelled like it too. But also, they oozed smugness. Will was sure they had found something.

He didn't have the quickest mind, but what he lacked in smarts he more than made up for in resolve. If they were going to offload the gold via boat, then they'd have to leave from Boat Harbour. It was too late today for them to do anything, and they'd talked about having to gather some equipment. Will was convinced he could return and pick up their trail the next day. He'd come back tomorrow after he had a chance to brief Brother XII and the others.

CHAPTER 22

As soon as Will docked the *Butterfly* back at Pirate's Cove, he went to find Jordan. He found him in the small hut where the meals were prepared, sitting with Anne and Molly. Anne seemed to have developed a more assertive streak over the last few weeks and she used it now. "Molly's told us some of what you overheard, but I don't think we fully understand what's going on."

Will was somewhat shy, and it took some tugging and coaxing by the other three to get the whole story. Jordan was still unsure of the entire picture. "So you're pretty sure they found the gold up north?"

"I'd bet on it. When they got back here, they couldn't wait to get off the island. If they hadn't found anything, I don't think they would have been in so much of a hurry."

Just then Brother XII showed up with the O'Malleys. "I was showing our guests around. When we got to the barn I noticed that my grandfather's Egyptian ankh was missing. Will, do you know anything about that?"

The time had come to spill the beans to Brother XII. Will was hesitant because he could feel how much this would hurt this gentle soul. He steeled himself and related the entire episode of the previous evening. He left nothing out, not even his desire to follow them and attempt to recover whatever they had discovered.

"Thanks for telling me everything, Will. That ancient hieroglyphic has been in that barn since my grandfather founded this place. It didn't have any special meaning to me except that my father used to be fond of it. I'm still shocked to find out that there really may have been some hidden gold here on the island. I guess all that research Daniel did paid off. It's too bad. If I had known about it we might have been able to upgrade some things here and provide a little better for those who have come to live with us."

"Well, I think so too, and that's why I've got my own plan."

"And what would that be?"

"After I take the O'Malleys back over, I'm gonna hang around and see if I can figure out when Marty and Daniel are planning to come back here. When they return with the gold, I'll find some way to get in their face and make them wish they hadn't fucked with us." Will was beginning to get worked up, but, perhaps due to his evolving social awareness, he caught himself. "Uh, sorry for the language, sirs and ladies. Those two just fucking piss me off."

Fred smoothed things out a little. "No problem, Will, it gives us all some degree of angst. I'm just not sure 'getting in their face' will do the trick."

"I've got an idea." Jordan's turn to speak up. "What if I go along with Will. We can take turns keeping an eye out for them and when they come back, we'll call the cops or something."

"If you're going, then so am I." Apparently Anne had some input as well. Her furtive glances at Jordan hadn't gone unnoticed. "I can help spell you two and, in a pinch, I can also drive the boat if we need to split up."

Fred, sensing the caper gaining momentum, was starting to feel like a bystander. "I'll let you people work this out. If we get to recover any of the money, it would be nice if some of it could help out our little place here. But please be careful, and if I can help, either use the radio or find some way to get word to me."

Kevin and Jenne were overwhelmed at the pace of things. They had come to the island partially out of curiosity, but mostly to be of moral support for Fred and his community. The speed of events left them feeling like the Coyote in a Road Runner cartoon. "Um, I don't know everything that's happening here, but Kevin and I have grown fond of you folks, so if we can help in any way, please let us know." Jenne, volunteering again, but in this case Kevin was on the same page.

Jordan took the lead among the trio volunteering their sleuthing skills. "Thanks very much, you guys. I'm pretty sure we can handle this, and we really appreciate the offer, but I think we'll be okay."

"How about this," Kevin suggested. "We'll go back with you now and find some place to spend a night or two. You're going to need some wheels over there, and you can take our Explorer. We'll be around if you need us. First thing we're gonna do when we get back, though, is pick up a couple of burner phones. I know there's no cell service here, but you'll need them over there, and we'll be able to stay in touch."

All present liked Kevin's approach, even his wife. "Gosh, Kevin, what a great idea." Even to Fred it sounded slightly sarcastic, but it was essential to the couple's intimacy, and they treasured how they were the only two on the same wavelength.

"Of course, darling, you inspired me to come up with it."

After stocking the *Butterfly* with some food, binoculars, and plenty of water, they left for Boat Harbour. When they were halfway through the channel, Jenne had a thought. "Hey, if those two guys are gonna leave from the same place we're going to, won't they see the *Butterfly?*"

Jordan started to think things through. "We'd have to dock there to drop off you two anyway, so if they happened to see us now it's no big deal."

"That's right, but they would get a little suspicious if they saw the *Butterfly* docked there overnight," Anne pointed out. "That's why you and Will are gonna get off with the O'Malleys, and I'm gonna find some place to stash the boat where it won't be seen. When you get a cell phone you can reach me on the VHF, and I'll let you know where to pick me up."

Jordy knew there was more than one reason Anne was part of the team.

With the outline of a strategy in place, the shipmates proceeded to their slip at Boat Harbour.

Howard Bories was not a happy man. He had just come from his general manager's office where she'd filled him in on the findings of the Apogee representatives. He had thought that maybe the excellent service and training could disguise the state of the furnishings package, but it was not to be.

No longer could he pull the wool over a prospective buyer's eyes. After the two birders got back to the home office, everyone in the industry would know. No operator worth their salt would touch the place. It would take millions to replace the finishes and the furnishings. To do that he would have to close the place. The advertising dollars, the big push in the travel magazines and flight brochures, all would be for nothing. Then, of course, there was the elephant in the room—and it wasn't Burton.

His plan to make a quick sale and pay off his blackmailing stoolies from the planning bureau was toast. He still had plenty of money stashed away but, at this point, he'd leveraged most of it to fund the refurbishment of the Tofino Inn and Spa. If he had to come up with that much cash that quickly, he would find himself in a deep hole. His only option was to try to buy some time. There was still a chance some rich idiot would come along and buy the place. The other alternative was to keep operating it and pay the bastards on the installment plan. Only one way to find out.

Rob Bensen and David Jeppesen were both of Scandinavian descent. Like many of their ancestors who settled in the Northwest, they prided themselves on being frugal. It had been a tough life for most of those who had gone before them. Most were fishermen and did not live to a ripe old age. Even today the fishing business was still one of the most dangerous professions in the world. It was passed on from generation to generation that some days the fish weren't biting, and you'd damn well better have money to get you through the lean times.

Because of their upbringing, and also because they were pretty sure they had Bories over a barrel, they were not inclined to offer blackmail on the installment plan. After Howard made the offer, they informed him immediately that it was not acceptable. If they were not paid in three days, the shit would be meeting up with the fan.

Howard tried to convince them otherwise. After all, if they ratted him out, they too would incur the wrath of the attorney general. Rob and Dave sorta figured they'd get to this point. Mutual destruction seemed an effective means of neutralizing the situation. They did have a contingency plan, however. They had always suspected Howard was not to be trusted. Shit, the guy was paying people to screw with the quality of life and the environment here in the Northwest. How could he be?

When their payment looked like it might be doubtful, the two civil servants paid a visit to the state attorney general's office. They met with Janet Slattery, one of the assistant AGs. Suppose, they offered, there was someone who paid off government employees to grease the skids for getting permit approvals. And suppose it had been going on for a long time. If the employees who had been paid off were to turn state's evidence against this person, would, just for the sake of argument, they, maybe, be given immunity? And if they were to really nail this guy, could they please keep their pensions?

Janet had seen and heard many proposals over her career, but this one was a doozy. She didn't much care for these two, but nailing a big-time developer for graft and bribery would send a message. That the Puget Sound area was a liberal bastion, there was no doubt. As such, the preservation of its environment and quality of life was paramount to her boss, and so it was to her. It took hours and hours to convince those upstairs to go along with the proposal, but they finally relented.

The kicker was when David said they just might have some recordings of Bories instructing them on how to approve several of his projects.

With the never-ending back-and-forth of all the negotiations, the bribes Bories had been paying to them were overlooked. Rod and Dave were going to skate on this with whatever monies they had squirreled away, *and* they were going to keep their pensions. Who said crime doesn't pay?

CHAPTER 23

Anne consulted the area nautical charts as soon as they docked. There was a tiny inlet just south of their current location that could work. She'd have to be cautious about getting in and out since there were hidden rocks that would become a problem at low tide, but it should work. They were between tides now, and it was ebbing, so she needed to get going. There would be plenty of time to leave when Daniel left for DeCourcy.

Will and the O'Malleys disembarked as soon as the *Butterfly* came to rest. Jordy would accompany Anne to the inlet she had identified. There, they would drop anchor and take the dinghy to shore.

As Kevin got behind the wheel, Jenne searched on her cell for a nearby place to stay. "There's a small sort of rustic collection of cabins just off Pylades Drive. It's called the Boat Harbour Inn, interestingly enough, and I can't imagine they'll be full up this time of year. I'll give them a call."

As it turned out there was plenty of room. She reserved three cabins, one for them, one for Jordan and Will, and one for Anne. The cost was forty-five dollars Canadian per night, so she didn't much care if she and Kevin ended up footing the bill. As an added benefit, the view from the cabin windows was of the very cove where Anne had anchored the *Butterfly*. It took all of ten minutes to drive from the slip to the inn and was such a short stretch that they got there well ahead of Anne and Jordan, who could just walk over from the dinghy.

The cabins were certainly rustic, but they were very clean. They were of log construction, each heated with a wood stove. The innkeeper made a point of telling them all seven of the cabins had indoor plumbing. Apparently some of the less desirable accommodations in the area weren't as well equipped. Lucky them!

About thirty minutes later Anne and Jordan showed up looking much happier than the situation warranted. "We had to make sure there was a solid hold on the anchor, so it took us a little longer," Jordan told them. "Great that you found this place, though. We can walk right down to the cove. How many rooms did you get?"

Jenne responded with three and asked if he minded bunking with Will.

Jordan did a few foot shuffles and got red in the face. "I don't mind at all bunking with Will. But Anne and I thought it would save some money if the two of us just stayed on the boat." Anne was quietly standing by, watching with interest.

Jenne and Kevin knew where this was headed, but they couldn't resist a little tease. "Geez, Jordy, I don't know, Will was counting on having you for a roommate, and we've already booked three rooms." Kevin had an impish smile on his face and was thoroughly enjoying himself.

Fortunately, Jenne showed a little mercy. "Go ahead, Jordan. I think Will won't have any trouble getting over it, and I'm sure we can cancel the extra cabin. Why don't we order in some pizza. You can have dinner with us and then you and Anne can go guard the boat. And gosh, think of the savings."

Jordan knew when he was being goaded and, this time, he actually enjoyed it. It was so refreshing, he thought, to be with folks who cared enough about him to make the effort to do so.

While making the short trip from DeCourcy to Boat Harbour, there was no reason to ever go below deck on the upscale trawler. The single stateroom there, however, was far better appointed than any of these *rustic* cabins, and he aimed to take advantage of the privacy it provided.

"Ya know, Jordy, I really am gonna miss you. I kinda thought we had something going." Even Will joined in the ribbing. He, too, was thrilled with the new room assignments, and this new side of him suggested evidence of his comfort level with the group. "Maybe we should run into Nanaimo tonight to pick up a couple of prepaid phones just in case Daniel leaves early in the morning."

"Good idea, Will. Jenne and I can take care of that. Why don't you three talk about how we're gonna keep tabs on those two while we're gone. We should be back in an hour or so."

The O'Malleys drove the six miles on Yellow Point Road to the southern outskirts of Nanaimo. Luckily, they happened upon a Home Depot before they got too far into town. The store carried almost everything, including a special on Huawei prepaid phones. Most of the local contractor subs used them instead of the more expensive Samsungs and iPhones. When these were dropped off a roof, they could just throw them away instead of being out nine hundred bucks.

While they were collecting their purchases, Jenne poked Kevin in the ribs. "Hey, that hurts," her husband whined.

"Shush, be quiet and look over there."

They were slightly behind an endcap of Ryobi power tools. Kevin looked where he was told and was startled to see Daniel and Marty at the checkout counter. "Holy shit, did they see us?"

"No, I'm certain they didn't. They're not being evasive or anything. Take a look at what they're buying."

It was as if Marty and Daniel were preparing for a mining excursion, which in a sense, they were. Menucci was wheeling a four-wheel heavy-duty wheelbarrow. Inside it were assorted pry bars, flashlights, and wrecking bars. Additionally, there were rubber boots and a dozen pairs of rubber gloves. If there had been any doubts about them locating the gold, they no longer existed.

Daniel was in line behind Marty and was pushing an orange flatbed. Piled on top of it were four two-by-four-foot PermaFloat drums. These were normally lashed together in multiples to form the foundation for a floating dock. They were incredibly buoyant modules, capable of supporting almost six hundred pounds of weight each. Along with the drums were three standard wooden pallets.

Kevin and Jenne hadn't yet moved from behind the power drills and saws, while a steady parade of annoyed contractors detoured around them. "Let's give them time to get their stuff loaded and leave the parking lot. It's probably not the end of the world if they see us, but I think it's best if they don't."

"I agree," Kevin said. "They would have no way of knowing that we're onto them. Still, I like your idea of studying these excellent power tools."

They allowed another ten minutes before they hustled through the checkout and then returned to the Boat Harbour Inn. When they got there, the balance of the team was still in their cabin.

"Glad you're all still here. Jenne, please proceed with the new information." Jenne narrated the details of what they had seen at the Home Depot. The others weren't totally surprised, but the details about the amount and type of gear left them wondering.

"I can understand the pry bars and boots and gloves, but the other stuff, I haven't a clue." Jordy was the first to guess.

"They talked about a cistern, so maybe they need to pry it open or something." Will was the only one with firsthand knowledge of the gold recovery, but he could shed no further light on things.

"It's getting late. Here are your phones. We should share numbers and then hit the sack. Let's meet up for breakfast at six thirty and decide how best to handle things tomorrow. I think they have bagels and coffee at the check-in counter." Kevin passed the phones and chargers to Will and Jordan. "See you bright and early. Good night."

Daniel had a difficult time finding a boat he could rent that would fill their needs. Because there were very few slips occupied this time of the year, the pickings were slim. There were several small craft, only suitable for joy riding and towing innertubes. The next step was all the way up to a thirty-six-foot Grand Banks trawler. This particular boat was available for charter only because the owner was in Europe, and the caretaker needed some fast cash. He'd let them use it for the day for five hundred. Daniel knew it was a rip-off, but he didn't have the time to quibble. The *Butterfly* would have been perfect but, for obvious reasons, that was out of the question. The Grand Banks was incredibly seaworthy but serious overkill for hauling a pile of gold back to Boat Harbour.

Sunday morning was shrouded in the gray foggy drizzle that was the primary weather pattern in November in the Northwestern U.S. and the southwestern corner of Canada. Visibility was no more than a few hundred yards, plus the gloominess had a way of dampening the sound. The F-150 was loaded with their Home Depot purchases as they pulled into the loading area just beside the gate to the dock that berthed the Grand Banks. They had looked the trawler over the previous evening to familiarize themselves with the controls and the location of the various safety devices. It had been dark then, and this was the first time they had noticed the name on the stern. "*Golden Buoy*, geez, should we take that as an omen?" Marty was amused by the coincidence.

"Maybe the owner has blond hair and a trust fund. It's either that or the stars really are in alignment for us. Let's get this shit aboard so we can take off." Daniel had already started with the pallets and the float drums. They weren't heavy, but they were bulky, so it called for several trips.

After everything was stowed away, they parked the pickup and boarded the *Golden Buoy* to begin, what they hoped, was their last trip to DeCourcy Island.

While Marty and his buddy loaded up, they were being observed by Will and Jordan, who were watching from the O'Malleys' Explorer. They had parked it on the side of the road, high above Boat Harbour. They knew what to expect after Kevin had reported their observations from the previous evening. Anne had stayed at the cabin with Jenne and Kevin while they tried to figure out where this was going next. Since they weren't one hundred percent convinced Daniel would be returning with the gold, they were in a holding pattern.

Over a fine breakfast of toasted bagels and coffee, they all agreed that if there was any treasure on the island, it belonged to Fred. Whether he was an oddity or not, he'd been providing moral and physical support to needy folks for a long time and his legacy should be paid forward. The challenge would be to intercept and recover the treasure without it getting dangerous. They all agreed it was best for the two men to observe and report back before committing to a plan of action.

Will called in just as the Grand Banks was leaving Boat Harbour. "They got everything loaded up and just took off. The weather sucks so it might take them a little longer to get over there. They've got that truck here, so we know they're coming back. Jordy and I are thinkin' it's gonna be at least until midday before they make it back. We're gonna make a coffee run and then just sit back and wait. As soon as we find anything out, we'll call you."

It was the most Will had said in one sitting since Kevin had met him. "Looks like the boys have things under control. Let's brainstorm about what we should do if they really do come back with something."

"I suppose we could confront them when they get back with the boat," Anne said more to herself than the others. "But I guess they'd just say, 'Fuck off' and tell us it was something they found, and it was theirs to keep."

"That sounds about right. Forget the fact that the only reason they found it was because they discovered the map behind Fred's grandfather's heirloom," Jenne offered.

Kevin put his two cents in. "Don't forget, they did this by trespassing on Fred's property while kidnapping Marty. 'Course they're buddies now, but still, if it ever ended up in court, I think Fred would come out on top."

They batted a number of ideas around, but no one was convinced any of them were workable.

"I got it." Both women looked at Kevin expectantly. "How about this? I give that RCMP guy a call, the one that interviewed me in Tofino."

"Yeah, so?" His wife wasn't that impressed. "Why does he care?"

"Jenne, Jenne, Jenne, so disrespectful. He cares, darling, because Daniel is the fucker that had those two goons kidnap me just before that bear had them for dinner. I think ol' Sergeant Preston just might have an interest, right?"

"Okay, I'll forgive the smart-ass remark just this once. It's actually one of the better ideas you've ever had. Do we wait until they get back or do it now?"

"Well, either way they'll want to know who's responsible for the kidnapping, so I think we call now. We tell him that we also suspect the guy is stealing something that rightfully belongs to Fred. Maybe the cops can find a way to stop them."

Anne must have thought it was a great idea as well. "I like it. We don't get in the middle of things, and Daniel gets what's coming to him."

With all the accolades being heaped upon him, Kevin took his time calling the Mounties. He was not able to reach Preston immediately, so left him a message suggesting he knew who initiated the Tofino kidnapping. He felt certain the sergeant would be calling shortly.

CHAPTER 24

The trip across Stuart Channel was tedious but uneventful. With the low visibility, the GPS and the radar were necessary to avoid any other traffic silly enough to be out in weather like this. The only way to access the small inlet at the northeast tip of DeCourcy was to navigate almost two hundred seventy degrees around the island. The passage at the north end between Link Island and DeCourcy was never really passable.

They rounded the southern tip, passed by Pirate's Cove, and arrived at the small inlet they had studied earlier. It was low tide so there was no concern about being grounded when it came time to depart.

The Zodiac tender was equipped with a fifteen-horse outboard that would serve them perfectly. The rear davits lowered the dinghy nicely, and they began the process of ferrying their equipment ashore. The pry bars and wheelbarrow were simple, and they would be taking them to the cistern site.

The float drums were clumsy but necessary. They dropped the four of them in the water beside the Zodiac. Daniel proceeded to lash them together with the accompanying hardware that the manu-facturer included. When the assembly was complete, he attached the three wooden pallets to the top of the drums. The finished result was a miniature floating dock measuring eight feet by four feet. Marty threw him a line cleated to the dinghy, which he attached to the front pallet of the floating structure. The wheelbarrow took up much of the space in the dinghy but that would be left here in the inlet for some future scavenger.

They motored into the small inlet until the tender bottomed out on the sandy beach. Their dock assembly was securely tied off to the Zodiac, which they muscled well onto the shore. Even as the tide rose their ticket off the island was safe.

Pushing the wheelbarrow over the wet, alternately sandy and rocky beach was a pain in the ass, but they finally pushed it up the dirt road to the entry point to the site. There were so few people on the island that the possibility of being seen was remote. Still, the sooner they were out of here the better. No sense having to come up with some story if it wasn't necessary. In any event the shitty weather was an asset.

They turned into the woods where the remnants of the old road were. Pushing the heavy-duty wheelbarrow through the years of accumulated organic matter was impossible. "Let's just leave this thing here. As long as it's out of sight, we can carry the gold bars from the cistern to here." Marty's plan made sense, although Daniel wasn't sure if the skinny guy appreciated how much a gold bar weighed.

They proceeded into the especially dark forest until they reached the old water tank. The pry bars made short work of lifting the cover and, once again, they were treated to the smell of ancient water and decaying anaerobic bacteria. Daniel donned the rubber boots and gloves, grabbed a flashlight, and let himself down into the opening.

The additional pry bars were used to dislodge the gold bricks that had become wedged together by years of mud and water. Daniel dug down with his gloved hands and lifted out the first bar. "Let's get them all out first, and then we can cart them over to the wheelbarrow."

One by one, Daniel lifted out the bars. Each one weighed approximately thirty pounds, and it wasn't long before the exertion and terrible breathing conditions had him exhausted. "Fuck, I gotta get out of here. Your turn. We should have brought a respirator. The air in there is awful."

After Daniel climbed out, Marty changed into the rubberwear and climbed in. They had twenty-five bars already stacked on the old concrete floor. Marty was able to hand out another fifteen before he threw in the towel. "I had no idea this stuff was so heavy. I can barely breathe."

"Marty, you're a pussy. Get your ass out here, and I'll get the rest of them." Daniel slowly sat on the edge of the tank and lowered himself in. With most of the gold removed, the tank opening was now just above his head, and breathing became very challenging.

While Daniel worked away, Marty did his part stacking the bars on the floor. "Maybe we've got enough, now. We can just leave the rest."

Daniel shouted out through the opening, "Marty, each one of these is worth almost seven hundred thousand. Maybe we should leave your share here, what do you think?"

Marty seemed stunned at this. "Shit, no Daniel. I had no idea, let's get 'em all."

"Here's the last one, he said as he handed it to Marty. Get me the fuck out of here so I can breathe again." With that he grabbed hold of the top and climbed out, exhausted.

The two of them sat there, dirty, sweaty, and physically depleted. Not a word between them as they stared at the fruits of their labor, fifty bars of pure gold. "Jesus, Marty, I can't believe we did it. So that's what almost forty million dollars looks like."

Marty suddenly looked alert. "I thought you said it was twenty million. Were you just bullshitting me, or didn't you know how much was here?"

Uh-oh. Daniel was so exhausted he'd forgotten that he had lied to Marty about the worth of the treasure. Right now he was too tired to fight, and he needed help to finish this journey. "Okay, Marty, you're right, I lied. I thought there was more here than I told you. I really don't want to have this come between us right now. How about this, you get twelve million and I get the rest. We've still got to pay ten percent to your money guy."

"Fifteen, just because you were a prick and didn't trust me." Pouting wasn't Marty's best look.

This was rich, thought Daniel. The guy's a fucking con man and a swindler, and he's upset that I didn't trust him. Thing is, right now he didn't give a shit. He just wanted to be done with things. "Okay, Marty, fuck it, you got your fifteen. Let's move this stuff."

They started carrying two bars each to the wheelbarrow but that changed quickly to one. The footing through the woods was awkward, and their already weakened state made things difficult.

"We can only move eighteen or so at a time because we won't be able to wheel this thing across the shore. It's downhill from here so that's good but, man, this is more work than I ever want to do again." Marty *was* kind of a pussy. A day's work for fifteen million dollars was apparently too much for the man.

The work was physically grueling, but finally they had relocated all the gold to the small cove. From there began the task of placing them on the pallets of the fabricated floating dock and then fastening them with nylon webbing to secure them for the tow to the *Golden Buoy*. The tender was stable and durable, but fifteen hundred pounds of gold would sink it in a hurry. The transfer of the bullion from the pallets to the trawler took another grueling hour.

At last, after the final bar had been transferred, they weighed anchor and departed DeCourcy Island, confident it was for the last time. It was almost 5:00 p.m., and the two pirates could barely move. Daniel was fifteen years younger than Marty, but even he was close to comatose. "Hey, Marty, I got an idea. We don't have to turn this boat back until tomorrow morning. I am fucking destroyed. There's two staterooms on this thing, let's just anchor over in Boat Harbour, spend the night on the boat, and take it into the slip in the morning. The thought of moving all this gold to the truck tonight is scaring me."

"I don't need any convincing. I can't even move, but I *am* starving. How can we get some food?"

"I'll take the Zodiac in and pick up some food and beer from the Crow and Gate. Shouldn't take long, and you can rest those old bones of yours. I still think we should anchor rather than pull into the slip. Way safer and more secure that way. Agreed?"

"Whatever you say. Just get me some fucking food."

It took until nightfall for Sergeant Preston to return Kevin's call. "Mr. O'Malley, I got your message about the guy who arranged your kidnapping. Please tell me what you know."

Kevin filled him in on the conspiracy that Daniel and Bories had hatched in order to get him out of the way for a while. The cop was not all that surprised at the Bories connection. Just recently there were rumors out of Seattle that there had been inconsistencies with many of the building permits issued to the Bories Corporation. It was startling how quickly some of these things tied together. For his part, Kevin was surprised that Bories' reputation had sustained such a blemish.

Preston remained quiet as O'Malley continued the saga of the rumored treasure and the possibility that Martin Menucci and Daniel Phillips had found it and were maybe going to leave the country with it. He left nothing out, including the part Will and Jordy were playing in the surveillance.

When the sergeant heard that *his* kidnapper might get away, he became seriously interested. "It will take us some time to mobilize on this. Usually these types of crimes are handled by the local jurisdiction. In this case that would be the Nanaimo detachment, but I would really like to personally be involved in this one. Have you heard anything from your friends who are watching for them?"

Kevin said he hadn't but would check in with them as soon as he hung up.

"I'm calling from my cell phone. Please get back to me as soon as you hear something, and I'll see what I can come up with."

Kevin was on the phone to Will right after he said goodbye to Preston. "So, Will, talk to me, what's going on?"

"We've been sitting here all day playing games. We were just gonna give you a call when their boat showed up. Funny thing is they've anchored out in the bay instead of pulling into the slip. One of them just took the dinghy into the dock and left in the truck."

"So what do you think is going on? I've already alerted the Mounties."

"I'm not sure. Maybe Jordy can tell you what he thinks."

"Hey, Kev, how's things?"

"Dandy. Anne says hi, by the way. Please tell me what's happening."

"The guys got back just a little while ago, and they dropped anchor in the bay. For some reason they don't want to put the boat in the slip tonight. My guess is they're gonna spend the night on that trawler and offload their cargo in the morning."

"Makes sense to me, Jordan. Why don't you two stay there until whoever left comes back. It doesn't make sense for them to do anything until first light. You and Will come back and get some sleep." "If it's all the same to you, I don't trust these guys. Will and I can catch some shuteye here in the car. He's been wanting to spend the night with me anyway." Will's glance was enough to know he'd scored some points.

"You guys are something. I'll let Anne know she's got some competition." Kevin signed off, secure in the fact that his two private eyes were at the top of their game. He immediately called Preston back and told him not to expect any further developments until the next day.

"That's good news. I'll get over there first thing tomorrow, but call me if something comes up." They hung up and waited to see what the next day would bring.

Daniel and Marty were up early Monday morning. They were still exhausted from the physical efforts of the previous day but recognized that they needed to get going. "So what's the plan, Daniel?"

"Well, I'm not exactly sure how we're going to get it done, but we've got to find a way to get three quarters of a ton of gold to your contact in Hamilton. I don't know how to get to Bermuda but, in any event, we first have to get out of this country. Once we're in the States we can come up with a plan to get to Bermuda. Maybe another boat trip or something."

"Do we drive south and cross over at the Bellingham checkpoint?"

"I don't think we can disguise this stuff enough to get through there."

"So, what? The ferries? I think the checkpoint in Sidney, going through the San Juans, is probably the easiest to get through."

"We would be taking a chance. I guess we can put the gold back in the bed and cover it with a tarp, but I would hate to take the chance that one of those customs inspectors would find out what we're doing. Forty million in gold bars isn't exported from Canada every day."

They batted ideas back and forth, losing confidence in their ability with every suggestion that failed to measure up and, soon, silence ensued. They had focused so much of their energies on finding the gold that figuring out how to convert it to actual spending money had not been high on the priority list. Now it was.

"Wait, I got it!" Marty erupted while jumping to his feet. "I did some business with a guy that owns an inn back in Carmel. He and a few of his buddies take an annual fishing trip to Campbell River every year."

"Well, good for them, who gives a shit?"

"No, wait. They use a float plane to take them there. Kenmore Air flies there regularly but this guy uses a private outfit. If I can get his contact, maybe we tell him to meet us there, and we get out of the country on his plane. I think the only customs inspection would be on the U.S. side, but we make sure he lands on a private lake somewhere so we can avoid it."

Daniel was quiet for a moment while he digested Marty's proposal.

"It might work. It's only a hundred miles or so to Campbell River. The big question is, can we get this private outfit to meet us there?"

Marty agreed to check with his former client. Luckily this happened to be one of the few he hadn't screwed over; it had been the early years.

He was able to reach his former client on the first try and scored the private charter's phone number. He immediately called and was greeted with fortuitous information. The pilot who usually flew the Campbell River route was dropping off three fishermen on Tuesday. He was going to be deadheading back to Seattle, and picking up two passengers would be welcome. Marty thought it prudent not to mention the additional cargo they would be bringing nor the issue of an alternate landing site. If the pilot took exception to any of these unusual requests, they'd offer him a bar. Who in his right mind could pass up almost seven hundred thousand dollars?

Daniel was very pleased that they now had a plan, but he still thought it prudent to get moving. "Okay, Marty, let's get this stuff in the truck and get going. I'm uncomfortable just sitting here. It's only a hundred miles to Campbell River, but I prefer to get on the road."

They pulled into the slip and completed the transfer of the gold to the pickup. They had to do it by hand, one or two bars each trip. After fifteen trips, with thirty to sixty pounds each, they were again winded. "I never realized how much work this was gonna be." Marty, again with the complaining.

"C'mon, Marty, *please* just be quiet. With any luck we'll only have to do this a couple more times." They had located their stash in the second row of their crew cab. With the seats folded back, the neat stack of gold fit perfectly behind them.

"Will, wake up." It was a little after six, and Jordan had been awake since four-thirty. He was monitoring any movement from down below, in the marina. "They're pulling the boat into the slip. Pretty sure something's going down."

They watched Daniel and Marty tie up and then begin the transfer of gold to their pickup.

"Well, I guess that answers the question of whether they found anything or not. Jesus, as many trips as it's taking, there must be a shitload of money there." Will's unique take on the situation was appreciated.

"Keep watching, Will; I'm calling the cabin."

Jordan filled Kevin in on things and committed to following their quarry if they left the marina. Kevin said he would get back to them after he consulted with the police.

While things were happening on the east side of the island, the Tofino Inn and Spa was quiet. Howard's strategy of mutually assured destruction with his blackmailers had failed spectacularly. The ungrateful pissants had squealed to the AG's office and now he was in very deep shit.

He had just received a notice from some Slattery bitch who wanted to "interview" him. Interview, *hah*, what a joke. What they wanted was to convict him of bribery. Howard was not a young man and spending any time in the slammer was not in his future plans. He had *some* money but most of it was tied up in the deal here in Tofino. He had had to leverage the property with a Seattle bank to fund the refurbishment. Now they held the first position on the place and unless some fairy godmother came to buy him out, he was fucked; they would foreclose on him.

At least for a short period he could just ignore the request. When they got serious, and they would, they would extradite him and charge him with bribery. He was furious with those two assholes. Hadn't he paid them extremely well through the years? There had to be some way out of this mess, but for the moment he couldn't see it. He was so used to getting his way, being in control. Damn, this was *just awful!*

CHAPTER 25

Kevin called Sergeant Preston's cell as soon as he finished with Jordan. "Sergeant, the two guys you're after are just loading up their truck now. Our friends who are observing them are positive its gold. I guess they found the treasure that was rumored to be on DeCourcy Island. It looks like they'll be leaving Boat Harbour very soon."

"We're on our way right now, but it looks like at least an hour until we get there. One of the officers who found the cabin that the kidnappers used is with me. If they are attempting to leave the country, there's a good chance customs might catch them. If they've done a good job hiding it, then maybe not. I haven't called in reinforcements yet, but I will if I have to. Please stay in touch with your friends."

Jenne thought it odd that the Mounties didn't just call in other officers, but she guessed that since it was originally on Preston's turf, he wanted the collar. She also figured the gold recovery would be one of those disputed issues, and it would take some time to settle. It wasn't like anyone had been murdered. Well, maybe those two kidnappers.

"Kevin, you better tell Will and Jordan to follow the gold if they leave the marina."

"On it. I'll tell them to be careful."

Sergeant Preston was riding in an unmarked charcoal gray Dodge Charger. The department had very few of these, and he was fortunate enough to be given one to use. They were driving the Pacific Rim Highway, just east of Clayoquot Plateau Provincial Park. PC fourth class Thomas Andersen, now driving, was still a rookie but showed outstanding promise for such a newbie. It was he who had discovered the cabin that Donnie and Jeff had used as a staging area for the kidnapping. Andersen was more than happy to be mentored by Preston whose reputation was that of a demanding but fair training officer.

Preston knew better than to apprehend suspects outside of his detachment, but this guy had made him look foolish. He was acquainted with a number of the Nanaimo officers, and they were certainly competent. Still, he felt the need to close this case on his own. If he needed help he could always call them at the last minute.

The constant drizzle made for poor visibility, and patches of the very wet pavement were slippery. This portion of the road was only two lanes so even though speed was of the essence, caution was called for. Andersen had been through both aggressive and evasive driving schools. Very few cadets had, but he felt it important for his posting. The roads on Vancouver Island varied from bare and dry to wet to icy to snowy. Any time of the year could produce any or all of these conditions. The drizzle was the worst. Visibility sucked, and although the droplets were small, there were zillions of them. Ten seconds outside was long enough to be soaked through. The wipers were on high speed and could barely keep up.

They had just pulled along Sproat Lake, which was due west of Port Alberni. There were several gradual turns along this stretch and one stretch of road that was described as the "S" curve. Thomas eased into the first portion of the "S" and goosed it a little, thinking it straightened out at that point. The road did not. When he saw the last loop of the "S," it was too late. The three hundred sixty-eight horses under the hood had instantly responded, causing the rear wheels to slide slightly to the driver's side. The slick pavement exaggerated the minor change in the vehicle's direction, forcing Thomas to make a small correction in steering the Charger toward the direction of the slide.

The oncoming SUV was a white Cadillac Escalade. The two couples inside were on their way for a holiday at the Tofino Inn and Spa, which had recently had a spread in *Condé Nast Traveler*. They were startled at the Dodge Charger that had taken half of their side of the road, but there was little they could do considering the size of their vehicle. At the last second the driver of the gray car swerved hard right to avoid a wicked collision.

Andersen's quick decision avoided the oncoming vehicle but sent them into an uncontrollable three sixty. The powerful police chase vehicle slid through the shoulder and collided with a five-hundred-year-old Douglas fir. Air bags deployed, glass windows exploded, the engine compartment buckled, and steam hissed. The Charger was destroyed. The tree was just fine. Probably good for another five hundred years.

The folks in the Cadillac, good citizens of Seattle, immediately pulled over to offer help. They came back to where the auto/tree collision had occurred to be of assistance. The first thing they noticed was that the occupants of the car were policemen. The air bags had stopped the two occupants from smashing into the windshield, but the speed of the collision had done serious harm to them. The driver was bloodied but moving; the passenger appeared to be unconscious.

"One of you call 911. Sean, give me a hand and we'll see if we can get this guy out." The operator of the Escalade and his friend were able to open the driver side door and managed to extricate the semi-conscious officer. He began mumbling, "Sorry, sorry," or words to that effect. The group decided the best course of action was to wait until the aid car arrived to let the paramedics deal with the other policeman.

"Looks like they're taking off, Will. Let's see where they are headed. Hopefully, the cops can get here soon and take over." Will fired up the Explorer, Sport Edition. They'd have no trouble keeping up with the crooks, especially with the added fifteen hundred pounds the bad guys were carrying.

"Ya better tell the folks back at the cabin what we're doing. They'll need to know so they can send the cops." Will was focused now. He kept a respectful distance from Marty and Daniel and tried to guess where they were headed.

Jordan called Kevin's cell phone. "Hello?" It was Anne. "Jordy, how's it going?"

Man, it felt great to hear her voice.

"Jenne and Kevin went to see the owner to make sure if it was okay if we keep the cabins a little longer. I'm staying here with them instead of on the *Butterfly*. It just feels better this way, you know, when you're not here."

"Of course, I'm glad you are. I'm sure the boat will be fine. Heck, you can see it from there."

"That's what we thought. Hey, what's going on there?"

Jordan proceeded to fill Anne in on their movements. He said he'd keep them informed so that the cops could catch up to them. They exchanged sweet nothings until Will got tired of it and told him to disconnect and pay attention.

After the O'Malleys got back to the room, Kevin tried to reach Preston to see what his ETA would be. "That's odd, it just went to voicemail. Maybe he's in one of those 'no cell' zones. I'll try in a few minutes."

Marty and his pal headed west until they reached Island Highway 19. This highway would take them all the way to Campbell River. Daniel was driving, Marty was complaining. "What are we gonna do when we get there? The plane doesn't get in until tomorrow so, what, we just hang around?"

"Marty, we'll figure something out. I just felt we needed to get away from Boat Harbour and Nanaimo. I'm not sure about Will, and if he starts telling people about me trying to find the gold, then maybe they'll start asking questions. I was supposed to return the truck yesterday, we broke the ankh, and I haven't communicated with Fred either. They'd have to be morons not to suspect something's going on. I'll just be glad when we get away from southern Vancouver Island."

"Okay, that makes sense. You think we stay on the highway the whole way?"

"We'll play it by ear. If there are lots of patrols on it, we'll take an alternate route. I'll make sure to stay around the speed limit for sure."

Kevin tried to reach Preston several more times without any luck. "I can't imagine what happened to him. We'd better let the boys know they're on their own for a while."

Jenne did the honors this time. "Hi, Jordan. Listen, we can't reach Sergeant Preston. I'm afraid you and Will are gonna have to keep tabs on those guys until we can get something figured out."

"It's no problem, Jenne. Your car's very comfortable, and it's got plenty of gas. Will and I have been stuck in it for over twenty-four hours though, and it's starting to get a little gamey in here."

Jenne couldn't help but laugh. "Well, open the windows for a bit, and we'll make sure to get it fumigated when you make it back."

Will gave Jordy a nasty look.

"What? I was just kidding, you smell wonderful." They continued following the Ford pickup, heading north, not knowing where they would end up.

CHAPTER 26

Karla was upset. She was also lonely. At six years of age, she still hadn't found a mate. The years in Strathcona with her mother and two siblings were idyllic, at least that's how she remembered it. She was the largest of her family. That she was the beneficiary of a recessive gene passed on through five generations was beyond her comprehension. All her ancestors were grizzlies. All except one, and the attributes of that gene were apparent.

There had been plenty of food, lakes of the purest water, and no predators. Until she had wandered south, she had never seen a human being. She had been on her own now for almost three years. Her size set her apart from not just the black bears, but also the grizzlies. She was enormous, nine feet tall and a few hundred pounds short of a ton. From the time she was twelve months old, she knew she was different. Most of the other bears, including her siblings, wanted nothing to do with her. Whenever she played with one of her species, she couldn't help but hurt them.

Brown bears, as they age, are primarily loners. Except for mating and raising cubs, they travel by themselves. They often range sixty miles or more. They can live in a variety of climates and geography and rarely congregate except occasionally in feeding areas along rivers where salmon thrive.

Karla spent the first five years of her life in Strathcona Provincial

Park. While grizzlies don't normally inhabit Vancouver Island, they sometimes swim over from the mainland to feed. Many, many years ago, the escaped Kodiak from DeCourcy Island had found his way to this park. He'd mated with one of the visiting grizzly sows and the resulting offspring populated this central section of the island. Until Karla was born, the Kodiak DNA had remained suppressed.

She'd wandered from the only home she had ever known in search of something she didn't understand. The Strathcona Park abuts the Clayoquot Provincial Parks, with only dirt logging roads meandering through them. The land varied from snowcapped mountain peaks to meadows to lakes and streams. Along her travels she frequently saw black bears, wolves, and cougars. None among these were a threat.

The closer she got to the west coast of the island, the stranger the sensations became. Her incredibly delicate sense of smell easily picked up the aroma of the sea air. Along with it came the sporadic smell of cooking smoke and of humans. There was also the sound of vehicles on the Pacific Rim Highway. The sound alarmed her terribly and she retreated inland to safety.

Basically a nocturnal animal, she slept during most of the day. During one of these naps she heard the sound that had frightened her earlier. She had been dozing in a tiny clearing on the side of an overgrown logging road and drowsily stood up to attempt to find the cause. She was facing the direction of the source when something that she had never seen before began threateningly approaching her. The smell of the metal creature was overwhelming and unnatural. As she roared to scare it away, the creature rammed into her.

She reacted immediately, smashing with her claws and wrestling the beast over on its back. She clawed at the belly of the thing, tearing out its innards. She grabbed what she could and ran off into the forest.

That had been a long time ago, at least in bear time. The experience had alarmed her so much that she'd headed back to the land of her birth. Maybe the familiar surroundings would calm her soul.

Kevin, Jenne, and Anne were clearly getting cabin fever. They had been cooped up for two days now. The last ten calls to Preston had gone to voicemail. "Obviously, something's happened. Let's call the headquarters or something." Anne, too, wanted something, anything, to happen. The strong feelings she had for Jordan had only increased her uneasiness.

"Jenne, you're a little better at this than I am. See if you can reach someone who knows something at the RCMP."

Jenne grabbed the cell from Kevin, looked up the number for the Tofino Detachment for the Mounties, and made the call. After asking to speak to Sergeant Preston, she was passed on to his commanding officer. She explained why she wanted to speak to Preston and informed his CO of the nature of his interest in the two kidnappers-slash-gold thieves. The superior was somewhat surprised at this information, admitting he had not been in the loop. "There's been an accident. Both Preston and his associate were involved in a crash on the Rim Highway. Andersen, his partner, was treated at the hospital and sent home. The sergeant has some broken ribs and a concussion. They're going to keep him for a few days to make sure there's no bleeding in the brain."

"Yikes, I hope he'll be fine. So what should we do now?"

"Preston was pursuing this outside of our jurisdiction. It would be inappropriate of me to get involved in this. What I will do is send this information over to our Nanaimo detachment for them to follow up."

Jenne had not informed the inspector that they were surveilling Daniel and Marty. She rightly assumed that he would insist they cease their amateur sleuthing. She disconnected, saying they would follow up with the local detachment and then filled Kevin and Anne in on the situation.

"It looks like we're on our own for now. Maybe if Will and Jordan find where they're headed, we can let the police know. They just don't seem that enthusiastic about catching these guys." Jenne was becoming frustrated.

"That's because they don't know what we know," Anne said. "Preston was determined to close the case because it was his to begin with. Now that he's out of commission, it's no longer a priority. Should I call Jordan and let them know that they have no backup?" Anne was anxious to talk to Jordy again.

Kevin nodded at her. "Go ahead. Tell them to keep in contact with us and, when they see where they're going, let us know immediately."

Daniel had been driving for an hour and a half, and Marty had been quiet for at least ten minutes. "Let's get some food. I'm hungry."

"Of course you are. Seems like all you do is talk, eat, and complain. We're almost to Courtenay. We'll find a McDonald's and do the drive-through."

"C'mon, Daniel, let's stop and get some real food."

"You think it's a good idea, like it's smart, to leave forty million in gold inside our truck while we grab a fucking bite? Really?"

"Oh, I guess I hadn't really thought about that. Sorry."

Daniel was growing weary of Marty. He wished he had a gun so he could shoot the fucker. As it stood now he still needed him anyway. He could maybe have found some way to convert the gold, but he really hadn't thought that far ahead.

"McDonald's is fine."

God, the guy was annoying.

They ordered their quarter pounders, fries, and shakes at the intercom station next to that stupid clown Ronald. Marty actually seemed a little afraid of the image. They pulled over to the farthest corner of the lot and munched their lunches.

"So, do we know where the plane lands in Campbell River?" Daniel was trying to think ahead.

"When I talked to the gal at the charter place, she said it's the same place all the float planes land. It's just north of town, right on Discovery Passage. I'm sure I can find the place."

"Do we know what kind of plane it is?"

"She said it was something to do with an animal."

"Animal?"

"Like a muskrat or something."

"Marty, there's no such thing as a muskrat plane."

"Well, it was something like that, I'll think of it. What's the difference? Who cares as long as it gets us out of here?"

"It'll only make a difference if it's too small, so try and think of it, okay?"

Will had pulled into the gas station on the other side of the McDonald's as soon as he passed the pickup. He'd had several cars between them, so he wasn't concerned about being seen. "Looks like they're gonna be there for a while. We should fill up while we can."

As soon as the car was turned off, the phone rang. It was Anne. "Jordan, it's me. We just heard that Preston was in an accident, and he's in the hospital. They were on their own so, at least as of now, you two are by yourselves. Kevin says to let us know as soon as you find out where they are going. I guess you'll know when you get there, eh?"

"Well, I guess so, yeah. There's not much we can do but follow them. I thought they might head for the ferries but they're not, they are headed north."

"You guys be careful; I'd hate to see anything happen to you. I mean it!"

"Don't worry, Anne, we're not Rambo here. I promise we won't engage with these chumps. There's really no place that makes sense for them to go if they want to leave the country, so I'll be anxious to see where they end up. As soon as we find out, I'll get back to you." With that Jordan ended the call and moved to the driver's seat to take over for Will.

The two-vehicle convoy continued north on Island Highway 19, the F-150 with a destination in mind, the Explorer still wondering.

Marty offered to drive but Daniel wasn't one to relinquish control.

"So, Daniel, we're gonna get to Campbell River in a half hour or so. What are we going to do until tomorrow afternoon?"

"I don't know. We'll have to find someplace to hang out for twenty-four hours. I'm afraid we'll have to sleep in the truck. That is, unless you want to get a hotel room and move this stuff into the room and then back out again."

"Shit, I hadn't thought about that. Fuck." Marty looked crestfallen. He hated the idea of sleeping in the truck with Daniel. Sadly though, carrying the damn gold both ways was unthinkable.

"Why don't you pull up Google Maps and find us a place we can park for the night that's not too far from the seaplane landing area."

Marty began his assigned duties.

They continued on Highway 19 until they reached Campbell River. This city, the third largest on Vancouver Island, is known as the Salmon Capital of the World. It sits on the east coast of the island and is considered the line of demarcation between the more populated southern territories and the wild and rugged northern regions. Sport fisherman the world over are flown in to catch their limit of wild salmon.

Lodges that range from luxurious and extravagant to downright rustic and spartan are kept full during the year-round fishing season. Every species of the delicacy from chinook to coho to chum, pink, and sockeye can be hooked from the Campbell River, on which the town sits. For many, it's a bucket-list excursion that, once experienced, is never forgotten.

The turnoff to 19A leads directly into the city itself. Daniel glanced over to Marty as they headed into town. "So did you find anything?"

"I say we head over to the marina. There shouldn't be much going on there this time of year, and it's close to lots of restaurants and things. We got the whole afternoon, tonight, and tomorrow morning to kill, so we may as well be comfortable."

"Makes sense. If there are any vehicles there, they most likely are long-term parking. It should discourage any suspicions about us being there overnight. If anyone says anything, we'll tell them the truth: we're waiting for a plane to pick us up tomorrow and didn't want to waste money on a hotel. Oh yeah, it's near restaurants too. Good get, Marty."

They found an obscure corner of the lot, parked, and waited for Marty to get hungry again. There was very little traffic here, a pickup or two and a Ford Explorer were the only vehicles they'd seen during the first half hour.

Jordan was surprised that their targets had exited in Campbell River. The only ferries here went to Quadra Island and there was nothing there. Will had thought their first objective would be to get back to the States and Jordy agreed. When he saw them pull into the marina parking lot, he kept going and immediately turned into a shopping center where they paused, idling.

"Whaddaya think, Jordan?"

"Not sure. From what I can see, they look like they're going to be here for some time. They have to be waiting for something, maybe a boat? I don't know, any ideas?"

"I've only been here once, so I don't know the area very well. Came up here with three other guys on a fishing trip. We came in on one of those float planes. Really cool comin' in here on one of those. We stayed in one of those cabins on the river."

"They fly out of here?"

"Sure, just watch over there. You'll seem 'em landing right on the water. They're loud as hell, big friggin' engines to get them up and outta the water, lotta drag. Member havin' to wear earplugs during the flight."

Will never ceased to amaze. "That might be it, Will. Maybe they're waiting for a plane. If that happens we're screwed."

"I dunno. I don't think a legitimate charter outfit would do it.

Besides, that shit's heavy. The planes aren't that big. I still think maybe a boat."

While Will and Jordan discussed possibilities, Marty got hungry again. "Daniel, I'm going over to that Starbucks to get something to eat. Want anything?"

"No, Marty, I don't. But go ahead. At least you'll shut up for a while."

Marty turned, walked a few steps, then turned back to the pickup. "Beaver, it's a goddamn beaver."

"What the hell are you talking about?"

"The plane, the gal said it was a beaver, not a muskrat. I knew it was one of those things."

"Go get your food, Marty. Let me look this up."

Daniel immediately did a search for "beaver float plane." What he found was slightly disturbing.

The DHC-2 Beaver, manufactured by de Havilland Canada, was manufactured up until 1967. It was still the most favored bush plane in Northern Canada and Alaska. Aviation historians consider it a Canadian icon. Daniel was encouraged by the rumored dependability of the plane. The troubling part, however, was the twenty-one-hundred pound weight limit. That could be a problem. He could only hope the pilot was a lightweight. Tomorrow should prove interesting.

Once Jordan was satisfied that Daniel and Marty were going to stay put for some time, he found a place to park in the nearby Discovery Harbour parking lot. From here they could keep an eye on the pickup and be prepared if it were to suddenly take off. They settled in for an unknown duration and called their friends to update them.

After Anne and the O'Malleys were brought up to speed, they sat around looking at each other, feeling helpless. Anne was the first to suggest a course of action. "I've got an idea. Whatever is going to happen with the crooks is most likely going to be in Campbell River. They think they're going to be there a while, right?"

"Yup."

"Well, how about we take the *Butterfly* and meet them up there. If Daniel is going by boat, we will be able to track them. If not, at least we'll be there for support for Will and Jordan. It should only take us five hours, so we can be there before dark."

"Great idea, Anne, let's get going. I'll check us out, you and Jenne pack us up, and we'll get out of here."

The threesome was at the dinghy in twenty minutes and on the *Butterfly* shortly thereafter. "I think we should bring Fred into the loop; he should probably know what we're up to. Kevin, why don't you bring up the anchor, and I'll get things underway here."

Anne started up the Cummins diesel and let it idle while the anchor was stowed. She grabbed the handset and called in on Fred's frequency. "Fred, it's Anne, here's what's going on. You better have a seat."

Fred was swiftly brought up to speed and, for a few seconds, Anne thought she'd lost him. "Fred, you there?"

"Yup. Come pick me up, I'm going with you. I may be old but not old enough to let my buddies down. If you and the O'Malleys, who barely know us, are gonna go to all this trouble, the least I can do is join you. See you in just a bit. I'll be at the dock."

Anne had started to protest, but she quickly realized how futile it would be. Jenne overheard, rolled her eyes, and said, "I think it'll be fun having the ancient one on board. Let's go get him."

Brother XII, aka Fred, dressed in his signature jeans, plaid shirt, Carhartt vest, and John Deere cap, was waiting on the dock when they arrived. When Kevin inquired about his missing spit cup he got a four-word reply. "I quit, bad habit." And then they were on the way to Campbell River.

The crew of the *Butterfly* connected with Will and Jordan whenever there was cell service. With nothing to report, save for Marty occasionally leaving for food, the general feeling was that it would be some time before anything happened. Anne was an excellent captain, and the rest of the crew was impressed by her seamanship. As the designated pilot for the *Butterfly* during her time on DeCourcy, she had considerable experience in good and bad weather. The drizzle and clouds had given way to cloudless cornflower-blue skies, and the scenery was spectacular. The beauty of this place was mesmerizing and even with the gravity of the situation, the crew of the *Butterfly* was impressed. Both Kevin and Jenne found the vistas stunning, as this was their first time this far north in Discovery Passage.

During their journey, Fred captivated them with stories of the early days on DeCourcy. Back then many of the residents were religious and were looking for salvation. Fred did what he could for them, but he was very young and made the mistakes that young people make. He tried his utmost to save those who were looking for guidance and even those who weren't. He learned the hard way that, while there may be some good in everyone, in some, it's extraordinarily difficult to find. Eventually, he understood that each soul needs to discover for themselves what works and what doesn't. He focused on providing a place to stay, comradery with others, and advice and consultation only when it was requested. While many people who knew little of the commune thought the place was run by some nut job, Fred just let them think what they would like. He did the best he could for his people; anything else was up to some higher power.

Fred's voice was hypnotic. When he looked their way with those eyes, well, it was easy to understand why some thought he was more than just a common man.

CHAPTER 27

Anne radioed the harbor master at the Discovery Harbour Marina, requesting a slip. They were assigned the one farthest outboard on "J" dock. It suited their purposes nicely since being seen by Daniel was out of the question. The *Butterfly* edged into its slip just as the last glimmer of dusk retreated.

Cell service was excellent here in Campbell River. As soon as Anne shut the engine down, she got Jordan on the phone. "Jordy, we're here, come down and see us. Can you do it without those two seeing you?" Anne sounded like a schoolgirl with her first boy crush.

"I don't think it'll be a problem cuz their truck is at the far northern end of the marina parking. We're south of your position, so unless they're out walking around, we should be safe. The last thing I want, though, is to miss out if they leave or do something else."

"You should be fine. Just in case, Kevin's been goofing around with his phone. He says the marina has webcams, and he thinks he's located their truck in the lot. Besides, Fred wants to say hi."

"He's with you?"

"Yup, said he wanted to be here with us."

"Okay, give me that site with the cameras, and I'll make sure it's Daniel's truck."

After making certain they had eyes on the F-150, Will and Jordan joined the others on the Beneteau Trawler. It was heart-warming seeing the heart and soul of the DeCourcy Island group together. The O'Malleys felt like interlopers for all of two or three minutes before Fred made certain to include them in the conversation. Will was somewhat shy at first when talking to Fred. He had always held the commune leader up as a father figure, and this new familiarity was taking some getting used to. Fred's personality was extraordinarily disarming, though, and soon Will was asking about Molly and how she was doing.

As the evening lengthened, they enjoyed some takeout from the marina restaurant, shared more stories, and speculated on the inhabitants of the pickup they frequently viewed on Kevin's phone. Anne and Jordan found a corner up on the freezing bridge and managed to steal a smooch or two before it came time to head back to the Explorer.

Sleeping arrangements were somewhat cramped but doable. The double stateroom below went to the O'Malleys, and the two single berths in the cabin were assigned to Fred and Anne. Not an idyllic situation, but heaps better than sleeping in a truck or a car.

Will and Jordan slept fitfully, each waking frequently to make sure nothing was going on with the Ford pickup. The webcam find had been a godsend, since their visibility had diminished, and the online camera quality was exceptional. By 6:00 a.m. both were wide awake, apprehensive as to what the day might bring. The overcast had returned along with a smattering of rain showers.

The gold pilferers were also up and about. They took turns visiting the Starbucks, bringing their sausage-and-egg sandwiches back to the truck. Marty had been told by the charter outfit to expect their ride to land a little after one o'clock. Anxiety was also pervasive in the crew cab. Daniel hoping that the pilot was a small man, Marty complaining about carrying the gold to the plane. "I hope this low ceiling doesn't screw up the plane getting here."

"I think we'll be fine, Marty. These guys fly in all kinds of shitty weather. Besides, the rain is supposed to stop by late morning. Just relax."

The *Butterfly* dwellers too were performing their early morning chores. The coffee was on and food had been purchased and shared. Fred looked fresh as a daisy. Kevin and Jenne had returned to the lower cabin to pull their things together. "That guy amazes me. He seems to have an endless reserve of energy. He's a dear and I'm really glad he's on our side." Jenne was smitten.

"Jenne, I was trying to figure out what their plan is. Common sense says it's a boat, but I don't think they'd choose that. It's too slow and they'd be sitting ducks, literally. Besides, if it was, they would have been gone by now."

"What are you thinking?"

"Gotta be a seaplane. It can land anywhere there's water, and they can avoid customs if the pilot's shady. They're camped out in the marina lot, and the seaplane landing area is just north of us here in the marina. My money's on a plane."

"Why don't we discuss it with those two up there and then get Jordy on the phone and tell him what we're thinking."

Scott Weber had flown anything with wings or props. From Hueys in Vietnam to turboprops for a small domestic airline. He had missed most of the action in 'Nam, mostly did mop-up stuff, but that was where he'd honed his skills. Now, at seventy years of age, he should have been retired. Thing is, he loved flying. Even when he wasn't working he spent his free time ferrying personally owned aircraft from airport to airport. Two years ago he got a call from one of his old army buddies. Seems the guy owned a small charter outfit serving the sportfishing industry and was short a pilot. Scott confirmed that, yes, of course he'd flown float planes. And, yes, he was quite familiar with the de Havilland aircraft. But, he told his pal, I'll only do it on a part-time basis. "I got grandkids, and I just don't wanna be gone that much."

Scott had been a skinny kid when he was in the army, and throughout his piloting career he worked hard at staying in shape. Now that he was a part-timer, he'd let himself go some. His wife of forty years loved cooking for her kids, their kids, and Scotty. Her Sicilian heritage contributed mightily to her culinary skills.

His six-foot frame had tipped the scales at one-eighty-five when he worked for Uncle Sam. Now, with a diet rich in pasta and wine, he was pushing two thirty. Scolding from his doctor did little to encourage him to change his diet. Cheating death for as long as he had reinforced his invincibility. Besides, he loved his wife's cooking.

He left Orcas Island under overcast skies with his three charter fares at noon. They had been staying in Deer Harbor for the weekend and were looking forward to scoring their limit of king salmon from the Campbell River. The Beaver he was flying was fifty years old, yet he had as much confidence in this aircraft as in any he'd ever flown. The powerful Pratt and Whitney radial engine generated four hundred fifty horses, plenty to overcome the drag on the pontoons. When he handed the earplugs to his passengers, he knew immediately this was their first time in a Beaver. "Relax, gentlemen, you're really gonna enjoy this. Just make sure you put these in before we take off." They were glad they did.

Flying underneath the thick ceiling the entire trip afforded excellent views for the three fishermen. It was a smooth, uneventful flight. However, never having flown in a floatplane before, the landing shocked them. The flight path was directly toward the marina, avoiding a painfully long taxi to the dock. Scott secretly enjoyed the hell out of landing with first timers. While float planes need excessively long straightaways to take off, they can land in a puddle, a very small puddle. Just when a crash into the marina seemed imminent, Scott dropped the pontoons into the water. With a whoosh, the Beaver came to a halt with three hundred yards to spare. Even though he'd flown these things for years, he was still amazed at how quickly they came to a standstill after hitting the deck.

Smiles all the way around, they taxied to the dock and then to the small customs office that welcomed visitors to Canada. Scott stayed with the Beaver, awaiting the two fellows he was supposed to take back to Lake Union in Seattle.

"Marty, we've got to find a way to get this gold down to the plane. According to the map there's a maintenance road that looks like it goes all the way to the seaplane dock. They probably use it to service the fuel tanks. I'm going to go find our ride out of here and see what I can work out with the pilot."

Daniel made his way past the marina until he reached the platform bordering the small inlet that served as the taxiway for floatplanes. Several planes were parked at moorings close by and a de Havilland Beaver was tied up at the dock. Standing by the plane was an older gentleman sporting a snow-white mustache on a ruddy, weathered face.

"Hi, I'm Daniel Phillips. Looks like you're our pilot."

"Yes, it does. I'm Scotty Weber. Are there two of you?"

"There are. Marty's coming down that road over there right now."

Scott turned to look in the direction Daniel was pointing and saw a Ford pickup heading toward them. The maintenance road terminated at the refueling tanks for the aircraft. Turning back quizzically to his passenger, Scott looked for an explanation.

"We have some baggage we need to load before we take off. That okay?"

"I guess, long as it's not too big."

"It's not too big, but it's a little heavy, and we might need some help loading it."

Marty had parked the truck and was walking toward them lugging two gold bars with him. "Thought I should start the process."

"What the fuck!" Weber's eyes bugged out of his head, his mouth wide open. "Where did that come from? Is it stolen?"

"Don't go jumping to conclusions. We found this stuff buried on a small island. You haven't heard of any gold heists lately, have you?"

"No, I can't say that I have. But what about customs when we get back to Seattle. How are you gonna handle that?"

"Well, that's what we needed to talk to you about. We thought maybe you could land somewhere else, you know, like a small lake or something."

"I don't think so. We have flight plans and my charter company to consider. You'll just have to figure out a way to handle customs when we get to Lake Union."

Daniel had expected some resistance. "Suppose we could make it worth your while?"

"There's nothing you can pay me to make it worthwhile. I like my job."

"What if you had enough to stop working, or maybe buy your own plane? Do you know what one of these is worth?"

"Don't know, don't care. We're landing on Lake Union or you're not coming."

The reluctance to skirt the law Daniel understood, but this guy couldn't be bought? He thought otherwise. Maybe he needed to up the incentive.

"Scott, let me be a little clearer. Each one of these is worth close to seven hundred thousand dollars. Would almost a million and a half dollars, tax free, make a difference? I want to assure you that this is *found* gold. We would just prefer to keep a low profile on this."

Marty finally put the heavy bars down on the dock while he observed the negotiations.

The spark of interest in Scott's eyes was confirmed when he asked, "Where would you want to land? It's not like just anywhere will do. It's possible to land anywhere. It's taking off again that's the challenge."

"We hadn't gotten that far along. We thought maybe you could suggest something."

"Let me think about it. I can always say something's off with the plane and I had to put it down. But explaining dropping you two off, that's a little more problematic." Scott looked as though he were trying to balance the small fortune with his law-abiding ways.

They began the arduous process of hand carrying the gold bars to the plane. The small but unbelievably heavy loaves occupied less than three cubic feet of cargo space when they were all on board.

Standing back to look in wonder at the precious cargo, Scott had an inspiration. "I got it! I know how to do this but it's gonna cost you another one of those little bars."

Daniel felt as though he were being taken advantage of, but he was out of options. "Tell us why we need to cough up another one."

"This is what we're gonna do. We land on Lake Union in Seattle…."

"Whoa, no, not happening." Even Marty appeared uncomfortable now.

"No, hear me out. Landing on another lake is too problematic. Too hard to unload the stuff, no transportation when we do. Too much to explain to everyone, including customs. My buddy owns this charter company, but he operates it on a shoestring. If you contribute another one of those little shiny things, then we'll have three between us. We'll each get a million and I can keep flying if I want to. I'm confident I can convince him. We go way back."

"Even if we agree, how do we get around customs?" Daniel asked hopefully.

"Hell, that's the easy part. You just leave the gold on the plane. We pull up to the dock, throw a tarp over it and call it trash. You two go through customs, declare some fish or something, then uber off to our maintenance hangar at the north end of the lake. We're in and out of the dock all the time, so they'll never check the plane. You can unload the stuff yourself—I'm not helping this time—when you get to the hangar."

Scotty smiled and looked very proud of himself. Daniel smiled at Marty and Marty smiled back. "Goddam, I knew we hired the right guy."

CHAPTER 28

As soon as the pickup left its location, Will and Jordy started the Explorer. They followed Marty until he turned off on the gravel maintenance road. With almost no traffic in the area, they were forced to pull into a deserted RV park to wait it out. They knew from their maps display that the road led down to the floatplane dock.

"Uh-oh, I think we're screwed, Jordan. Looks like they got a plane ride outta here. What should we do?"

"Let's get the *Butterfly* on the phone. Maybe they can see what's going on from their slip. I know they have some field glasses on board the boat."

Kevin had seen Marty take off while studying the webcam. When his phone rang, he knew it was the boys. After getting some idea of the general location, he was able to locate the floatplane area. The charters had been taking off and landing all morning and, as he suspected, this was to be the escape plan for the offenders.

"I can see the plane, Jordan. Why don't you and Will get over here, and we can come up with something."

They showed up just as the last of the gold was being loaded aboard the charter. "I was able to copy the tail number of the aircraft, but I'm not sure what else we can do. Let's contact the Mounties who man the Nanaimo detachment and give them the details. They may have some means to connect with the Seattle cops and inform them they have a kidnapper headed their way. As for the gold, I just don't know how to go after that. Fred, any ideas?"

"The gold was donated by my grandfather's followers. I don't know what he planned to do with it, except in some way I think it belongs to the island and the folks who live there. As for me, heck, what would I ever need the stuff for." And so, the proprietorship of the gold was somewhat dubious.

With the last brick stowed away and Marty and Daniel in their seats, Scott Weber taxied the de Havilland Beaver out to his takeoff position. Scott gave the powerful engine one hundred percent throttle, and they headed into the northerly breeze. The ceiling had lifted, and puffy white clouds dotted the sky. When the plane failed to reach takeoff speed as it passed the final windsock, Scott looked only slightly concerned. After another thousand feet, he was still ten knots under recommended liftoff velocity, ratcheting up his anxiety. He'd run into the rocky shallows in another thousand feet, so this was it. Weber was an outstanding pilot who knew the limits of his airplane. "C'mon you fucker, lift," he shouted as he jerked back on the yoke.

The yellow and white Beaver clawed its way out of the grasp of the waters of Discovery Passage. Even free of the water's clutches, the plane was sluggish and the controls balky. "What the hell is going… shit, we've got too much weight on this thing."

The realization hit Daniel simultaneously. Now he remembered why he had hoped for a smaller pilot. This tubbo, along with the weight of the gold, more than exceeded the twenty-one hundred pound payload capacity of this fucking muskrat, beaver, whatever.

Scott, wrestling with the controls, had the altimeter over two hundred feet now, but the concentrated weight of the gold was fighting him every step of the way. As he initiated a long turn to port to get them headed in the right direction, he dropped down to thirty feet over the river to take advantage of the ground effect. Until he got into some denser air he would try to keep them over the relative flatness of the water.

Trish had heard the rumors. Although she wasn't privy to the particulars, she was aware of the demise of Howard Bories. Camped out in his robe, he did nothing but wander around his suite during the day. Trooper that she was, Trish did her best to keep the operation on an even keel. The Tofino Inn and Spa was still operating at almost capacity with none of the guests aware of the impending foreclosure by Howard's lenders. Janet Slattery had notified the authorities in the province of British Columbia, which had initiated the extradition procedure of one Howard Bories.

Howard had two more days of freedom before he had to return to Seattle to face the music. It appeared as though his future travels would be limited. Even if he fessed up and appealed to the mercy of the court, it was doubtful he would be out anytime soon. Maybe they'd put him in some low security place where he could stroll around the grounds. How ironic, he mused. Presently he hosted guests, provided them food and beverage, and took care of their every need. Now the state would be doing the same for him.

Trish had put out some feelers and had made it a point to contact Apogee. They were excited at the prospect of having her as an employee and vowed that she could have her choice of any open general manager position in their portfolio. The birders promised they would be back to visit within the next two weeks to discuss things.

Those aboard the *Butterfly* saw the gold take off in the DHC-2 along with its three escorts. It seemed odd that the seaplane barely escaped the protruding rocks at the end of its takeoff run. That it had only risen a couple hundred feet was puzzling as well. They watched as it dropped down and made the wide sweeping west turn to head back to the south. The stiff tail wind created less lift than expected, and the plane was forced to follow the Campbell River to avoid the foothills of the mountains of the Strathcona Provincial Park.

"Seems like they're goin' the wrong way," Will offered.

"They're too heavy, all that gold is holding 'em back." Fred appeared to know these things. "I'm thinkin' they're gonna follow that river until they find a place to land. Now that they're in that valley, they can't get high enough to turn around."

"Somebody pull up a map. Let's see if there's a road that parallels the river." If there was any way to track them, Will was all for it.

As quick fingered as ever, Kevin pulled up his map app. "Looks like the Gold River Highway runs alongside the water forever. Not sure how long those guys will be in the air but maybe it's worth a try."

"C'mon, Will, let's see if we can find them." Jordan hopped to the deck with Will in close pursuit. "We'll keep in touch as long as the cell service holds out." They bolted to the O'Malley's Explorer and fishtailed out of the lot to try to chase down the floatplane.

The highway did parallel the river, but the road was nothing but a jumble of twists and turns. They could get the SUV up to forty-five occasionally but just averaging thirty-five was a push. After six or seven miles, the river dumped into Campbell Lake and the road turned inland. Had there not been such a sense of urgency, the scenery would have taken center stage.

While Jordan managed the driving chores, Will got Jenne on the phone. "We're doing the best we can, Jenne, but no sign of anything yet. We'll just go until we see something or until we have to give up. Have you heard anything?"

Her response was broken words and static, then nothing. "I guess that's it for phone service for a while, Jordy. Let's just keep going." After another ten miles of hairpins and right angles, a break in the forest revealed the grandeur of Upper Campbell Lake. At ten miles long and almost a mile wide, it was extraordinary. For the last half hour there had been no sign of human activity that could attempt to diminish this unspoiled wilderness.

Jenne stopped talking when she realized that whatever cell tower they were using could no longer reach Jordy and Will. "We've lost them."

"I know they're on their own, but I feel good about those boys. They'll know what to do when the time comes." Fred's confidence was contagious. The man had an uncanny knack for delivering positivity in the face of doubt. It was no mystery that lost souls seeking direction often ended up on his doorstep.

"There isn't much more we can do here but wish them well. I don't see any other way out of those mountains unless they come back through here, so I guess it's a waiting game until we hear something." Kevin sat back on a deck chair and suggested Jenne run up to the marina for a six-pack of Labatt's.

"What's the matter, what are you doing?" Marty screamed as Scott lowered the plane to just above the water.

"We're overweight; I should have realized how heavy that gold is. I'm flying low to use the ground effect to keep us in the air. We can fly along the water until either I find some denser air or we have to land, but the farther inland we go the taller the mountains will be, so there's no turning around."

Daniel appeared not very happy now that Scott had to figure out a way not to crash this thing. The sound in the cockpit caused by the screaming four-hundred-fifty-horsepower radial engine was deafening. Without headsets and an intercom, the only way to be heard was by shouting or screaming. "What do we need to do?"

"What we need to do is lighten this load. We should start throwing some of your goodies there out the door."

"No fucking way. Come up with something else."

"I don't know any other way to do it. We *have* to lighten this thing up."

Daniel was quiet for a moment as the mountain peaks towered

above them. "Can you land this in one of these lakes and then take off again?"

"Sure I can. I need two things, though. First, we should lose about five hundred pounds. Second, we need a long enough lake to take off from."

"Okay, let's do that. Look for a lake that will work and then land this thing. If you can get us close enough to the shore, we'll take twenty of these beauties and hide then where they can't be found. We'll continue on to Seattle, then come back for the rest of it."

Scott wasn't keen on spending any more time with these bozos than necessary. He supposed, though, he could hit 'em up for another of those seven hundred grand loaves for his trouble. The flight was only an hour and if they found the right body of water, it would be a piece of cake. "Daniel, I'll do it for another one of those little gold thingies. I hate to be a dick about this but we're gonna have another customs visit that we have to deal with and there's more risk, and my buddy will have to let me take the plane again. See where I'm goin' with this?"

"I do and I don't like it. You *are* being a dick."

"Yeah, I know, but see I'm the pilot, and you really, really need me."

"Okay, asshole, find a deserted lake and put this sucker down. We're good with the deal."

"We're over Upper Campbell Lake now, but I can't turn this thing around to land it here. I'm pretty sure this next lake to the south is called Buttle Lake. It's a long one, maybe fifteen or sixteen miles. It's remote too, surrounded by the Strathcona Park. You shouldn't have any trouble finding a place to hide your little treasure."

"Go for it. Just get us as close to the shore as you can."

"All right. There's a small river that dumps into the lake called Wolf River. Lotta sand washes into the lake there so I'm fairly certain we can bottom the pontoons out, so you'll only be knee deep. Once we shed five or six hundred pounds we'll just float off. We should have another eleven or twelve miles of lake to use for takeoff."

Since the Beaver was flying extremely close to the ground anyway, there was no need for a long approach. They saw the long, narrow Buttle Lake just as soon as they passed Upper Campbell; in fact, the two lakes were connected by a narrow passage. Weber remembered the Wolf emptied into the lake about four miles south of this passage. Regardless of how heavy they were, it still took only a few hundred yards to land. Just as soon as he saw the river delta to the west, he dropped the plane into the lake. All three were thrown into their shoulder straps when the pontoons were grabbed by the resistance of the water. Scott turned them toward the western shore and taxied until the aircraft glided into the sandy bottom. He shut down the engine while all three exhaled a sigh of relief.

CHAPTER 29

It had taken some time, but Karla had found her way back to her birthplace. Her mother had moved on and her siblings had started raising families of their own.

It was less a conscious feeling, more a sense of comfort and belonging that this land provided. Although her experiences on the west coast were frightening, they gave her a new appreciation for the untouched spirit of this place. Never again would she venture beyond the mountains, meadows, and valleys of the Strathcona Provincial Park.

The miles she had traveled to return here had taken their toll. The cold season was approaching, and her instincts dictated she put on sufficient weight to carry her through the coming period of hibernation. Often bears spent over four months at a time in their lairs. Less frequently though, they slept for long periods, recovered and wandered, and then returned to their dens. In either case, fall was when they needed to store up calories to carry them through the winter. The nighttime hours were spent foraging for berries, rodents, and kill from other predators to satisfy her need for nourishment. She mostly slept during the daylight hours to recover from her exhaustive efforts searching for food at night.

The few hours of the day when she wasn't sleeping were spent preparing the hollowed out remnants of a giant cedar that had crashed to the ground some thirty years ago. This part of Vancouver Island received frequent visits, during the winter months, from strong low pressure systems born in the Gulf of Alaska. The massive specimens of Douglas firs, Sitka spruce, and western red cedars still standing were testament to both the fury and resilience of Mother Nature.

Not just any old log would do for Karla. Her enormous size required something special. She found it in the excavated crater created by the gnarled roots of the ancient tree. The root ball would provide protection from the elements when she had removed enough of the forest detritus that remained in the pocket where the base of the tree had been ripped out of the earth. In addition to her shovel-like claws, she made efficient use of her prodigious strength, scooping out cubic feet of earth in a single swipe. After several days she deemed the earthen cave sufficient for a winter's nap. The final chore before retiring would be to load up on calories. She had chosen well. The den was located near fresh water with an ample supply of salmon and far away from anything smelling of humans. Looking forward, perhaps the spring would bring with it a mate of suitable quality.

At this point the Gold River Highway, Highway 28, traveled the length of Upper Campbell Lake, hugging its eastern shore. Here too, the absence of civilization was startling. "Keep your eyes peeled, Will. If they have to land that thing, and I'm pretty sure they will, then it would have to be a good-sized body of water. They would need it to take off again."

"Maybe they'll just start throwing the gold out of the plane."

"Guess it's possible, but those guys have gone to a lot of trouble to get this far. I can't see that happening. If they do end up going that way, we're screwed, so let's just hope they don't."

Will nodded in agreement. "When we get to the south end of this lake, the road turns back up the west side. I don't think it makes sense to go that way though. It gets narrower as we get into these mountains and I doubt they'll be able to turn around. There's a small road that continues south along the east side of something called Buttle Lake.

It's really long. After that, there's nothing but mountains. If they're gonna land, they won't have any other possibilities."

"I'm good with that. Let's just keep going. We're only about fifteen minutes from there."

After the deafening engine noise and the screaming in the cockpit, the complete absence of sound was eerie. Save for the rhythmic lapping of the lake water against the pontoons and the labored breathing of the travelers, there were no other sounds. It was as if each were reluctant to intrude upon the quiet.

Finally Daniel unclipped his harness and broke the trance triggered by the sudden silence of the place. "Okay, Marty, let's get going. We need to decide how much gold to take off the plane and where to stash it. Looks like Scott, here, was right about the sand. There's only a couple of feet of water to wade through."

"We're gonna get wet. I'm not sure I wanna do that."

"Marty, get your ass out of the plane. May as well grab a couple of bricks too. No sense in wading to the shore empty-handed."

The duo clumsily picked up sixty pounds of pure gold, over a million dollars' worth.

Marty was first out the door, straining not to drop his booty. "Goddamn, this water is absolutely freezing."

"Of course it is, you moron. These lakes are fed by mountain snow. They never get warm, even in the summer. Move along so I can get out." Daniel's patience with Marty was wearing thin.

They trudged through the shallow water, sinking in the sandy bottom from the weight they were carrying, eventually reaching the wooded shore just south of Wolf River.

"I gotta put this down. My back is killing me." Marty grimaced as he dropped the heavy loaf on the soft earth.

Daniel dropped his as well. No sense in carrying all that weight until they were sure where to hide it. They hiked into the wooded area just off the shore. "We're coming back tomorrow morning so it's not like we need to go very deep into this woods. See what looks good. Make sure it's out of the way, just in case a hiker is crazy enough to come over this way."

Marty wandered off a little closer to the river where some of the larger trees grew. Daniel headed a little farther south, searching for an out of the way place. "Daniel, over here," Marty yelled from about five hundred feet to his left.

"Looks like when this tree fell over it left this hole. We can put the gold in there and cover it with dirt and needles. Even if there are hikers in the area, they'd never see it. It's gonna be less than twenty-four hours, anyway. Plus it's only a short walk to the plane."

"Marty, you're smarter than you look. The place smells a little funky but maybe this *will* be okay. We only need to move about twenty of those bars so let's put them on the shore first and then move all of them to this hole under those roots. I can't imagine anyone looking over here, but we'll cover it up anyway."

Scott Weber was happy to be on the ground. Well, the water in his case, and he was even happier to have some quiet time for himself. He'd gotten caught up with how much the gold was worth at the expense of his moral compass. This escapade just had to be sketchy. His passengers weren't the kind of guys he'd like to be friends with; there just was too much left unsaid, too many knowing looks. He'd love to figure a way out of this without leaving them here. Maybe after they unloaded some of the excess weight he would take them to Seattle and just deliver them to customs, tell the authorities they were trying to sneak gold into the country. He'd be out over a million bucks but, screw it, what would he do with it anyway? Yes. He'd feel better about himself, he'd keep doing what he loved, and he'd be done with these assholes. If there was fifteen million dollars' worth of gold hidden here in the woods, then fine, let some hikers discover it.

Highway 28 gave way to Westmin Road, a much smaller two-lane affair, that went the entire length of the eastern shore of Buttle Lake.

Though it was much narrower than the Gold River Highway, it was also much straighter, and Will and Daniel were making excellent time. There were occasional breaks in the wooded cover between the lake and the road. When these occurred, the lake gleamed magnificently in the afternoon sun. Six minutes after turning onto Westmin, Will erupted, "Jordy, stop! Back it up. I saw something on the other side of the lake. You still got those glasses we borrowed from the boat?"

Jordan pulled over to the gravel shoulder, still facing south. Through the break in the trees, he could easily see the floatplane. As soon as Will could focus the binoculars, he could make out the plane and two men wading into the shore. "It's them, Jordan. Looks like they're taking some of the gold to the shore. Probably like Fred said, they're too heavy, and they're gonna take some of the gold off to lighten the load. What're we gonna do?"

"I think all we can do for now is watch. Cell phone's no good here, no service. We can take pictures with the phone camera, it's got a good zoom on it. At least we'll have something to document what we're seeing."

Both felt helpless watching Marty and Daniel carrying gold bars to the opposite shore. There was no road on the western shore, not even a dirt logging road. It was nothing but forest leading up to the higher elevations where early snows covered the peaks.

Karla was tired; tired and sleepy. Her foraging the previous night, combined with putting the finishing touches on her winter resting place, had left her exhausted. After the last paw full of earth was tossed to the side, she ambled over to a small clearing and collapsed. She needed some rest. In a matter of seconds she was in dreamland.

She dreamt of her mom and her siblings. She dreamt of the places she had traveled and how much better she felt being back where she belonged. She dreamt also of the awful, foul-smelling mechanical animal that had run into her. There was that terrible smell too, of the creatures inside the animal, the ones she had killed because they had hurt and surprised her. For some reason that creature smell had haunted her. She could almost smell it now.

She squirmed in her sleep at the memory. She woke up, afraid again at the memory, but the smell, it too was in the air. She had instinctively positioned herself downwind of the lake and the river. The slight breeze carried with it the awful stench of humans, something she had hoped to never again experience. It almost seemed to be coming from the area where she had prepared her winter den, but she had just finished her work there and had smelled nothing. She shook herself awake and quietly investigated.

What she saw frightened her and angered her. She had spent days preparing a place to rest during the cold winter. Now, these humans were doing something to it, ruining it with their smell.

"Marty, let's put these two in the hole first, then we can go get the rest."

"I thought we were gonna pile all of 'em here on the shore and then put them in there."

"I wanna see how it looks, how deep that hole is with how much this stuff weighs. Come on, it'll just be a few minutes." They each carried a thirty pound bar to the cavity left by the giant cedar and placed them in the center of the earthen crater.

"There, satisfied?"

Daniel nodded his head, admiring their cleverness at finding such a perfect repository for the gold bars that needed a home for the evening. Because he was smiling at the shiny bars, the ones he had researched and investigated and sweated for, he failed to recognize why Marty began screaming.

"Holy shit, Jesus H Christ, Daniel, let's get the fuck out of here!" Daniel raised his eyes but not nearly high enough to see the ferocious muzzle of the largest bear in existence.

"Go, go, go, run, Marty!"

Marty needn't have been told. In fact he was reminded of that old joke about how fast two hunters needed to run to escape a bear attack. The answer, of course, is "not that fast, just fast enough to be ahead of your buddy." In this instance, even at his advanced age, he was faster than Daniel.

Any bear can easily outrun a human. They can achieve thirty miles per hour in short spurts. Even the smaller black bears weighing five or six hundred pounds are incredibly powerful and fast. This bear, though, this bear was an altogether different animal. Being the genetic offspring of a monster Kodiak male and an overly aggressive grizzly put Karla in a category especially her own. A bear that was nine feet tall and weighed eighteen hundred pounds, one that proved three men and a truck were no impediment, one that was extraordinarily pissed at someone messing with her own personal bunkhouse, was a bear to avoid at all costs.

Marty headed for the Beaver. Daniel was lagging but still on his tail. Karla bellowed a roar that shook the primeval trees and scattered the forest dwelling creatures. Her single other experience with these beings was not one she'd soon forget, and this one was going to be the end of any future possibilities. She started thirty feet behind Daniel and made it up in four strides. With a mighty forward thrust of her two-hundred-pound right arm, tipped with razor-sharp six-inch claws, she swiped at Daniel's back, ripping a gash from his shoulder through his opposite hip. So deep and powerful was the wound that internal organs and intestines spilled through flayed muscle tissue and severed spinal cord. Daniel Phillips ceased his retreat without a murmur.

Looking back over his shoulder, Marty was stunned at the sudden violence of the attack. An extra burst of adrenaline propelled him to the edge of the lake and into the shallow waters. With only two dozen feet to the plane, he felt he was home free.

Scott had heard the thunderous roar and now had a front-row seat to the animal who had caused it. He had seen much in his life that shocked him, especially in Vietnam, but this was something otherworldly. His preparedness as a pilot enabled him to start the engine without a conscious thought. As soon as it fired he attempted to boost the power, hoping to dislodge the pontoon from the sandy bottom.

Marty, now reaching for the nearest float, began to pull himself up and out of the water. Karla had other plans. She splashed through the short distance in seconds. Another bellow, another swipe of her awesome weapon, and Marty's head became one with the right pontoon of the aircraft. There was still a small section of cervical vertebrae that kept Mr. Menucci's head from floating off on its own.

Scott had seen enough. Luckily, the damaged float forced the plane to tilt away from the shore, freeing the aircraft. He could no longer take off, but he could sure as hell get away from this monster. With full throttle applied, he was able to steer out to the center of the lake. It looked as though the bear was satisfied with only two fatalities.

To say Karla was upset would be the consummate understatement. Here she was, minding her own business, getting prepared for a long winter's snooze. A nice warm den had been established, plenty of carbos loaded, and all she wanted was to grab a little shuteye before heading out to graze on whatever came her way. Just when things were going so smoothly, fate delivers two smelly creatures who defile her winter home for absolutely no reason.

Now, after the fact, she felt she may have overreacted some. But, shit, these fucking humans had damn well better leave her alone. Did she ever go looking to intrude on their turf? No! Did she go to their homes and fuck up their beds? No! Did she throw heavy yellow lumps of shit in their beds? No!

Please, could they just leave her alone? Now, she would have to find another place to spend the next few months. She'd make sure, this time, that it was deeper into the mountains. It would be a little colder so the den would have to be a little deeper. But she was strong, she could handle it. She waded into the place where the big flying animal was and scraped up the skinny human, his head dangling off his body. On her way back into the woods she picked up most of the pieces of the other one. She huffed over to the den she would never use and tossed all the garbage into it, on top of the two yellow stones. Then she shoved piles of dirt over it with her enormous hind legs. She supposed she could have used the human debris for nourishment, but she just couldn't get past the smell. If other inhabitants of this forest wanted it, they were welcome to it.

Her tidying up complete, she shuffled off into the depths of the Strathcona Provincial Park. Somewhere, in the deepest darkest pockets of this territory, there would be a place of rest, of safety. She'd create a new and better den for the winter. When spring came and she awakened to greet her world, she would have lost a third of her weight. Maybe she'd be more attractive then, and just maybe a new mate would come calling.

CHAPTER 30

Jordan was watching the events happening on the opposite shore when a tremendous roar echoed across the thousand yards separating them. "Will, you hear that?"

"Shit yes. That's gotta be something really big."

"Uh-oh, that's a scream. Something awfully scary is going on over there." He tried to focus the field glasses as sharply as possible. "I don't know where Daniel is but Marty's running towards the plane, and it looks like he's yelling and screaming. I think something is after him but I— *holy mother of God, what the fuck, Jesus, unfuckingbelievable,* Will, you're not gonna believe this."

"I believe it. That thing is so big I can see it without the glasses."

In horror, they watched as Karla swiftly dispatched the former owner of Interiors by Martin. The seaplane had started up as soon as Marty splashed into the lake and was now slowly turning away from the carnage. The ginormous bear, standing on its hind legs, bellowed at the aircraft. Jordan knew nothing of aeronautics, but he was fairly certain the severe listing of the aircraft would prevent it from taking off. The pilot was doing his best to evade what had to be the biggest, scariest bruin on Earth.

"Will, lean on that horn, I'm gonna climb up on the hood and try to get his attention. He won't be going anywhere but maybe we can help him."

Scott Weber was still shaken by the slaughter he had just witnessed. There was nothing he could have done; even his escape had been doubtful until the bear had dislodged that starboard float. Thank God those pontoons were compartmented, otherwise the plane would be lying on its side right now. He managed to get out into the deeper part of the lake, so he felt safe for the moment. The bear appeared to be headed back into the forest, so other than being in a crippled Beaver stuck deep in a provincial wilderness, all was well.

As he brought the engine down to an idle, he thought he heard the faint beeping of someone's horn. Glancing to his left, he saw a gray Ford Explorer on the opposite shore. A guy was on the hood, waving his arms. Scott tacked for the east side of the lake without hesitation. He didn't get this far in years by ignoring a life raft when he saw one.

The eastern shore of the lake was not as sandy as the Wolf River delta on the west side, though there were areas where the plane could bottom out successfully. When the two rescuers recognized that they had the attention of the pilot, they drove a few hundred yards down to where there would be an easier beaching for the aircraft.

Scott followed what his rescuers were doing and quickly adjusted his slow taxi to the shore. When the mangled pontoon and the intact one scraped the bottom simultaneously, he shut her down and breathed a hesitant sigh of relief. "Jesus, am I glad to see you guys. You have no fucking idea what I've just been through."

"Well, I think we do. We've been chasing you since Campbell River, and we saw enough from here to have some idea what happened over there. I'm Jordan and this is Will, by the way."

"Scott Weber here. Why were you chasing us? And you may think you know what happened over there, but unless you were ten feet from that *thing,* you can't imagine it's strength."

They tied off the airplane while Scott hopped out and splashed through the water to the shore. Both men could see the pilot was still shaken from his recent debacle.

Will had been quiet until now but apparently saw the need for all to get on the same page. "How about this. We sit here in the car where it's nice and warm and then we share stories. This isn't bullshit time, it's fess up time. We'll know if you're lying cuz we've been after those two for four days now. In fact, we know more than you do, so you go first." Will may have had some shortcomings, but being crystal clear with his messaging was not one of them.

And so the three of them shared their stories with no untruths spoken nor any intent to deceive. Scott relayed everything from his initial meeting with Daniel until and through the bear attack. He held nothing back, including his complicity in coming up with the customs caper. He was adamant though, that he'd intended to come clean when they landed in Seattle and would have refused any payment.

Both Will and Jordan's looks of acceptance suggested that they believed Weber was telling the truth. They relayed the botched kidnap plan of Kevin O'Malley by Daniel, proving Scott's instincts were accurate regarding his shady activities. At this point Will interrupted, "This might sound stupid but what a coincidence. Kevin told us that story of a giant bear attack when he was kidnapped, and now this happens. Funny, huh?"

Yes, it was funny… sort of, but they weren't done sharing information. Jordan told Scott the history of DeCourcy Island and of Brother XII, aka Fred. He continued with how Daniel had ingratiated himself into the community in order to continue his search for buried treasure; with how the original gold was contributed to Fred's grandfather; how in a fit of anger Daniel had brought Marty to DeCourcy and ended up collaborating with him. He still wondered what Marty was contributing to the enterprise. It couldn't just have been help with the heavy gold bars.

He kept the narrative going, including how Anne and Fred had thought the O'Malleys coming to DeCourcy would help with encouraging Daniel to leave them alone. He let Scott know that their friends were still back in Campbell River, waiting to hear from them.

After the three had admitted all they knew about the gold, Marty and Daniel, and DeCourcy Island and the Farm, they took a collective breath. Scott was drained from all that had happened over the last three hours; Will and Jordy were too, just from the realization that the chase and the conspiracy had finally concluded.

"Here's how I see it." Scott broke the silence. "This gold belongs to that island and to this Fred or Brother guy, whoever that is. Those other two got more than they deserved. Just goes to show you, when a real big bear is pissed at you, you're fucked no matter how much gold you have. If you'll give me a hand, I think we'll load this stuff up in your car here. You'll make sure it gets to the right place, right?"

Will looked at Jordy. "Scotty, you're a standup guy. Let's get 'er done."

They transferred the heavy gold bars into the Ford, the rear springs sagging with the additional fourteen hundred plus pounds.

"You can't fly that thing, Scott, not with that bad float. Why not come back with us, and we'll figure out how to get your bird home tomorrow. Lots of floatplanes land at Campbell River. I'm sure they'll have parts or additional floats there. We can always bring you back and give you a hand."

"Ya know, that sounds good. I'm really tired, anyway."

They secured the de Havilland Beaver as best they could, turned the O'Malley's Ford Explorer, Sport Edition, around, and headed back north, then east, to Campbell River, to their friends, and to Jordan's girl. It took them a little under an hour to cover the thirty miles to the marina. They were able to pick up cell service when they were twenty minutes from town. Will did the honors. Jenne answered the call.

"Hey, Jenne, what's shakin'?" Will was enjoying this.

"Don't give me that shit, Will, tell me what's happening. We're all worried about you two. Did you find out where the plane was headed?"

"Actually, yes, we did, and we have a story to tell you that you're not gonna believe. Seriously, we're all okay but it'll take too long over the phone. We just wanted you to know we're fine, and we'll be there in just a little while. Could you do the three of us a favor though?"

"The three of you? Who's the third one, what are you talking about?"

"We'll get to that. First the favor. We need lots of beer and maybe some pizza. I think you can get it up at the marina store. And please, none of that lightweight pilsner shit. Get us one of those local IPAs. They're my fave." Both Scotty and Jordan smiled at Will. Each offered a fist bump.

"Will, you're pissing me off. Tell me what's going on. Who's number three?"

"Sorry, Jenne, losing signal, gotta go."

Jenne turned to her husband, Anne, and Fred, who were all looking on expectantly. "It was Will. He said they're okay, and the three of them were going to be here in just a little while."

Anne wondered aloud, "Three, what three?"

"He wouldn't answer. Just said that the *three* of them needed lots of beer and pizza. Will said he doesn't want shit beer either, wants some local IPA. Also said they had a story to tell us that we wouldn't believe. What do you guys think?"

"What I think is you'd better get up to the store and get some damn beer and pizza. Better be that IPA stuff too, whatever that is." Fred had a grin a mile wide. He was thrilled his peeps were coming home, and he didn't care who the third guy was, he'd be just fine. "That Will fella's growing on me, I believe."

The next several hours were spent reliving the harrowing events of the day. Scotty was welcomed by all and took an exceptional liking to Fred. It might have been the age proximity or more the depth of life experiences, but either way they engaged in lengthy discourse throughout the rest of the afternoon and evening. Jordan and Anne were reunited, it seemed after years apart. The O'Malleys thoroughly enjoyed sharing this time with new, and they were certain, lasting friends. Will's time with Jordan and his contributions to his friends and community had not gone unnoticed. To know that he was an integral and appreciated member of the group gave him a sense of belonging that he had not known before.

"There is one thing," Will said. "We've got all that gold in the car. I sure as hell don't want to spend another night sleeping in that thing, but we can't just leave it in the parking lot."

Jenne was quick with a solution. "We'll all help load it here in the boat. It won't take us very long, and it'll be safe here with you and Anne keeping guard. Right?" She delivered this while smiling slyly at Jordan.

"Absolutely, great idea, we'll make sure to watch it carefully."

"The rest of us can grab a room at the Comfort Inn down the street, and we'll be ready to take off in the morning. Scotty, I'm pretty sure you can get the mechanics at the shipyard on the other side of the fuel dock to give you a hand with a new float, and you'll be back in Seattle before we are. Will and Fred, I guess you'll be heading back to DeCourcy with our gold guards here."

All agreed and the gold transfer commenced. Within fifteen minutes the *Butterfly* was loaded with approximately thirty-five million dollars in gold. "Fred, have you given any thought to what you're going to do with the gold?" Kevin was curious.

Kevin never got used to the little guy in the John Deere cap with the voice of God looking at him with those piercing eyes. "No, I haven't given it much thought. It's more DeCourcy's than mine, so I'll have to consider it for a bit. We'll be in touch, of that I'm certain. I'll let you know."

When Fred said he was certain of something, he was. He turned to Scotty. "Scott, do me a favor. Take one of these here bars and use it to patch up your plane."

"Shit, Fred, that's way more than the plane will cost."

"Yeah, I know. Give some of it to your buddy at the charter to help him get along. Tell him from time to time I might need a plane ride somewhere. That's how he can thank me."

Scotty smiled at him, gave him a big hug, and said, "I'll do that Fred and thanks so much. For everything." As he left the *Butterfly*, the pilot brushed his eyes with his sleeve, like maybe there was something in them.

All said their goodbyes with the promise of reuniting sometime in the near future, not expecting it to be anytime soon.

CHAPTER 31

It was unseasonably warm on Wednesday, the week before Thanksgiving. The O'Malleys had been back in Bellevue for several weeks since returning from their "trip of a lifetime" to Vancouver Island. With only Ilene, their office manager, to hold things together, the work had piled up significantly in their absence. Now that they had caught up, Kevin had found an urgent need to resume his assault on par with his buddies at the club. Jenne and Ilene were reviewing finish schedules to be included with the construction documents for a hotel refurbishment in Seattle when the phone rang.

Ilene answered and immediately pulled the phone from her ear when the caller spoke. "Yes, she's right here, hold on a sec." She turned suddenly serious as she transferred the phone call to Jenne. "I'm pretty sure it's that guy, Fred, you were telling me about. Geez, the voice on that one!"

Jenne, looking slightly surprised, picked up. "Hello? Hi, yes Fred, great to hear from you. Where are you calling from?" She was aware that cell service on DeCourcy was notoriously absent.

"I'm over here in Nanaimo with Jordy and Anne. We needed to pick up some supplies, and I borrowed their phone."

"Well, it's nice to hear your voice. Tell those two I said hi."

Since Ilene could only hear one side of the conversation, she could only interpret that something odd was being relayed by the expression on Jenne's face. "Well, no, we didn't have any plans. Is it anything you can tell me over the phone? Then, sure, we'll be happy to. We'll both look forward to it. Bye."

"What was that all about?" Ilene was never bashful about getting the lowdown on things.

"You were right, that was Fred, the little guy from DeCourcy. He says there have been some *developments* relating to us and his friends on DeCourcy, that's the word he used, *developments*, and he wants Kevin and I to come up next week to have Thanksgiving with them. He sounded somewhat evasive, which is unlike him. So I told him we'd be there. Now I'll have to let Kevin know, hah!"

That evening during a quick dinner at the club lounge, after Kevin had gone over his round in detail, of course, Jenne filled him in on their Thanksgiving plans.

"Sheesh, how come you didn't tell me right away. What's going on up there?"

Jenne gave him that look, the one teachers give misbehaving fifth graders. "Gosh, I'm not sure why I didn't spill the beans immediately. No, wait, yes I do." Another teacher look, then, "He wouldn't tell me what it was all about, only that it involved us and his friends on DeCourcy. Said we were all going to share Thanksgiving dinner and that Anne would pick us up in the *Butterfly* at Boat Harbour on Thursday afternoon at one sharp."

"Sounds strange, but you know Fred. The man never does anything without a damn good reason. I guess we'll find out when we get there. We can go up Wednesday, spend the night at Marie's in Brentwood Bay, take the little ferry across the bay, and be there on time for Anne. Good for you?"

"Perfect. I'll tell Ilene she has the week off."

For their drive up to Anacortes on Wednesday, they had another gorgeous fall day, with promising weather on Thanksgiving as well. The ferry ride through the San Juans to Sydney, B. C., was both beautiful and relaxing. Kevin and Jenne were equally comfortable with silence as they replayed their own memories of their last trip to Canada.

"Jenne." The drone of the big diesels on the ferry had made her drowsy and Kevin had startled her.

"Yes?"

"Sorry, I was just thinking about Bories. Man, hard to believe we were on the fringes of that thing."

"Yeah, saw that he got five to ten. Plus he has to make restitution on all the environmental stuff he skirted. He'll probably be out in three years or so, but he'll be broke and too old to cause any more grief by then. Looks like the inn will be foreclosed on too. Glad we didn't do any work on that thing."

"Yeah, me too."

The rest of the trip proved uneventful and very pleasant. Marie was glad to see them and very happy with her new artwork. It made their day when a client was satisfied.

After picking up the requisite lattes at a nearby Starbucks, they proceeded to Boat Harbour, arriving early. They saw the *Butterfly* approach the dock, sun gleaming off the snow-white roof of the bridge. Anne was at the bow, waving happily at the couple. Jordy was at the helm.

When the *Butterfly* pulled alongside the dock, the O'Malleys climbed aboard with hugs for each of them.

"So glad to see the two of you. What's Fred got up his sleeve? He wouldn't say much on the phone." Jenne wasn't much for small talk.

Anne replied with a wide smile. "Well, I think we need to let Fred fill you in. There have been a few developments since you were last here and, you know Fred, it's difficult to disrespect his wishes."

Kevin piped up, "Okay, so we wait for Fred." What he was thinking was, there's that word again, *developments*.

They reached Pirate's Cove in twenty minutes and were met by Will and Molly, both with wide beaming smiles. Will's grin even made him look presentable. "Hi, you two, great to see you. Molly and I can take you up in the Jeep while Anne and Jordy tie off the boat."

Kevin looked at Jenne with a WTF look in his eyes as they made it up the hill to the Farm. They pulled up to the barn where Fred stood, in his standard attire. He, too, looked like the cat who ate the canary.

"Kevin, Jenne, thanks so much for coming and sharing your holiday with us. C'mon inside."

They followed him inside the barn, which was set up for the event. Several long tables with folding chairs at the sides sat parallel to the large open doors. A smaller table for seven or eight sat over to the side, just under the loft.

Oil lamps were spread generously throughout, supplying more illumination than the place had seen in a century. The O'Malleys greatly appreciated the efforts made by the group, knowing full well that the Canadian Thanksgiving was six weeks earlier than the U.S. version.

"The rest of the residents will be here soon to join us for dinner. I thought maybe we sit and chat for a bit before, if that's ok?"

"Of course," Jenne replied, still a questioning look in her eyes.

When the three of them pulled up to the table, Will, Molly, Jordan, and Anne walked into the barn and also joined the group.

"This seems like some sort of intervention," Kevin uttered, nervously looking at the other faces.

"No, no, not at all. We just have some news to share with you." This was Fred's show, and they all turned to him expectantly.

"About a dozen years ago a young man came to live with us. He was extremely intelligent, even a Harvard graduate. At the time, though, he was disillusioned with the greed and cutthroat activities he'd witnessed as an investment banker. He was lonely, never having taken the time to form any real relationships. He quit his very lucrative job and became mired in a deep depression. He spent most days in his New York apartment, reading and sleeping. He stumbled across an article written by a former resident here, extolling the beauty of this place. Less about the Farm, just about this area. He flew to Vancouver, took a ferry, then hired a local to take him to DeCourcy."

Kevin gave Jenne a nudge under the table, his raised eyebrows indicating, "Where the hell was *this* going?"

Fred continued, "Jim, that's not his real name, stayed here for the better part of four years. We talked a lot, he worked very hard in the fields, and he spent many hours in meditation. He got physically stronger as well as mentally. During one of our last chats, I told him I thought he was ready to move on, that he had much to offer to someone. He left here eight years ago and moved to Seattle. He's got a lovely wife and twin daughters now. He went back into banking, but this time in a place he can help minority business owners get started. He's with one of the big banks in the city.

"Funny thing is, it happens to be the same bank that provided the loan to Howard Bories for the refurbishment of the Tofino Inn and Spa. It's not his department, of course, but he's very well respected there. We've become close over the years, and he dearly loves this place for how it's helped him. He knows we operate on a shoestring, at least we did, and he read something about the gold that was found. He came to me with an idea, and I think we like it and we're gonna do it.

"He tells me that if we cover Bories' note and make the bank whole, we can have the place before the bank forecloses. Sorta like a short sale."

"So, *you* are going to buy the Tofino Inn, *you*?"

"Well, don't say it like that, Jenne, it won't be just me. We've established a foundation that will be the owning entity. I can't tell you all the details, but Jim has assured me that everything has been done properly."

"But why?" Kevin looked stunned.

"Lotsa reasons. Mostly cuz it's a hell of a deal." Fred rarely swore but he felt the emphasis was needed. "And the profits will go directly to funding our community here. Additionally, the inn will help us transition folks back into society by providing them a place to work."

"But you've no experience running a hotel."

"Yes, you are correct. You remember Trish, the manager, the one with the dog?"

"Yes." Jenne was paying attention now.

"Well, that Apogee outfit hired her. They just bought a hotel in Seattle, where her family is, and she'll start there in a couple months. Point is, she's offered to show the ropes to the new managers."

"Have you found anyone yet?" Kevin asked.

"Yes, he has," Anne answered with a huge grin. "Jordan and I are the new managers. We've already met with Trish, and she's promised to help us through the transition period. She says we're naturals at it, and Burton stays with the inn. She loves him but says he's not a city dog, he belongs in Tofino."

"Wow, these certainly are some *developments*." Kevin was excited for them.

"That's not all." Will spoke now. "They can't take care of that place without an outstanding operations manager and that would be me." He actually beamed while staring at Molly.

"Apparently they're gonna need a new food and beverage person too. I got myself enrolled at a culinary school in Vancouver that will teach me the ropes. It'll probably take a couple of years, but Trish said we can keep her guy until I'm ready. She says he'll always have a home with her. Also, the chef said he'll stay, and he'll help me out along the way. I'll be able to work there when I'm not in school and, of course, Will's gonna be there."

"Whew, all I can say, you guys, is congratulations. Kevin and I are very happy, for all of you."

"Hold on there, Missy," Fred interrupted "You're not getting away that easy. We're gonna hire you two. We've got enough left over to replace all that junk that Marty put in there, the floors and carpets and stuff. We'll do a few rooms at a time. You just tell us the right materials to put in there and we'll be fine."

"Fred, I don't know what to say. We'll be thrilled to help, and we can't wait to get started." Kevin, too, had a smile from ear to ear.

Many of the residents started filing in for the turkey dinner. As they were seated they looked over to Fred, who made certain to look at each one individually, with a nod of his head, a twinkle in his eye, and a smile.

A SMALL FAVOR

Thanks very much for purchasing this book, I hope you enjoyed it. If you have a few seconds can I ask you to leave a review on Amazon? It's the best way for me to get feedback and also helps prospective readers find stories that interest them. Rest assured, your candid comments are appreciated.

See you on down the road…

Ted

"TEED UP FOR TERROR"

Join the O'Malleys as their private golf club becomes the target of a fringe white separatist group. In a new adventure, Jenne and Kevin become enmeshed in a plot involving jewel thieves, terrorists, drug traffickers and hero dogs. The fun continues in Ted's new book, *Teed Up for Terror*, available now on Amazon.

ABOUT THE AUTHOR

Ted has lived throughout the US, mostly in the Pacific Northwest. He's an Army vet, sales and marketing VP, entrepreneur, business owner, avid reader, one of nine children, former caddie, and lover of dogs and golf. The last twenty-five years he spent in partnership with his wife, Patte, as the owners of a highly respected and published hospitality interior design firm in the Seattle Area. They're now back to living on Whidbey Island and loving it!